GONE ROGUE SERIES

Rogue PROTECTOR

PATRICIA D. EDDY

If you love sexy romantic suspense, I'd love to send you a short story set in Dublin, Ireland. Castles & Kings isn't available anywhere except for readers who sign up for my mailing list! Sign up for my newsletter on my website and tell me where to send your free book!
http://patriciadeddy.com.

CHAPTER ONE

January

Austin

"He'll see you now, sir," the uniformed airman says as he nods towards Commander Ivan Clarke's office door. My boss, the head of the Special Operations Command Unit, summoned me here with an early morning phone call and then made me wait for two hours.

Two hours I spent sitting on an uncomfortable couch, back stiff, hands on my thighs, staring straight ahead at the photographs lining the wall behind the airman's desk. I'm in some of them. As are the President, the Vice President, and the Secretary of Defense. Photographs that used to represent the pinnacle of my career. Everything I ever wanted and more. But now... I don't know.

Standing, a quick tug on my coat hem smooths away the wrinkles, and I give the younger man a nod of thanks.

I shut the door behind me, then march up to the Commander's desk, stopping three steps away and giving him my best salute before standing at Attention, my gaze fixed just over Clarke's shoulder.

"Pritchard," Commander Clarke says. "You weren't due back here for another month."

The judgement in his tone doesn't surprise me. Nor does his lack of an At Ease command. He's pissed. In his position, I'd probably do the same damn thing.

"Sir. I had a family emergency—"

"You'll want to shut your trap before you dig that hole any deeper."

"Yes, sir." Clarke has the power—and every right—to end my career. Or worse. Leaving my post without warning or permission, going AWOL—especially at my level—was a stupid move. But one I'd make again without hesitation. My sister and my best friend needed me, and if I hadn't dropped everything to go to Venezuela, Trevor might be dead. And Dani...Trev's death would have killed her too.

But the real offense? At least from Clarke's point of view? Engaging with hostiles on foreign soil without orders. If I was seen, recognized, recorded by a single traffic camera, I'll be stripped of everything. My job. My rank. My pension.

My freedom.

Clarke could convene a court-martial with the snap of his fingers. From the look on his face, he just might.

"Morales called me. Passed on your vague excuses for disappearing in the middle of the fucking night and not contacting anyone for three days."

The commander runs a hand through his thinning hair before muttering, "For fuck's sake, Pritchard. At Ease."

I lock my thumbs behind me and track the commander's

movements as he turns to stare out the window at the rain that's been hammering Fort Bragg all morning. "You're one of the best, you know. Or were. When I tapped you for JSOC commander, I knew—*knew*—it was the right decision. You wanted more and you deserved it. But now?" Shaking his head, he says, "I don't know. Maybe you've been riding a desk too long."

Fuck.

His gray eyes focus on me, and I can see the exhaustion in them. Not much different from the look in my own every morning. "It's like you're *trying* to get court-martialed. Explain yourself."

I can't. Not and walk out of here a free man. So I settle for pleading my case.

"There's still a lot of good I can do here, sir." I don't believe that. Not anymore. But it's what I'm supposed to say. All the conversations I've had with Clarke over the past year have been full of everything I'm *supposed* to say. "I can be on a flight out before the end of the day to rejoin Morales and the others."

"No." Commander Clarke leans back in his chair and shakes his head. "You're goddamn lucky you chose your friends wisely, Pritchard. And you better hope there's no fucking evidence you were *ever* in a foreign country without authorization."

"There isn't, sir. Because I wasn't." Again, what I'm *supposed* to say. He's not buying my bullshit. Not for a second. But this is the game.

"You went rogue," he says. "And I can't have that on my watch. So you're headed to Pakistan. We've set up a dozen Grey Fox listening posts across the country to monitor for terrorist chatter. You'll oversee them until I have some fucking confidence you can do your job and follow orders."

I swallow hard and force myself to look him in the eyes. "So, I'm out. Sir."

Clarke snorts. "You should be. Without question. And if it were up to me, you would be. But the President doesn't want any official churn right now. So, until he's ready, you're going to Pakistan. Officially, you wanted to get back into the field for a few months. To put your finger on the pulse of the men who risk their lives every day." The commander flattens his hands on the desk, and his voice roughens. "If you tell anyone otherwise, I will put an end to your career so fast you won't know what hit you."

"Give me a timeline." I shouldn't say a fucking word. His tone tells me how thin the ice is. But I have to ask. Going to Pakistan without knowing when I'll be back? I can't do it.

"You're dismissed, Pritchard. Get out of my sight."

No amount of anger and frustration can overrule more than twenty years of training, so I shove my feelings down so deep, they'll never escape. "Yes, sir. Thank you, sir." Snapping to attention, I execute an about face, then march calmly out of his office.

Pakistan. I'm so fucked.

TWENTY-FOUR HOURS LATER, I'm in fatigues on a military transport plane headed to Pakistan. I didn't call my parents. I couldn't. Dad's going to see right through Clarke's manufactured excuse, and I'd rather be halfway around the world when that happens. Steve Pritchard might be over seventy, but he doesn't miss a beat.

My sister Dani texted me this morning, but I haven't opened the message yet. She doesn't need to deal with my shit right now. Or even worse, be reminded of Gil and his betrayal. She and Trevor need to heal.

My parents adopted Dani and Gil when Dani was only nine. When Gil turned on everything—our family, the CIA, his entire fucking country—we lost so much. Hell, he tried to kill me five years ago, and last week, Dani almost lost Trevor for the second time. The first time, they were just kids. This time? I can't even think about what almost happened in Venezuela. At the Crypt.

I rub my thigh as the plane levels out. The hundreds of cuts Gil used when he captured and tortured me five years ago cover my chest like latticework, but other than the pain and blood loss, none of them were serious. Until he plunged a knife deep into my thigh. I didn't lose any motor function, but it still aches from time to time. A dull pain that won't let me forget how I failed him.

Closing my eyes, I can still picture Gil as he was. The boy my parents brought into our house. Angry. Extremely protective of his little sister. Wary. But harmless. We were the same age. In the same class at school. Even...friends for a short time. Or so I'd thought. He and Trevor were closer, but the three of us were practically inseparable for a couple of years. And Dani always tried to tag along. Most times, we even let her.

The vision of him as a teenager morphs into what he looked like when he lured me to Caracas on a containment mission then ambushed my team, killing everyone but me.

That day? That first terrible day? When I woke up bound and gagged in an abandoned office building? My brother looming over me, wielding a knife, his face so full of pain and rage, there was nothing left of the man I'd once known.

"This is all your fault, brother," he says as he twirls the *switchblade in his hand. "You could have stopped this."*

I shake my head so hard the room spins. Gil's been flaunting his crimes to the CIA, the NSA, so many U.S. allies...anyone who will listen. He'll never see the light of day again. That is if Trevor can do his job.

Forcing out a deep breath, I stretch my legs to ease the ache. I could have stopped him. I should have. Because I should have known what he was planning. Maybe down deep, I did.

"Commander Pritchard? You okay?" The kid next to me looks like he should still be in college. If not high school. Except for his eyes. Wisdom, intelligence, a healthy dose of cynicism.

"Fine. And you are...?"

"Hargrove. Griffin Hargrove."

I give him the once over, studying his mannerisms, the practiced casual air, trying to figure out who he is and whether or not I can trust him. "First time in Pakistan?"

"Yes, sir." His blue eyes dart around the plane before he clears his throat. "I'm on your security detail. Sir."

Great. And he's never been to one of the most dangerous regions in the world? This is going to be one hell of a clusterfuck.

Clearly, I do a piss poor job hiding my displeasure, because Hargrove rushes to continue. "I'm the junior member, sir. I spoke to the team leader this morning, and he's been in Islamabad for two years now. So has the rest of the team."

Well, that's something, at least. "Good to know, Hargrove."

"Griff. No one but my SSO calls me Hargrove." He offers me a sheepish smile. "Always makes me feel like I'm about to be singled out in front of the class."

I arch a brow. "CIA?"

"Yes, sir. My previous posting was in Afghanistan. And I speak some Urdu."

Offering him a firm handshake, I force all thoughts of Gil from my mind. This mission might be punishment, but it's one I deserve. If I wallow too much in my own misery, I'll put this kid—and the others working with me, for me—at risk, and that's unacceptable. "Let's hope the next few months are uneventful," I say, regaining some of the composure and authority I lost in Venezuela.

Fake it till you make it. One of Dad's favorite sayings. Time to put it into practice.

CHAPTER TWO

August

Mikayla

The freak summer rainstorm sounds like hundreds of tiny pebbles hitting the roof of my car as I pull out of the garage at Baltimore/Washington International Airport. Next to me in the passenger seat, my mother sighs.

"You look so tired, Mikayla. How late did you work last night?"

Thank goodness I'm driving so I don't have to meet her gaze. "I left around 2:00 a.m." My mother clucks her tongue, and though she only wants the best for me, she doesn't understand why I do this. "Mom, the World Horticultural Society needed supporting documentation for the fellowship application, and I had to get it right."

"At the expense of your health?" my father asks from the back seat. "If you had gone to medical school—"

"That was *your* dream. Not mine." My eyes dart to the rear

view mirror briefly, finding his, then I return my focus to the road and merge onto the freeway. "I *love* what I do, Dad. My work... There's an orchid that only grows in Guatemala and on one mountain range in Mexico. It produces a rare phytotoxin in its roots and flowers, and one of my colleagues at Johns Hopkins thinks he can use it to help create a treatment for Parkinson's." I pause, hoping they'll recognize the importance, but despite losing my grandmother to that horrible disease, Mom's still giving me the side eye. "The orchid's in danger of extinction. Most of its habitat has already been lost to coffee farming, and it's so rare, poachers make a fortune selling it. Without proof it has more value than being one flower amid a host of others, it'll be gone in under a decade."

"We did not leave Syria and seek asylum in America so our daughter could risk her life studying a *flower*," my father says.

Anger flares up, bright and hot. This is his favorite argument, but it's also one I can refute easily. "No. You left Syria so your daughter could decide for herself what she wanted to do with her life. I want to study this orchid. Preserve its existence."

"And how does working all hours of the day and night help this?" The judgement in my mother's voice grates on my nerves, but despite her nagging, she's always come around in the end to be my biggest fan—as long as I could justify my actions. She convinced Dad to stop pressuring me to go to medical school, supported me when I told them I was moving from Mountain View, California to Edgewater, Maryland to take a job at the Smithsonian, and I know I can sway her now too.

"If I get this grant, I'll be able to take a team of graduate students with me down to Mexico and study the orchid in its natural habitat. With the information we'll get there, we might be able to find a way to reliably grow it in the lab or cross-breed it with a hardier variety so it'll thrive in more than these two specific regions. And we'll bring back enough samples for Johns Hopkins to work towards a clinical trial."

My words spill out over one another in my excitement, and I know I'm rambling in ways my parents didn't fly across the country to hear. They just wanted to spend a long weekend with me. But I can't help myself. "If we visit the grow sites, we can take air, water, and soil samples, install equipment that monitors all those variables year-round, and maybe even convince the Mexican government to do more to stop poachers from stealing the flowers and selling them illegally."

"You want to study *poisonous* plants? In the mountains of Mexico?" my father asks. "Mikayla, that does not sound safe."

"It is. I promise. The poison is only active when the flowers and roots are dried, and we always wear protective equipment to handle the samples. And it's not a *poisonous* plant. It's a plant that could potentially help millions of people. That just happens to be dangerous when dried."

"You would be hiking? Up in the mountains? Alone?" My mother rests her hand on my shoulder. "I do not like that idea."

Traffic grinds to a halt. A heavy summer rainstorm combined with rush hour doesn't make for ideal conditions, and as I stop the car, I lock eyes with each of my parents in turn. "This is a once-in-a-lifetime opportunity. The research papers I'll be able to publish alone will make my whole career. And if I can work with Dr. Branch—he's my colleague at Johns Hopkins —on *his* paper... Mom, I could save lives."

She's softening. I can tell from her expression, and emboldened, I take a deep breath. "I promise I'll be careful. I've started using the stair machine every day to get my lungs in shape, and my graduate students...they're working their butts off designing experiments and thinking up new ways we can possibly save an *entire species*. They deserve this as much—if not more—than I do."

For a full minute, no one says a word. Traffic starts crawling slowly, and I return my focus to the road just as my father clears his throat. "You know we love you, Mikayla. We are simply worried. It's what parents do."

Mom settles back into the passenger seat. "Your father is right, Mika. We worry because we love you."

I flash her a quick smile, and the tension in my little Prius evaporates almost immediately. "I know. I love you too. I worked so late last night so I wouldn't have to go in again all weekend. And I bought all of the ingredients for *kibbeh bil sanieh*. Tomorrow, we can cook together."

"You mean tomorrow I will cook and try to stop you from eating all the pine nuts." Mom huffs out a breath, but her lips curve into a smile.

I laugh, letting work fade into the background for now—and hopefully for the rest of their visit. "You won't have to. I bought double what we need, so I get to eat as many as I want. Dad can too. And I picked up a box of those chocolate caramels you love. We all get to indulge this weekend."

They only visit twice a year, and my work has kept me so busy, I couldn't fly out to see them during Ramadan. While I'm not a practicing Muslim, Mom and Dad are, and I know they were hurt when I couldn't even make it for a weekend trip during the holiday. For the next few days, I'll do my best to put work out of my mind and enjoy my time with them. And hopefully, in a couple of weeks, the grant will come through, and so will my dreams of making a difference.

Austin

Standing in the doorway of my empty apartment should stir more of a reaction. I want to feel...*something*. Anything besides this hollow, restless sensation that's haunted me for weeks. Since the attack in Islamabad.

We were targets from the moment we stepped foot in Pakistan. For six months, my security team worked their asses off. Until the United States Ambassador showed up for an unannounced visit. We scrambled. Mistakes were made. And when we escorted her back to the Embassy, they boxed us in on a narrow street. We were sitting ducks.

I managed to get her and her teenage son out of their burning vehicle and laid down cover fire until her security team got her to a mosque down the street for shelter.

But the second blast killed three members of my detail and left Griff, the only one who survived, with permanent hearing loss and only half his left arm.

"Pritchard. I can't feel my fingers," he'd croaked as I'd *dragged myself over to him and tried—despite three bullet wounds to my shoulder and back—to keep firing until help arrived. "Shit. I can't...there's something wrong with my ears. It's so quiet. Fuck. Am I dying? Don't let me die, man."*

Every night when I try to sleep, I hear him. See him. His arm crushed under the remains of that heavy stone wall. Blood covering the left half of his face. The desperation in his eyes.

Outside of Ryker McCabe—a retired Special Forces detachment commander—and his team, Griff has the best damn instincts of anyone I've worked with in more than twenty years, and now...he'll be lucky to ride a desk, let alone go out in the field again. Nothing will fix his hearing. And while I called in some favors to get him consults with the best prosthetic clinics in the country, it's not going to give him back his arm.

He saved my fucking life. Shoved me out of the way of a collapsing concrete wall—only to be trapped himself. I wish my gratitude could do him a damn bit of good. But I'm out. Clarke pushed my retirement papers through while I was still recovering, and now...I'm a civilian for the first time in more than twenty years.

At least I kept my pension. Wren—Ryker's wife and the best damn hacker I've ever met—carefully scrubbed every single piece of video evidence tying me to Venezuela and the fall of their government. Without her help, I'd be in a military prison right now.

Training won't let me leave a single footprint on the carpet I meticulously vacuumed after I cleaned the place top to bottom, so I stand at the threshold, wishing I knew what to do next.

A couple of days with Mom and Dad in New Haven. That's a given. Dad knows everything now. My sister, Dani, told him while I was in Pakistan. The weekend she brought Trevor home for a visit.

Dad will hammer me with questions. Mom will bake brownies and tell me I need to eat more. I give it all of a week before I have to get out of there. I love my parents. Don't think I could have asked for better ones. But I'm numb. Every damn day. The military is all I know.

Even with two Master's degrees, I've never worked in the private sector. And though some pompous ass named Smith from the CIA has called me every other day for a month, that's the *last* place I want to go. Not after Gil's death. After what happened to Trevor.

Hoisting my duffel, I stifle a grunt. One of the bullets tore through my rotator cuff. The physical therapist cleared me to resume all normal activities, but it still hurts like a son of a bitch if I move without thinking about it.

I need to go somewhere no one can find me. Dad used to talk about hiking the Maya Trail. He did it when he was eighteen. Came back and enlisted in the Air Force Academy after some transcendent moment of clarity.

I could get lost in Mexico. See if I find what I'm looking for. Escape. Purpose. Peace. Fifteen hundred miles? That'll keep me busy for a while. Maybe by the time I'm done, I'll know who Austin Pritchard, civilian, really is.

CHAPTER THREE

Mikayla

After I step back into the air conditioned halls of the Smithsonian Environmental Research Center, I feel like I can finally take a deep breath. The greenhouse door closes and locks behind me, and I lean against the wall for a moment. The Blushing Note orchid only grows in high altitude climates with over seventy percent humidity. We've recreated those exact conditions here, and the warm, wet air is hard on my asthma.

Almost two years ago, we obtained one of the plants for study—after contentious negotiations with the Mexican government—and I spend ten to fifteen hours a week now in conditions that could trigger an asthma attack with little to no warning.

You're training yourself, Mik. Acclimating in case this grant comes through.

At least two or three times a day, I have to repeat those words to steel myself before I head in to take samples, care for the orchids, or supervise my grad students who are mixing different soil combinations, testing out new fertilizers, and handling the cross-breeding.

We've separated the plant five times, grafted it to other, hardier orchids in the hopes we could preserve it, but so far, our successes have been limited at best.

Resting against the cool, white plaster wall helps calm my lungs and release the tight band wrapped around my chest. My daily inhaler works wonders, but it's not a cure, and if I have to break out my rescue inhaler, I'll be jittery and useless for hours afterwards.

Li, one of my graduate students, rushes down the hall, an iced coffee in each hand. "Hey, Dr. Mik. I brought you a pick-me-up."

I'm so grateful, I'd hug her if she didn't work for me. She's young—all three of my students are—but so bright, eager, and driven that most of the time, I leave her in charge of the greenhouse after I finish the morning rundown of the day's planned duties.

"You're a mind reader," I say before I take a sip. "And a life saver. I have a meeting with Dr. Lowenstein in fifteen minutes to talk about next year's budget. There's no way I want to do *that* without caffeine. Thank you."

Li blushes and stares down at her bright red flats. "You were still sending emails at 2:00 a.m. I thought Corey was supposed to help you finalize the budget spreadsheets?"

"He had to fly back to Los Angeles last night," I say. "Family issues."

"Oh." Li scuffs the ball of her dainty foot against the linoleum. No one talks about Corey's home life, but everyone knows. His dad gets picked up for drug possession with intent to sell once a year or so, and Corey flies across the country to bail him out, then deals with the man's verbal abuse for days.

"It's all done and submitted now. Nothing to worry about," I say as I force a smile.

At least I hope not.

Lifting her lab coat from the row of pegs outside the greenhouse door, Li frowns, which is so out of character for her, I almost do a double-take. "I love this internship, Dr. Mik. When I graduate next year, I want to work here if there are any openings."

"Oh, Li." This is the most vulnerability I've ever seen her display. She and Isaiah—the third student I supervise—started dating six months ago, and they're open and affectionate with each other when they think I'm too distracted to notice, but otherwise, they're all business all the time.

My gaze drops to the iced coffee, and the corners of my lips turn up slightly. "I'd hire you in a heartbeat. Your work has been amazing from your very first day. I have to believe we're going to get our full funding again. The work Brian Branch and his team at Johns Hopkins are doing shows real promise to help Parkinson's patients. They're depending on us. We *need* to continue studying the Blushing Note. Cross it with hardier varieties, do...*something* to keep it alive and existing in this world."

I don't need to tell her all of this. My sales pitch. It flows off my tongue so easily. Of course, I've practiced it in front of a mirror every night for a month. Now, the words are so second nature to me, I can't stop once I start.

Li's exceedingly polite, listening patiently until I realize what I'm doing and shake my head. "I'm sorry. I'm keeping you from your work. And the rest of your coffee. It's Friday. Leave a little early. Go have some fun this weekend. And tell Isaiah to do the same."

"Isaiah's on his way in," Li says, her cheeks pinking as she tries to hide behind her coffee cup. "I'll let him know."

I wish I felt comfortable reassuring her that she'll find no judgment from me for moving in with him. I heard them talking a couple of months ago, agreeing they'd always drive in separately to "keep up appearances." Her parents are even more conservative than mine from what I've gathered.

Raising my coffee cup and thanking her again, I head for my office to prepare for the meeting with Lowenstein. The drink helps steady my nerves, and the caffeine chases away the last of the tightness in my chest.

For the past two years, this orchid and its potential have been my life. I've seen the damage Parkinson's can do to a person. My grandmother died from it, and just a month ago, my mentor and boss revealed his own battle with the disease. Saving the Blushing Note and finding a treatment is more important to me than anything besides my family and friends. I can't fathom a world in which I fail, and there's no way I'm letting anyone take this work from me without a fight.

FIFTEEN MINUTES LATER, I knock on Dr. Howard Lowenstein's door, my heart beating a little too quickly for my liking. No matter what, I'll still have a job come January. But the Smithsonian studies all kinds of plants, animals, and insects in danger of going extinct, and I could easily be assigned to work on sea grass in Florida. While I'd do it without question—all endangered species need to be protected—I just *know* my work with the Blushing Note will make a real difference for so many people. If we can just get that grant...

Focus, Mik.

"Come in!" Howard calls, and I cradle my tablet to my chest, all the recent test data ready and waiting if I need to justify keeping all three of my grad students on this project. I've played the *what if* game time and time again, asking myself all the questions I think Howard—or anyone else on the board—will throw at me.

"Mikayla, it's good to see you," Howard says with a warm smile. "Put that tablet away. You won't need it."

Hope tugs at the corners of my lips as I shove the device into my messenger bag. "Does that mean we have our funding for the next year?"

My boss waits for me to sink into the chair across from him. "The budget decisions won't be made for another week, but I think I can safely say yes. I cannot imagine any reason why you wouldn't get full funding next year."

"You're killing me, Dr. Lowenstein. If the committee hasn't finalized everything, why call me in?" My fingers are tingling, as are my cheeks—they always do when I'm excited or nervous —and I force a couple of deep breaths.

"Is your passport up to date, Mikayla?" His brown eyes twinkle, and he pulls a piece of paper from under a folder on his desk.

"Y-yes. Why—? Oh! The fellowship? Please tell me we got it!" I'm practically vibrating now, anticipation racing up and down my spine, but Howard just sits there, the paper clutched in his hand, a wide smile on his face.

I want to shake the man, because he's letting me jump to all sorts of conclusions that might be totally wrong, except he's my boss and that would be inappropriate. "Tell me!" I say, leaning forward and squinting to try to read the embossing on the letter.

Lowenstein laughs, a rich, deep belly laugh, and slides the paper across the desk. "The Mexican government just approved VISAs for you and your team, and the money from the World Horticultural Society was wired to the Smithsonian today. Congratulations, Mikayla. You and your grad students have three weeks to study the Blushing Note orchid in the Chiapas mountains. The grant will fund a full mobile lab unit, hotel rooms in San Crisóbal del las Casas, meals, and incidentals. All yours. You earned it."

I jump up before he finishes his sentence, hugging the acceptance letter to my chest and beaming, tears pricking my eyes. "Oh my God. I can't tell you what this means to me. I have to call Dr. Branch at Johns Hopkins. And tell my students."

The long list of everything we have to do runs through my mind, and I start pacing the small office. "When do we leave? When *can* we leave? Do I have to make the travel arrangements myself? What about the Mexican government? Have they detected any poaching activity lately? If so, will they authorize additional patrols? How do we send samples back here?"

Howard shakes his head and chuckles. "Slow down, Mikayla. We'll talk about all of that on Monday. The final details are still being worked out with the authorities. For right now, go celebrate with your grad students. Oh, and make sure everyone has a valid passport. That's the most important thing. Ideally, you'll leave within the next three weeks, but the exact date is up to you." Pushing to his feet with a groan, he offers me his hand. Despite the early-stage Parkinson's he was diagnosed with last month, his grip is strong, and his eyes clear. "All of your hard work is paying off. I'm not naive enough to count on any sort of treatment from the Blushing Note to be available in time to help me, but because of you and your work, there's hope for the next generation. You deserve this honor more than I can say."

"I couldn't have done any of it without you. Thank you for believing in me."

"You made it easy. Now get out of here! Go celebrate."

I float out of his office feeling like my entire life finally makes sense. The ten years I spent in college. All those hours writing my dissertations. Fighting my way into this job—beating out a dozen other applicants—all of them men—and finding a home here. With colleagues who support me. Students as zealous as I am—if not more. And then, my partnership with Brian Branch and learning I had a chance to make a *real* difference...

So many times, I was rejected or dismissed out of hand because of my last name—Salim—my boobs, the color of my skin, my parents' refugee status.

Now, it's all worth it. Practically skipping down the hall, I head for the greenhouse to tell Li and Isaiah. It's too bad Corey's across the country, because I'm taking the other two out to celebrate.

CHAPTER FOUR

September

Austin

The cool, damp air of the *Grutas del Malmut* cave system is a welcome change from the heat of Palenque. The cave floor is slippery and wet in spots, and I take my time, running my hand over the rough rocks that bear the shape of long-extinct beasts, and planting my feet carefully with each step.

There's something visceral about this place. Something real.

For almost three weeks now, I've hiked my way along the Maya Trail. Old temples, ancient settlements...history. People who lived and loved and fought and died, were forgotten and rediscovered again. Yet, even here, I don't feel like I'm real.

My entire trip has been full of *real* experiences. Ones that make me wonder if I ever want to go back to the United States. What the hell would I do? Work for the CIA? I can't take another job that asks me to sacrifice so much. That puts other people in danger.

For the first time since Gil died, I feel something akin to peace. It's not. Not truly. But it's closer than I've been in five years. Maybe even longer.

What if I stay?

Losing myself in Mexico feels...right. My Air Force retirement pay is enough to make a good life here. I could find a job—something simple. Handyman. Though I don't know much about construction. Gardener? I know even less about plants. But I could learn.

I spend hours in the cool, dimly lit caverns until I realize a life without responsibilities just isn't me. I'd last a month. Maybe two. Hell, I already spend my days pushing my body to its physical limits and my nights drinking just enough to fall into bed and keep the nightmares away.

Less than two minutes after I emerge from the cave, my cell phone buzzes in my pocket, and I check the screen. Fuck. Trevor's the last man I want to talk to. Every time I think about him, I see Gil's face. Feel his blade slicing across my chest or driving deep into my thigh. But I have to answer. I owe him that much.

"Trev. Been a while."

"Whose fault is that?" Trevor's voice holds an edge I haven't heard in ages. Not since we were teenagers. "Dani's called you half a dozen times in the past few weeks, and you've ignored her every fucking time. Sent three or four word text messages back. What the hell is wrong with you?"

"That's none of your goddamn business," I snap and pull the phone away from my ear so I can end the call.

"You're hurting her," Trevor says, and that's enough to keep me on the line. "You know his fucking birthday is next week.

And Dani wants—*needs*—the only brother she has left to get on the phone with her and have an actual conversation."

"Shit."

"Shit is right. She'll be home in two hours, and her phone better ring in under four. You hear me?"

"Yeah. I do. I'm sorry, Trev. I haven't been in a good place." Finding a bench under some trees where I can watch kids kicking soccer balls and families enjoying tacos and gathering around fire pits, I stretch my legs, the tight muscles reminding me I'm getting...older. Too old to keep running away from my problems.

"You don't think we know that? That *I* know that?" His irritation fades, leaving only weariness in his tone. "You went to Pakistan because of me. You got hurt because of me. You were driven out of the Air Force *and* JSOC because of me."

"No." The single word escapes, harsh and rough, and I slam my hand down on the wood slats. The gesture stings my palm, but the pain is better than feeling *nothing,* so I do it again.

A woman passing by with her young daughter shoots me a look, and I blow out a long breath. "You're not...wrong. But you're not right either, Trev. For years, JSOC was all I wanted. Hell, they groomed me for it. And I probably would have made National Security Council or even Secretary of Defense one day if I'd actually *wanted* it. But I didn't. I haven't for a long time. Pakistan was a shitshow, and yeah. I went there to avoid a court-martial. I was damn lucky Clarke didn't decide to hold a grudge. But I knew what I was doing when I left my post and flew to Venezuela. And I don't regret a goddamn thing. You and Dani—and Mom and Dad—you're my family."

"Then why go dark?" he asks.

The lump in my throat shouldn't be so hard to swallow.

Trev's my brother in every way that counts. And was long before he and Dani found one another again. Fell in love. I have to tell him. If only because I can hear the pain in his words. He's blaming himself for everything broken in me, and none of it is his fault.

"Because something in me died when Gil...fuck." Trev's the one who had to put a bullet in my adopted brother's brain, and here I am whining about his death. I search for something to say that won't drive more of a wedge between the two of us, but I can't find a single damn thing that isn't pure and utter bullshit. "Because I have a lot to figure out. Can we just leave it at that?"

"Yeah, man. Sure. Just...call Dani. You have four hours." Trevor hangs up without saying goodbye, and I stare at the phone for a full five minutes before I can even think about moving again.

We may be family, but our friendship? Pretty sure I just tossed that out like day old trash. And I don't know if I'll ever be able to close the rift between us again.

***

Mikayla

The heavy mist cools my cheeks as I follow Isaiah up the steep, narrow trail. We've been in Chiapas for two weeks now, and it's rained every single day. At least halfway up the mountain where the grow sites are.

We were prepared for the rain. The wind, not so much. It whips my poncho around my knees, and I've already lost two hats.

The two kilometer trek through steep, uneven terrain takes

us over an hour to navigate. Our mobile lab unit sits at the base of the mountain, and every day, two of us make the climb to one of the five designated grow sites. They each sit in a little mini-caldera, scattered around the mountain like massive salad bowls, full to the brim with lush trees, moss, and of course, dozens of Blushing Note orchids. The plants cling to the massive trunks, wrap their roots around fallen branches, and I can only imagine what it looks like when they flower. If we'd been able to come two months later, we could have seen them in bloom, but by then, the weather would make hiking up here impossible.

Ahead of me by a hundred feet, Isaiah braces his hand on the side of the crevasse that leads to Site One. Something shifted in the weather last night, and today...the air is thick and oppressive, despite the high winds, and as I adjust my back-pack, my chest suddenly feels like someone kicked me and then dropped a twenty-pound weight directly onto my lungs.

"Isaiah," I wheeze, but he can't hear me. It takes me precious seconds to shrug out of my backpack and sink to my knees in the mud. The zipper doesn't want to cooperate, and my heart pounds faster and harder as I search desperately for my inhaler.

One. Two. Three. Four.

I try to slow my breathing, but this attack came on so fast and hit me hard enough that my vision has already started to tunnel. Breathing through one of those little coffee straws the hotel uses would be easier than this.

There it is. My fingers brush the hard plastic, but they're trembling so badly I drop the precious medicine twice before I get a good grip on it. Shaking the small cylinder takes every-thing I have, but I need to mix the Albuterol with the propel-lant or it won't do me any good.

Breathe out. All the way. Force it. Come on. You can do this.

My chest is so tight, and I can't hear the wind anymore. The burst of medicine doesn't feel like it makes a bit of difference, but I know it's helping. Or will, once I get my second dose in. But waiting even thirty seconds feels nearly impossible since each one stretches out before me like it's a year long.

Mud soaks through my khaki pants now, and I rest my head on my backpack as I bring my inhaler to my lips a second time.

Breathe in. One. Two. Three. Four. Five.

"Dr. Mik!" Isaiah's voice reaches my ears through a long tunnel, and then he's at my side, his hand on my shoulder. "Breathe. Stay calm. I'm here."

He knows what to do. All three of my grad students know. Unless it looks like I can't lift my inhaler at all, they're to just monitor my breathing and make sure I don't pass out.

After the world's longest minutes ever, the weight sitting on my chest lessens, and I lift my head to meet Isaiah's concerned gaze.

I nod, hoping he'll understand I'm okay. Or at least heading in that direction. Talking is still kind of risky, and there's no way I can continue the hike. My entire body feels like it's shaking, even though I know I'm not.

Isaiah pulls out the two-way radio and flips it on. "Li, can you suit up for measurements?" he asks. There's no cell signal up in the mountains, but the radios work until we go through the crevasse. "Dr. Mik had an attack. Tell Corey to come too. He can get her back to the hotel while we take today's readings." He rattles off our coordinates, then helps me to my feet and over to a flat rock just off the trail. "Do you need a doctor?"

"No." My voice is hoarse, but audible, and my cheeks catch fire as I realize just how much mud seeped into my pants. "Sorry. Don't know why today—"

"We got this, Dr. Mik. It'll all be fine." Isaiah is always optimistic. There's something about being twenty-six that makes guys feel like they're on top of the world. Indestructible. He's not even wearing a light jacket under his poncho. Just a base layer over hiking pants. "How's your heart rate?"

Checking my watch, I take a slow, relatively deep breath and wait for the number to flash on screen. "Ninety-three. Passable after an attack. I'll be fine. I can set up the slides while you and Li download the day's readings and take photos."

He shakes his head. "Nope. Corey's driving you back to the hotel."

"I don't need—"

"Yes. You do. Taking one afternoon off won't put us behind. Once Corey drops you off, he'll come back here and we'll stay until we get everything done. You're the boss, Dr. Mik, but we can handle this. I promise."

All three students are geniuses. Isaiah and Li have the highest grades in their respective programs, and while Corey's GPA isn't quite as impressive, he's driven in a way I've rarely seen.

I'll take the afternoon. Rest. Maybe try to read a book if I can focus on the words. And once my body calms down, run some of the numbers from the past few days.

"Fine," I mutter, dropping my head into my hands.

Ten minutes later, Isaiah pushes to his feet and peers down the side of the mountain. "There they are."

Li and Corey scramble up the last few meters, both breathing heavily, and Li hands me a travel mug of coffee. Instant, but at least it's caffeine. And hot.

"We'll handle everything," she says with a reassuring smile.

I can only nod, and Corey picks his way over a patch of loose rocks in the center of the trail before offering a hand to help me to my feet.

I groan, but they're so dedicated, it's hard to be angry with them. Still, I can't let them take on all of my work. "When we get back to the lab, transfer this morning's readings to a USB drive so I work after I take a nap."

"You don't have to do everything, you know. That's why you brought us with you." Corey holds a branch out of the way so I don't have to duck under it, and I nod my thanks.

He's right. And I should have known better than to push myself today. My breathing was slightly strained when I woke up this morning. The particular combination of temperature and humidity we're currently experiencing in Chiapas is risky for me, but I hate not being able to be out in the field myself. And my students know it.

The trip down the mountain takes forever—both because the mist has turned to rain and because I don't have the energy to keep up any sort of decent pace. Corey offers me his arm from time to time to help me over a fallen branch or slippery patch of mud, and I can tell there's something on his mind.

"You okay?" I ask when we reach the trailer that's served as our temporary base camp for the past ten days.

Corey shrugs as he grabs the keys for the Land Rover. "Sure."

"That's not an answer." My backpack feels like it weighs fifty pounds, and before I climb into the vehicle, I spread my poncho out over the seat so all the mud caking my pants and plastering them to my skin doesn't destroy the rental car.

Ick. The feel of sludge seeping deeper into my butt crack makes me shudder, and I can't wait to get back to the hotel so I can shower. And then try to sleep off these jitters.

We don't speak again until we turn onto the main road fifteen minutes later. "How are things at home?" I venture when the silence gets to be too much.

He clutches the steering wheel so hard, his knuckles turn white. "Quiet."

Underneath the pounding headache and nerves, warning bells go off. Things with Corey's father are never quiet. "You know I understand, right?"

"No, you don't," he says sharply. "Not really." The venom in his voice shocks me, and I turn to stare out the window, the lush green landscape practically untouched save for the two lane paved road and the occasional small house or old barn. So much of Chiapas is undeveloped, though it boasts some of the most interesting ruins and caves in this region of Mexico.

Eventually, he sighs. "That was out of line."

"A little. But you're not wrong. I've never been afraid of my parents. My cousin has, and when she came to live with us, she told me all about the hell she went through. But I never lived it."

"Why did you give me this internship?" Corey asks with a quick glance across the Land Rover. "Li and Isaiah I get. But me? My grades were barely above the minimum required."

"Because GPA isn't always the best indicator of how smart or motivated a person is." The set of his jaw tells me he's not buying it, so I let out a sigh. "Your essay. That's why. Because I knew you'd seize this opportunity and make the most of it. It's great to be the best and the brightest. But it's just as important to be the most driven and dedicated. And maybe...I saw a chance to help you like my parents helped my cousin."

"I'm just going to let you down," he says quietly.

"Why would you say that?" You're the one who cross-bred our most successful hybrid." The largest orchid in the Smithsonian greenhouse is growing like no other, and Corey nicknamed it "Queenie."

"That plant... It was a mistake. It was all a mistake."

"Corey? I don't understand." I wish I knew what to say to

him. Five days before we left, he had another *family emergency,* and when he came back, he was different. Sadder. Less...himself.

He fixes his eyes on the road and doesn't say another word until he pulls up in front of the hotel. "Rest up, Dr. Mik. We got this."

CHAPTER FIVE

Austin

Back in my room at the Hotel Centro in San Cristóbal de Las Casas, I sink down onto the double bed and pull out my phone. I made a promise, and no matter how much it hurts, I'm going to keep it.

"Hey, squirt," I say when Dani answers the call.

"Where are you?" The hurt in her voice sends a knife twisting through my heart, and I flop back and stare up at the ceiling. "Are you coming back before...Gil's birthday?"

"No." I should soften the blow, say something reassuring, explain. But I don't have the words.

"Austin, please. I've never asked before, but this year...after everything we went through in Venezuela, it's...important to me."

"I can't, Dani. I need to be alone for a while. Figure out what the fuck I'm supposed to do with my life. If I came back... I'd just make things worse."

She stifles a sob. "Worse than what? Than learning just how broken Gil was before he died? Than seeing Mom and Dad blame themselves for not loving him enough? I had one brother disappear on me, Austin. Are you trying to make it two? Because it sure seems like it."

"Way to make a guy feel like the biggest asshole in the world," I mutter. "You and Trev went through hell, Dani. You don't need *me* around to remind you of...all of it. Think about how hard it would be for Trev to see me broken up about Gil's death. *I* wasn't the one who fired the shot. *I* wasn't the one who trained with him. Who fought with him. Hell, I wasn't even his target five years ago. No. I was his pawn to get to Trevor." I'm practically yelling now, and someone in the next room pounds on the wall. Squeezing my eyes shut, I try to come up with something...anything that will make her understand why I have to stay so far away. At least for right now.

"Trevor doesn't blame you. Not one bit. He never has. But...hang on." A door shuts, and Dani's voice takes on a hushed tone. "We're okay. Better than okay. Most of the time. But you know his history. Some days, he still feels alone. *Really* alone. Despite Ryker, Rip, and the rest of the folks out in Seattle at Hidden Agenda, his family at Second Sight. And me. Those days...I think they'd be easier on him if the two of you sat down and just...talked. Honestly. About Gil, about Venezuela, about everything."

Fuck. Guilt socks me in the balls, and I roll onto my side, not sure I can even take a deep breath for several seconds.

"Austin?"

"I...I have to go." At her exasperated groan, I add, "I can't come back yet, squirt. I'm sorry. But I'll call you in a few days. Trev too. I'll be...better."

"Please try, Austin. I love you."

"Love you too." Tossing the phone on the nightstand, I punch the pillow a few times, sending feathers floating through the air. I can't keep hurting the people I care about, but that's about all I know how to do these days.

Something has to change. If only I could figure out what.

THE BRIGHTLY PAINTED hotel restaurant is quiet, which suits my mood after talking to Dani. I order a plate of tacos, a beer, and a shot of tequila. I'll need at least three shots before I'm done tonight. If not more. Anything to stop the constant refrain going through my head.

You failed. Gil. Dani. Trevor. Everyone.

Every single hike, all the nights alone, each solitary meal... they should have helped me figure out who I want to be by now. Who I am. Instead, I've spent almost every minute rehashing my mistakes. All the signs of Gil's betrayal I missed. The secrets he kept from me. From Dani. From Mom and Dad.

The lies.

I knew every time he deflected. Every time he kept something from us. Every time he bent—or fractured—the truth to suit his needs. Hell, I was trained to read people. Micro expressions, body language, tone of voice. But I didn't want to believe what I was seeing. Gil was CIA. It was his job to lie. To keep us in the dark. To protect us. At least that's what I told myself. Wrote off his behavior as being "on mission."

Why didn't I push harder?

Could I have saved him? Or saved Trev and Dani from the hell they both went through?

"Excuse me?" The sultry voice holds an edge of impatience, and I shake off the thoughts pinging around in my head and turn as she continues, "Lost in your own world, huh?"

The woman with her hand on the stool next to mine carries her exhaustion in the bags under her brown eyes, and her wariness in the stiffness of her shoulders.

"Sorry. Been a day," I reply. "Can I help you…?"

"Just wanted to know if this stool was taken," she says and gestures to the main seating area of the restaurant. In the twenty minutes I spent nursing my beer, reliving memories of Gil and all my other failures, apparently the rest of the hotel decided it was time to grab a drink.

"Nope. All yours."

"Thanks." She sinks heavily onto the well-worn leather seat and runs a hand through her sleek, dark brown hair. It's cut short, with a few tendrils falling onto her forehead in gentle waves, and I catch the scent of lilacs as she leans over slightly to reach into her purse. A moment later, she coughs into her elbow a couple of times.

"You okay, miss?"

After a wheezing breath, she grabs the bottle of water the bartender set in front of her, nods, then takes a sip. "Fine. Stupid asthma. Someone was smoking just outside the lobby doors." She doesn't meet my gaze, instead focusing on the menu in front of her.

"Sorry. Didn't mean to pry." Staring at my beer, I try to forget the pain in Dani's voice when I called her.

I had one brother disappear on me, Austin. Are you trying to make it two? Because it sure seems like it.

With a flinch, I drain my first beer and signal for another. The woman beside me glances over as I curl my fingers around the bottle, and something in her eyes is too alluring for me to turn away.

"You didn't pry." Her hesitant smile fades as she sets an inhaler on the bar top. "You were being a gentleman. Or…at least a halfway decent guy."

I snort. "Can't say I'm either. At least not anymore." The alcohol is clearly going to my head, and I crack my knuckles to help me focus. "My mom has asthma. It only bothers her during ragweed season, but she has a couple bad attacks every year."

"It's the humidity for me." She tilts her head and holds out her hand. "Mikayla."

"Austin."

Mikayla's grip is solid, as is her stare, stripping me of my defenses layer by layer until I release her fingers and reach for my drink again.

"Not a whole lot of Americans in San Cristóbal de Las Casas this time of year," she says. With a quick glance at the menu, she signals the bartender, then orders a taco plate and returns her focus to me. "Outside of my team, you're the first one I've met. Or...at least the first one I've talked to."

"Your team?" Curious, I shift on my stool and take her in. Petite. Maybe five-foot-five at most. Curvy, but compact. Flawless, tawny skin, high cheekbones, perfectly sculpted brows, delicate fingers.

Another smile, this one full of pride. "My graduate students. We're researching an endangered orchid that only grows up in the mountains outside of Las Ollas."

"An endangered *orchid?*" I almost choke on my beer, but Mikayla's completely serious, and bright streaks of copper shine in her eyes as she narrows them at me.

"Yes. An orchid." With a huff, she reaches for her napkin and unfolds it across her lap. "What's so unbelievable about that?"

"Nothing." Holding up a hand, I duck my head so I can meet her gaze. "I'm sorry. I haven't been around people in a while. I guess I forgot how to be—"

"Not a jerk?" Mikayla asks.

"Something like that." I go for another sip of beer, then pause with the bottle halfway to my mouth. Alcohol won't stop me from chewing on my boot again, and it's been a long time since I actually *wanted* to talk to someone. "Can we start over?"

The bartender returns with two plates of tacos and slides one in front of each of us. "Anything else?" he asks, and Mikayla eyes my beer.

"Any good?" At my nod, she adds, "Then I'll have what he's having. Also another bottle of water, please."

As soon as the guy turns away, she holds out her hand again. "Dr. Mikayla Salim. But most people call me Mik."

"Major General Austin Pritchard. United States Air Force." The formal introduction rolls off my tongue like it's second nature, and it is. Except that's not who I am anymore. Flames crawl up my neck to my cheeks, and I quickly add, "Retired."

Mikayla's brows shoot up, and she gives me a short whistle. Her fingers are warm, and I don't want to let go, this sudden, unexpected wave of intense connection barreling through me so hard and fast, I worry it's going to knock me off my stool. "And I thought doctor was an impressive title."

"Well, I never got further than a couple of master's degrees, so..." It feels good to smile. Like I'm reclaiming a piece of myself I lost long ago. "Doctor sounds pretty damn impressive to me."

"So what are *you* doing in San Cristóbal de las Casas, Major General Austin Pritchard?" Mikayla settles a little more solidly onto her stool, and the wiggle of her ass draws my gaze for a split second.

Eyes up, Pritchard. I focus on my plate as I answer. "Just Austin. I retired a little over a month ago. Needed a break.

Losing myself on the Maya Trail for a while sounded like a good idea."

After a generous bite of a taco, she studies me, those wide brown eyes taking in every detail. "Sounded?"

I chuckle. "Picked up on that, huh?"

"Maybe."

Her smile makes me want to tell her everything. Just start talking and not stop, but that's probably because I haven't spoken more than a few words to anyone in since I left the United States.

"Well, turns out, spending six weeks alone with only your thoughts for company isn't the best idea when those thoughts are pretty damn insistent that you relive all the mistakes you've ever made in your life."

I wash the bitter admission down with a swig of beer, shocked at how easy it is to share my failings with someone I don't know. Dani tried to get me to go to therapy when I was sent home from Pakistan. Said it helped her—and Trevor. Maybe I should have listened.

"Oof. Well, I don't drink very often," Mik says as she lifts her bottle and tips it towards mine, "but I've found when I do, my inner voice tends to take a hike."

"Shit. That's what got me into this mess." When Mik's brow furrows, I snort. "Taking a hike?"

"Oh, crap." She lowers her eyes to her beer, then bursts out laughing. It's the sweetest sound, full of abandon, and I finally pick up my bottle and touch the neck to hers.

"To hiking?" I ask.

"No. No, no, no." She shakes her head, and her bronzed cheeks take on the hue of a summer sunset. "To a meal with a stranger who'll hopefully forgive me for making a complete fool of myself."

"Nothing to forgive, Mikayla. Mik. This is the best meal I've had since I arrived in Mexico."

Her blush deepens, and fuck. I wish this didn't have to end with dinner. But it does, because no one deserves to see my damage in the light of day. For the next hour though, I plan on enjoying every minute of my time with the gorgeous Dr. Mikayla Salim. Because why the hell not?

CHAPTER SIX

The four-hour nap I took after Corey brought me back to the hotel was amazing—and desperately needed—but it doesn't bode well for being able to sleep tonight. Which is why I'm still sitting in the hotel bar long after midnight chatting with this handsome, retired Air Force officer.

Austin's short, dark hair narrows to a widow's peak, and every once in a while, the light catches a strand of gray. He wears two or three days' worth of stubble along his jaw, and I think his hazel eyes have seen too much. Tattoos cover his right arm from his wrist to his elbow, with words I haven't yet been able to read. They're not in English, that much I know. But languages were never my strong suit. Beyond Latin.

"Mikayla?" Austin leans a little closer. "Did you hear me?"

I fiddle with my napkin, fighting the embarrassment racing up my neck to my cheeks. "Sorry. I was trying to figure out what those words mean," I say, gesturing to the ink.

A mix of pride and sadness plays across his features.

"Loosely translated, they say, 'We won't give up, weren't born for that. We'll throw ourselves into the battle for honor.'"

"That's beautiful."

Silence stretches between us, and I stifle a yawn.

"I'm keeping you from a good night's rest," Austin says as he finishes off his tequila. "You probably have an early wake-up call."

Offering him a sheepish smile, I nod and take the last sip of my beer. I don't normally drink, but after an attack, the meds often leave me so wired, a beer is about the only thing that lets me fall asleep. "We have another five days to finish up our research, and I put us behind. After my asthma attack, one of my grad students had to take two hours out of his day to drive me back here, plus, they had to do my share of the work today."

"You couldn't exactly help it," Austin says, and when I meet his gaze, I find understanding, sympathy, and a hint of encouragement.

"No, but I'll have to make up for it tomorrow." Reaching into my cross-body purse for my cash, I pull out four hundred pesos and drop them on the table. Hours ago, when the restaurant started to empty, we found a corner booth where most of the noise faded away and it was just the two of us, talking about...nothing really. Casual conversation. Movies. Books. Music. "My treat," I say when Austin frowns and reaches for his wallet.

"You can't really expect me to let you pay?" He straightens, his broad shoulders stretching the black t-shirt across his chest. "Dr. Salim, where I'm from—"

"Mik. Or Mikayla, remember?" I brush my fingers over his wrist, and he stares down at the contact, where the heat of him seems to burn my skin. I'm not usually so brazen. No. Scratch that. I'm *never* this brazen.

When he looks up, the storm of emotion in his eyes shocks me.

Pulling away, mortified, I stammer, "S-sorry. I...I'm tired, and I wasn't thinking."

"Am I'm supposed to be angry? That was...nice." Austin catches my hand in his, holding on as he stands and helps me to my feet. "When I came to the bar tonight, I was in a shitty mood, and my entire goal was to drink myself out of it. Or at least, drink enough I could forget about...a lot of things. Instead, I traded what would have been half a bottle of tequila for conversation with a smart, beautiful, and fascinating woman I really want to see again."

I don't know what to say to him, and the silence doesn't do anything for my nerves. Because I want to see him again too. If only we weren't two strangers in a tiny hotel in the Mexican highlands. There's *zero* chance this will be anything more than what it's been. One of the best evenings I've had in a very, *very* long time.

"You said you have another five days?" Austin asks, taking a step closer. Close enough I have to tip my head back to see his eyes.

"Y-yes."

His smile warms me down to my toes. "I don't have anywhere else to be just now. Losing myself on the Maya Trail, remember? The best part of getting lost? No one can find you—unless you want them to. I like San Cristóbal de las Casas. I think I'll stay a few more days. Maybe...five more?"

"Oh. *Oh.*" The butterflies in my stomach are starting to drive themselves into a frenzy. "I work all day. We leave before sunrise, and I don't know what time we'll be done. It all depends on the weather. It's been so wet lately, hiking up the trail to the grow sites takes twice as long as it should. We might not get back here until after dark—"

"Mikayla?" Austin squeezes my hand, and I snap my jaw shut. Anything to stop myself from rambling on and on and on... Oh, crap. He said my name. And I'm just standing here like an idiot. "Back with me?" he asks.

"Um...sorry. I spend a lot of time in my own head. Like, I have whole conversations with myself in there. Long ones. Kind of a risk of the job." I don't know how I manage to say all of that without tripping over my own words, but I don't care at the moment, because all that's good in this world can't hold a candle to Austin's smile.

"I'm staying in Room 236. When you get back, no matter what time it is, give me a call. Or come and knock. We can at least have a drink together."

"I'd...I'd like that." Shock at my admission settles the butterflies—or maybe it just kills them—and I smile. "Um, I should go. Get some sleep." I don't want to release his hand, but if I stay here any longer, I'm going to make a fool out of myself, so I pull away, but then his room number registers somewhere in the back of my head, and I stop. "You said Room 236?"

"Yes."

It's a good thing the lighting in this bar is so dim. Otherwise he'd see how mortified I am. "I'm in 234." There goes any chance of making a graceful exit.

His hazel eyes take on a brilliant sparkle, and he shoves his hand into his pocket, then offers me his elbow. "Then may I walk you to your room, Mikayla?"

I can't do anything but nod and tuck my hand in the crook of his arm. The hotel isn't large, and it doesn't take more than five minutes to reach our rooms, but I spend every second wondering what's going to happen when we get there. I want him to kiss me, but I never kiss on the first date, and was this even a date? We ate dinner *next* to one another. Not *with* one another.

Austin waits until I have my key in hand and turn, staring up at him. "Well, this is me."

Stupid, Mik. Of course this is your room. It's literally right next to his.

"Sleep well, Mikayla," he says, his voice rough and his eyes dark. "I haven't had a night this...perfect in a long time."

Perfect? It was just...dinner. And a beer. And hours of conversation.

Except, despite my inner voice trying to convince me otherwise, he's right. Everything about this evening was perfect. Casual. Easy. Fun.

"I'd like to ask you something." He skims a knuckle along my bangs, and the intimacy of the touch makes me want more, so I nod. "Can I kiss you?"

"Yes," I whisper.

Strong fingers cup my neck, but he doesn't touch me beyond that. Simply leans down and presses his lips to mine. His stubble sends shivers through me, and I brace my hand on the wall so my knees don't buckle. It's a chaste kiss by any standards, as is the second. And the third. But still, there's something very intimate, very possessive, and very raw flowing between us, and I don't want it to end.

But it has to. And does, when Isaiah and Corey stumble around the corner, talking too loudly, clearly inebriated, and I jump back before they see us with our lips locked together.

"Good night, Mik," Austin says quietly as he backs away. Right before he disappears inside his room, he stops and pierces me with an intense stare. "I'll see you tomorrow."

As soon as I lock my own door, I rest my back against the wall we share, unable to wipe the goofy grin from my lips. "Good night, Austin."

BETWEEN THE AFTER effects of my meds and the intensity of those kisses, I'm still wired and a little shaky two hours later. I caught up on all of my data entry, wrote up the experiments for the next day, and...yes...Googled Major General Austin Pritchard.

He's exactly who he said he was. And a hell of a lot more. The man has a Wikipedia page, complete with a photo of him in full dress uniform. And crap on a cracker, does he clean up nicely.

Commander, Joint Special Operations Command

I don't know what that is, but it sounds impressive. Another ninety minutes pass, and I have to shut my laptop and try for at least a couple of hours of sleep. When I close my eyes, though, visions of Austin doing all sorts of heroic things play in a loop in my head.

Though my parents were right in the middle of the fighting in Syria in the seventies, they came to the United States as refugees with my grandmother before I was born, so I was spared all those painful memories. All I know about war is what I see on the news. But Austin...he's *lived* it.

Is that why he wanted to disappear for a while? So many questions run through my mind, and I stare up at the hotel ceiling until my lids are too heavy to keep open any longer.

STIFLING a yawn as I adjust the microscope, I wish I'd moved just a little faster this morning. A second cup of hotel coffee would have been really nice. Instead, I have to make do with instant. Li and Corey are at Grow Site Five, and Isaiah works at the table across from me, cataloging the photos he took yesterday.

"Leaf rot on the ferns surrounding Site One's grow zone,"

he mutters to himself. "Heavy concentration of spider mites in the area, but I don't see any on the orchids…"

"What did you say?" I stumble as I slide off my stool, spilling my coffee all over the work bench. "Crap. Get some paper towels!"

Panicking, I reach for the slide tray, but grab it awkwardly, snapping one of the thin pieces of glass in half with my thumb. A drop of my blood stains the shard, and my heart shoots into my chest. If that was one of the dried pieces of orchid root…I could be in trouble.

"Dr. Mik?" Isaiah's next to me in three steps, staring down at the blood. "Shit. What was on that slide?"

"I…what number is it?"

Breathe. There are a hundred slides in that tray. Only ten of them are potentially poisonous.

With a pair of tweezers, he gingerly pulls out the broken glass. "Fifty-three."

"It's okay. I'm okay." Staggering over to the sink, I turn the water on full blast and hold my hand under the spray, squeezing the fleshy pad of my thumb to help flush out any mold spores from the razor thin piece of fern that had been preserved under glass on slide fifty-three. "Totally harmless. The orchid roots were on slides one through ten."

"Thank God." Isaiah mops up the spilled coffee while I wash my hands thoroughly and then wrap a bandage around my thumb.

That was a stupid mistake. Amateur. One that would have earned any of the grad students a stern lecture had they been in my shoes.

That's it. No more coffee in the lab. But after being up half the night thinking about Austin, I was wiped. As he tosses the soaked towels in the trash, Isaiah says, "The spider mites leave the orchids alone. That's what I was saying. If I didn't know better, I'd say the plants were being sprayed, but we're the only ones up here."

"The Mexican Ecological Foundation assured us that they'd leave all five grow sites alone for at least three weeks before we arrived. They wouldn't even set foot in them, just have their security patrols make sure no poachers entered the area. Show me the images?"

He projects them onto the largest monitor we have. The first day, we did nothing but tour the five sites, and I pull up those pictures for comparison. "That's really weird. You can see evidence of spider mites on the photos we took weeks ago. There's no reason for them to *not* be there now."

"Li and Corey won't have time to visit Site One today," Isaiah says. "But we should go tomorrow and take fresh samples. Then we can check for pesticide. I wish I'd noticed this when I was up there yesterday. The rain was intense, and it took all of my focus to keep the camera dry."

"If someone *is* spraying up there, half the data will be useless." The idea that we've wasted the majority of our time in Mexico leaves a sour taste in my mouth, and now I don't want more coffee. I just want answers.

Isaiah radios Li and tells her to swab at least twenty-five percent of the plants at Site Five and bring back cuttings from another ten percent. Even with the walkie-talkies, communication halfway up the mountain is spotty, and she asks why, but when he tries to explain, there's nothing but static on the other end of the connection.

"I need some air," I say as I cover the ninety-nine remaining slides and put the tray in one of the lab fridges. "I'll be back in twenty minutes."

"Okay, Dr. Mik. You're not going far, right?" Concern crinkles around his dark brown eyes. Of my three graduate students, he's the most empathetic, and every time I have an asthma attack, I swear he gets more overprotective.

"Just down to the river. And I have my radio and my rescue inhaler." I show him the tube, then shove it into the pocket of my khaki pants and pull my windbreaker over my head. It's not as wet today, but the weather can change on a dime this time of year.

"Be careful. It's still slick out there," he says as he returns to his work. I can tell he doesn't want me to go, but tough. I'm the one in charge here. And I'm *fine*. Except for making a stupid, rookie mistake that could have left me in need of medical attention.

The phytotoxin produced by drying the Blushing Note's roots is so powerful, I haven't let any of the students even touch the slices I cured last week. And yet, I'm the one who almost stabbed myself with one of them.

With only my own petulance as a companion, I stalk out of the trailer. This is my dream. Has been ever since I interned with Dr. Brian Branch while I was working on my dissertation. He knew about the orchid, and when he told me about its potential therapeutic properties, saving it became my mission. I've applied for this grant three years in a row, and now, if our research is compromised, I'll lose all credibility in the academic community, but the real tragedy will be the loss of a chance for a real, legitimate treatment for Parkinson's.

The air holds a chill, even though it's well over sixty today, and I wrap my arms around myself tightly as I pick my way down towards the river. Autumn in this part of Mexico is unpredictable. One day can be beautifully sunny with ninety percent humidity, and the next, fifty degrees with rain that feels like it's driving into your skull.

The river, only a trickle in June, flows swiftly, and I lower myself down to a large, flat rock I discovered our second day here. It's big enough to stretch out on—even do a few sun salutations—and it's high enough above the river that even now, after several days of rain, I won't get wet.

Crossing my legs and leaning back, I stare out over the lush landscape. Despite how awful this weather is for my asthma, the air is so fresh this high up in the mountains, and there's a purity to the flora and fauna that's been lost in so many of the world's industrialized areas.

Places like Chiapas are why I decided to study endangered species in the first place. Sitting here, listening to birdsong so loud, it almost drowns out the rushing water, I feel like my life has meaning. Like I'm making a difference.

I just hope whatever we find tomorrow doesn't shatter that illusion completely.

CHAPTER SEVEN

Austin

Pushing myself to my physical limits helps drive my demons deep inside where they can't hurt me—or more importantly, damage others. And if I'm going to have dinner with Mikayla tonight, those demons need to be well hidden.

Kissing her rocked me down to my toes, and I was so hard when I returned to my room, I couldn't sit down for fifteen minutes. Now, after hiking seven miles to the ruins of an old temple, then climbing the hundred and twenty steps to the top —and back down, twice—my body feels like it's been wrung out and left to dry in the sun.

I know how to recover, though. Electrolytes, beer, and an hour's nap, and I'll be able to push myself all night if I have to. And fuck, do I hope I have to. I'd love to take Mikayla into town for a proper date. I might never see her again after this week, and I have no business starting anything *serious* with her given my current mental state, but I don't do things halfway.

Within minutes of stretching out on the bed, I'm asleep,

but peace? That's harder to come by. In my nightmares, Gil finds me, and his taunts, his blade, his betrayal...they're still just as fresh as they were five years ago.

"The United States government wants me dead," he says as he drags the knife across my chest. *I hang from an exposed ceiling beam, my wrists secured with a thick zip tie. Blood drips down my abs, soaking into my pants. My hands went numb hours ago. "I knew they'd send you."*

Another cut, but I don't let myself react. Pain can be controlled. To a point. The ribs he broke when he captured me are much more concerning at the moment. Each breath is harder than the last.

"What...do you think...torturing me...will get you?" I force out through clenched teeth. "You're a traitor, Gil. You'll be lucky...to live...another day."

"Oh, I think I'll last longer than that. My father owns this country." Gil laughs and waves the knife in front of my face. "You'll never defeat the Loma Collectivo, Austin. When they send Trevor—and they will—I'll make him watch as I gut you."

I jerk awake, my hand automatically moving to the thick scar just below my ribcage. I never told Trevor, but an hour before he showed up in Venezuela to rescue me, Gil had stopped playing around and his blade had come within half an inch of piercing my liver.

Sometimes, I forget. The pain. The fear I'm not supposed to admit to anyone. The failure.

Giving up on sleep, I shower, wrap myself in a towel, and stand in front of my rucksack for way too long, trying to figure out what the hell to wear on the first date I've had in three years. Assuming Mik shows. For all I know, I could have scared her off.

Dr. Mikayla Salim is full of contradictions. Last night, there were moments she was bold, outgoing, funny as hell, and others, like after she touched me at the end of the evening, she almost disappeared inside a shy, demure shell. I want to know more about her. Everything about her.

Ten minutes later, three shirts laid out on my bed, I'm only half dressed when someone knocks. Shit. In my rush to see her, I don't even grab one of the shirts before I fling the door open.

Mikayla takes a quick step back. "Oh, crap on a cracker. I'm...um..." Her gaze locks onto my chest, and her cheeks flush a dark crimson. "I can come back. When you're not all..." she waves her hand up and down, "muscles."

"Not all muscles? You do realize they don't go away when I get dressed, right?" My laugh feels good. *Normal.* But Mikayla covers her face with her hands and groans.

"I know how muscles work," she says, her voice muffled as she retreats. "I'll, um, be...in my room."

"Mikayla." The single word stops her in her tracks, and I snag the closest shirt from the bed and shrug into it as she drops her hands and risks a second glance at me. "I'm sorry. I didn't mean to be inappropriate. Or make you uncomfortable. I just need to button up and grab a couple of things. Come on in."

"I can wait in the hall." She lowers her gaze, shoulders hunched, feet cemented to the floor.

I want her in my space. Leaving her scent in my room. But she's definitely *not* budging from that spot, so I give her a quick nod, then head for the dresser. The hotel's old enough the doors don't shut automatically, so I can see her start to relax slightly as I fasten the last button. "Are you up for a little adventure?"

"Adventure?" Her eyes narrow. "I thought this was just...dinner."

Sliding my wallet into a zippered pocket inside my jacket, I offer her what I hope is a reassuring smile. "It can be. But I spent some time wandering the town a couple of days ago, and I thought if you weren't too tired...maybe we could find a little outdoor cantina, watch the tourists go by?"

Relief softens her features. "I'd like that. I've only been into San Cristóbal de las Casas once, and that was to pick up a prescription refill. I need to get a jacket, though. Be right back."

While she's gone, I slide a folding knife into a sheath on my belt. It sits at the small of my back, easily accessible, but almost completely hidden by my blue linen shirt. This is a safe town, but I've been in too many *safe towns* that suddenly weren't, and even though we've spent all of four hours together, I already know. Mikayla is definitely someone I want to protect. Even if only for this one night.

My phone, hotel key, and passport go in another secured pocket, and I meet Mikayla at her door when she emerges with a small cross-body bag at her hip, barely visible under her windbreaker.

"Are we walking?" she asks.

"Unless you'd rather not." The small elevator doors close, and fuck. I want to take her in my arms and kiss her, but after what just happened, I shove my hands into my pockets. "We can call a cab."

"No. It stopped raining on our way back to the hotel. As long as I don't have to run anywhere..." She offers me a sheepish smile. "The humidity isn't great for my lungs, but I hate being trapped inside all day."

"Then we'll walk. At a leisurely pace."

She's right about the weather. The air smells like passion fruit and wood smoke, and a gentle breeze ruffles Mikayla's hair. She peers up at me when we stop at the corner, confusion in the set of her brow, but then quickly looks away as we start walking again. I'm about to ask her if she's all right when she curls her hand around my left wrist and holds on.

The contact makes me think I didn't totally fuck up back at

the hotel, and I quickly adjust so I can link our fingers. "Wasn't sure you wanted—"

"I was raised...by very conservative parents," she says, the words tumbling out like she's about to lose her nerve. "And it's been a while since I've dated anyone. Seeing you earlier threw me a little."

"Hey." I stop and, with my free hand, nudge her chin up slightly so she can see my eyes. "You don't have to explain, Mik. We're not getting married. Not getting naked. Yet, anyway." Her lips form a little *o*, and I cup the back of her neck, but don't step any closer. "And not ever unless you decide you want to. Tonight, I'm yours. Whatever you want to do, whatever you want *me* to do. Nothing more. Nothing less."

Even though my dick hasn't fully relaxed since she came to my door, I won't push her. Hell, for all I know, she could be a virgin.

Her eyelids flutter closed for a breath, and when she opens them again, the setting sun catches the golden flecks in her irises, turning them into tiny flames that make me want her even more. Just as I start to release her, she swallows hard and licks those perfect, bow-shaped lips. "I want you to kiss me again."

That does it. I'm now turned on enough she's going to notice. Any second. But I made her a promise. Whatever she wants and whatever she wants me to do. So I dip my head and taste her.

I never believed in sparks. Kissing a woman...well, it can be about the best damn feeling in the world—maybe even better than great sex, because with a kiss, there's a connection. If you're doing it right. But as soon as she parts for me and her tongue starts a slow, lazy dance with mine, there are definitely sparks. If not a raging inferno.

A tiny moan escapes her throat, and I slide my hand up to

tangle in her hair. The short strands are soft and thick, just the right length for me to hold onto. I can tell when I move too close, though, because she tenses at the feel of my length against her stomach. "Sorry, sweetheart," I say as I break off the kiss. "Can't help what you do to me. Give me a minute."

"Don't apologize." Her voice cracks, and she nestles herself against my chest, her arm around my waist as we start walking again. "There's nothing to be sorry for."

"I made you uncomfortable."

"No. You surprised me, that's all." With a sigh, she shakes her head. "I'm not...completely inexperienced, Austin. It's just been a while. And this?" Her sultry laugh as she gestures between us does nothing to calm me down. "This isn't something I've ever done before. Pick up a guy in a hotel? Lie awake half the night thinking about a kiss that...well...was *nothing* compared to that one?"

"You weren't the only one."

"But I don't sleep with guys on the first date," she says. "Or the second."

"No sleeping. Got it."

"No sex." With a chuckle, she twists out from under my arm and flashes me a smile. The move pulls at my shoulder, and I can't stifle my wince, or the quiet grunt of pain. "Austin?"

"Just an old injury." I drive the heel of my hand into the center of the throbbing ache, and after a few seconds, it fades enough for me to shove it into the background where hopefully, it won't bother me again tonight.

"What happened?" She approaches warily, like she's afraid she'll break me, but I sidestep her and tuck her under my good arm where it only takes a few steps for her to relax again.

"It's an ugly story," I say quietly, then press a kiss to the top of her head. Her scent helps chase away the demons floating so close to the surface. "And tonight...let's stick to the good ones. That okay?"

"On one condition." Mik peers up at me, her long, dark lashes framing eyes full of concern. "If we have a tomorrow, will you let me ask you again?"

"Yes, sweetheart. I will."

Mikayla

Dozens of tourists wander the streets amid the colorful buildings and open-air stalls of the public market. It's relaxing with Austin at my side, his fingers wrapped around mine. "What did you do all day?" I ask. "And just how many hiking trails are there around here?"

A laugh rumbles in his chest, smooth and deep and sexy as anything I've ever heard. Steering me towards one of the booths selling freshly cut flowers, he points to a blushing red rose. "*¿Cuánto questa?*"

After handing over five pesos, he accepts the bloom, brings it to his lips, and then to mine before he offers it to me. I don't know what to say other than, "Thank you," and he gives me a quizzical look.

"Not here." Scanning the area, I point to a little cantina with outdoor tables and clear lights hanging overhead. There's a table for two at the edge of the patio, and when we're facing one another with my rose between us, I stroke my fingers over the velvety petals. "No one's ever bought me flowers before."

"You're kidding. Who are these guys you've been dating, Mik?" Austin cups his hands over mine, and the contact makes those butterflies in my belly flutter to life again.

This is a much more personal conversation than I thought

we'd be having tonight. But there's something about this man I trust, and it's not just his collection of medals and commendations. "Well, there have only been three of them," I admit.

"Shit. Mikayla. Why? You're smart, fucking gorgeous, and incredibly sexy. Men should be falling at your feet and begging you to spend time with them."

My cheeks catch fire, and I pull my hands from his when the server comes to take our order. "Margarita?" Austin asks.

"I've never had one." His brows shoot up, furrowing his forehead, and I stammer, "I-I don't usually drink. Just a beer... uh, once in a while. I'll take an Agua Fresca."

Alone again—or as alone as we can be on a patio full of people—I fiddle with the tablecloth. "I'm not good at relationships. I study *endangered orchids*. I have two Ph.Ds. I'm much better with microscopes and soil acidity, and...*numbers* than people. I spent the day analyzing the cellular structure of half a dozen root samples from the grow sites we have access to, then entering data for three hours."

"Three hours?" He frowns, then rubs his hand over his jaw. "Shit. Sorry. That came out wrong. But I don't know anything about orchids. Or most plants, for that matter. What's there to study?"

"The Blushing Note orchid is one of the largest in the world. Some of the plants weigh close to fifty kilograms. And its roots and flowers...they're poisonous. A self-defense mechanism it developed. The dried particles are a powerful phytotoxin, but there's a researcher at Johns Hopkins who thinks he can use that phytotoxin as a component in a treatment for Parkinson's. But the orchid's endangered. Almost extinct. And...I'm babbling. You really don't want me to bore you with all the details. This is my passion, and even *I* think a lot of what we're doing here is...well, dry as all get out."

There's that laugh again. The one that sends those butter-flies all the way down to my toes. "All get out?"

"I...I don't swear much either. Or at all. Crap on a cracker was the most vulgar phrase my parents allowed when I was growing up." My cheeks warm, and I do the quick mental math. Four hours last night. Another hour tonight. Five. Yep. About the length of time most men take to figure out I was raised Muslim. Then run away.

"Oh. Shit." Austin's eyes widen. "Shoot?"

Now I've done it. "It doesn't offend me when other people swear. And no one should have to change their behavior because of how I was raised. Really, I almost wish I *did* swear. But my parents don't allow it in their house, and keeping things...clean makes it easier when I see them."

"That's..." Austin gets a faraway look in his eyes for a moment, then focuses back on me, "actually sweet. But I have to ask. You rarely drink, rarely date, and don't swear...?"

Taking a deep breath, I hold his gaze. "I was raised Muslim. My parents are devout, and while I'm not, I respect their choices. If that's a problem for you, please tell me now? My last boyfriend didn't tell me for weeks. James the Jerk just wanted to get me into bed. Once he did, he called my parents terrorists, and I never saw him again."

Tears prick at my eyes, and I blink them away. I won't let James ruin this night for me. Assuming I haven't ruined it all on my own.

Austin sits back in his chair and stretches his legs under the table so the outside of his thigh touches mine. "Mik, I'm not that shallow. Or judgmental. Or...any of those things James the Jerk apparently was. In fact, if you want me to find him and punch him into next week, I will. Or at least threaten him a little."

He's completely serious. Now, I'm the one who's shocked.

"But you're... I Googled you," I say as I stare down at the rose. "You fought in Afghanistan. Iraq. My parents are Syrian. They applied for refugee status before I was born, became citizens ten years ago or so, and they love the United States. They're the most peaceful, kind people you'll ever meet, but still—"

"Hold up right there, sweetheart. Any man who would walk away from you because your parents are Muslim is a fucking idiot." He takes my hand and rubs his thumb over the sensitive skin on the underside of my wrist. "I used to be damn high up in military intelligence. Which means I've been trained to read micro-expressions. Tone of voice. Body language. You don't have to convince me of anything. Being Muslim doesn't make your parents terrorists. Or anything other than two people I hope I get to meet someday."

I relax a little, letting his gentle touch soothe my pounding heart. "You're too good to be true."

Austin snorts. "If I were..." With a shake of his head, he releases my hand. "You don't get where I was without a whole lot of bad disguised as good." The sadness in his voice makes my heart hurt, and I want to ask him to explain, but the server drops off two plates of tacos and our drinks, and he looks so relieved, I let it go.

For now.

Austin

"So, tell me about your family," Mikayla says when we've finished our meal and have a dish of flan between us.

"Mom and Dad live in New Haven. I was an only child for almost thirteen years, and then they decided to adopt. Dani was nine, and Gil—" I swallow the lump in my throat, "—he was my age."

"Was that hard? Suddenly having to share your parents?" Mik drains the last of her Aqua Fresca and grins. "My cousin lived with us for a couple of years, and I was *horrible* to my parents for at least six months. Until they grounded us both for sneaking out of the house—separately. We had to spend all weekend cleaning out the garage together and she told me what her home life had been like before. We bonded after that."

Running a hand through my hair, I pin my gaze over her shoulder, unable to look her in the eyes. "Nah. Dani was too cute to resent, and Gil...he and I were close for a while."

"Just for a while?" Her delicate fingers slide over mine, and I want to pull away, but there's something magnetic and calming about her touch. Something that frees the words stuck in my throat.

"When I enlisted...things went south pretty quick." Shaking my head, I force the words out. "He died five years ago."

"Oh, Austin. I'm sorry." She squeezes my hand, her eyes shining, and I pick up my spoon, needing to turn the focus of this conversation away from me. And Gil. Before I can no longer keep everything he did to me bottled up inside where it belongs.

"What about your cousin? Are you two still close?"

"We talk on the phone at least once a month. But she moved to France a few years ago. Fell in love with a great guy. So we don't get to see each other as often as we'd like."

"New topic," I say, forcing a smile. "This or that."

Mik's brows draw together. "I don't understand."

"What do you like better? Ice cream or chocolate? This? Or that?"

"Chocolate. Definitely chocolate."

IT'S close to nine when we leave the restaurant. Three hours passed in the blink of an eye, and I need more. Much more.

"I don't want to go back to the hotel yet," Mik says as she winds an arm around my waist. "Tomorrow morning is going to come way too early, and we have to take a boatload of samples. I'm worried someone's been spraying pesticide at the grow sites, and if so...all of our research will be worthless. And," her voice takes on a wistful tone, "we'll have to pack up and head back home."

"Wait. Tomorrow? You'd leave tomorrow?" Fuck. I'm not ready to say goodbye. Stopping in my tracks, I frame her face with my hands, tracing her cheekbones, memorizing this moment.

"No. Not tomorrow." Her lips curve into a sad smile. "But the day after. If we find evidence of pesticide. If not, I still have another four days."

"Then so do I. I want to see you again, Mikayla. Tomorrow. And the tomorrow after that. And the tomorrow after that. If you'll let me."

"What are we doing?" She searches my face as I still hold hers. "I work twelve-hour days. Even at home. I never take vacation. I haven't been on a date in three years. And you're—" Mik runs her hands down my chest, "—like Captain America, James Bond, and Indiana Jones all rolled into one."

"You're wrong, sweetheart." Dipping my head, I kiss her, tasting the single sip of my margarita she asked for—the last sip —that I handed over without a second thought. I keep it light, because I can't—I won't—scare her off. "You're on a date now."

And I'm none of those guys. Not even close.

"As for what we're doing?" Another kiss, this one deeper as I slide my hands down her back to rest just above her ass. "I don't know any more than you do. I'm not a smart bet, Mik. Too many ghosts hiding in my closet. You should walk away from me right now. Run even. But I can't bring myself to let you go."

Mik rests her cheek against my chest. "I want a tomorrow. I can't promise you more than that."

Wrapping my arms around her, I savor her curves, her scent, something fresh and clean with that tantalizing hint of lilacs. "Then we'll start with just one tomorrow. And see what happens."

***

UNWILLING TO LET this night end so soon, we walk through the outdoor bazaar—a permanent marketplace with everything from jewelry to wool blankets to cheap trinkets designed to catch the eye of tourists searching for a quick memento to bring home with them.

A year ago, I wouldn't have been caught *enjoying* something like this if my life depended on it. And then it hits me. A year ago. That's when everything changed. Last September. When Trev came to me and asked me to look into two JSOC guys hassling Ryker and Dax. And Ripper. That visit dredged up all the memories from the week Gil tortured me. I thought I'd banished them. Dealt with them. I was wrong.

"Hey. Where'd you go?" Mik asks, giving my waist a squeeze. "The look on your face...it was like you were seeing ghosts." When I don't reply, she frowns. "Talk to me, Austin. What's haunting you?"

We're standing next to a booth selling beaded bracelets, and rather than answer, I peer down at her and smile.

"What's your favorite color?"

In her confusion, that furrow between her brows begs to be kissed. "Purple. Why?"

Guiding her to the closest wall, out of the way of the crowds, I smooth my hands down her arms and kiss her as I gently turn her so her back is to the booth. I don't know why. It's not like she didn't *just* see the rows and rows of jewelry. "No looking over your shoulder. I'll be right back."

"Austin, what—?"

I cut her off with my lips on hers, and this kiss sends pure, overwhelming *need* shooting straight south of my belt, and Mik grabs on to me, her hold desperate as she offers me more. Her hips grind against me, and I know the exact moment she realizes how hard I am. Her heart is beating so fast, I feel it in my palms on her back, and I break away before I do something she definitely wouldn't be comfortable with—like cupping her breasts and running my thumbs over the tight nipples straining under her tank top.

"Trust me, Mikayla. I'll only be two minutes."

She's breathless, and nods before she pulls a water bottle from her bag and tries—with unsteady hands—to unscrew the cap. "I don't know why I should," she mutters. "Trust you, that is. Not when you keep doing *that*."

"Maybe *that* is the exact reason." Giving her shoulder a quick squeeze, I stride back to the booth and haggle with the vendor until she cuts the price of a raw amethyst and tourmaline bracelet by a third.

Mikayla's still facing away from me, so I call her name before I touch her, and the look on her face when she turns is part relief, part impatience, and...fuck. Part lust.

I take her hand and press the bracelet into her palm. "I don't know what happens after tomorrow, Mik. Maybe we never see one another again. But you should have something of this place. Of this night. Of me."

Her eyes shine as she looks from the polished stones to me.

"I'll say it again, Austin. You're too good to be true. Put it on me?"

"With pleasure, sweetheart."

An undercurrent of guilt churns in my stomach as I fasten the clasp. I didn't lie to her. I do want her to have something to hold on to from this night. From whatever this is we're sharing. But I can't get her words out of my head. *"Talk to me, Austin. What's haunting you?"*

She thinks I'm a good man. Maybe that's true. Or could be. But I'm also a fucking coward who used a pretty thing to avoid answering a serious question.

CHAPTER EIGHT

Morning comes too soon. I stayed out with Austin until close to eleven, and when we got back to the hotel, we retreated to a corner of the bar and talked until the staff kicked us out.

Before he said goodnight, he pressed me up against the wall and kissed me so thoroughly, I felt it down to my toes. When I got back to the room, I ached to touch myself. He featured in every single one of my dreams. Well, at least his face and *very* well-muscled chest.

But for all the hours we spent together, I still don't feel like I know the man. We danced around all the deep topics. His brother's death, his injury, the haunted look in his eyes.

Every time I asked him a serious question, he deflected. Maybe it's his military training, but I think there's more to it. Not that I was much better. I don't have a lot of experience to draw from, and ever since James the Jerk dumped me *after* talking me into bed, I've been too afraid to trust anyone with my body—or my heart.

Yet, when Austin and I kiss...it's like he understands me in a way no one else ever has. And he never once pressured me for more than I was willing to give. When we finally managed to step away from each other very early this morning and he had to go back to his room? The way he was walking looked very, *very* uncomfortable.

In the lobby, I fill my travel mug with coffee from the breakfast bar and wait for my students. But ten minutes after they're supposed to meet me, Li's the only one here.

"Where are Isaiah and Corey?" I ask.

Rolling her eyes, then dropping her gaze to the floor, she sighs. "Corey talked Isaiah into going out to a bar in town. Drinks and karaoke. I told them there was no way I was staying out as late as they wanted." Her voice drops to a whisper, "And Isaiah didn't come to my room last night."

Whoa. They insisted on separate rooms when we booked this hotel, but Li's staying next to me—on the opposite side from Austin—and the walls here? They're pretty thin. I've heard him sneaking into her room every night.

"I can go knock on their doors," she says quietly.

"I'll do it. They *knew* we had to get an early start today so we could hit up Sites One *and* Four." Frustration edges my tone, and I blow out a breath. "Sorry. I shouldn't take this out on you."

"No. You're right. They were irresponsible. Corey said he wanted to blow off some steam, but that's no excuse." She fiddles with the hem of her t-shirt. "I'll load up the bags." Li grabs the rolling sample case and holds out her hand for my backpack. Flashing me a shy smile, she says, "This way, I can pick the music."

"Oh, that's sneaky. You're learning," I say before rushing back to the elevator. My sports bra feels too tight across my ribs. Staying up late two nights in a row, 6:00 a.m. wake-up calls, and all those dreams about Austin? Not smart. If I don't slow down, I won't be able to get more than halfway through the day without needing my rescue inhaler.

Breathe, Mik. If you have an attack, you're going to feel like crap when you see Austin tonight.

Except if we find evidence of pesticide use, or if we have to wait another day to take samples, I'll feel like crap anyway. Knocking on Isaiah's door, I force myself to breathe slowly and put on my sternest "Ph.D boss" face.

The shuffling from inside only spurs my frustration on, but I wait, hands on my hips, until he opens the door. "Isaiah. Crap. What happened to you?" He looks like death—if death had gotten into a bar fight and spent the night in a gutter. And the smell. I cover my mouth and nose and take a step back. "Oh, God. Open a window or something."

"Sorry, Dr. Mik," he croaks. "I...food poisoning." He turns, racing for the bathroom, and the distinct sound of vomiting makes my stomach do backflips and sends nausea crawling up the back of my throat. I can't handle other people throwing up. It's a sure-fire way to activate my own gag reflex.

"Isaiah?" I call when the sound fades and the toilet flushes.

He braces his hand on the wall as he makes his way back to the door. "We went to this bar. And fuck. I've been up...all night. I can't go more than," he swallows hard, his skin turning greener and a sheen of sweat breaking out over his brow, "a few minutes without the bathroom."

"Do you need a doctor? Or to go to the hospital?"

"No. Just...shit." He tries to laugh, but then his face twists into a grimace and he doubles over and holds his stomach. "We'll get...to Site One tomorrow... Oh God." Isaiah shuts the door in my face, and a few seconds later, I can hear him throwing up yet again.

Corey looks marginally better, and his room doesn't smell,

but when he tries to tell me he'll be okay in an hour, I wave him off. "No. Rest. Li and I can handle some of the analysis from yesterday's samples and head out to Site Four on our regular rotation. Just...don't ever do that again, okay? We only have a few more days to finish up all of our experiments—and that's only *if* the sites are clean. We can't afford another delay."

He nods, and the look on his face is one of pure and complete shame. He knows he screwed up, and I soften my tone. "Lots of water. Call down and have the restaurant send up some apples and toast. Nothing else. At all. And check on Isaiah. He's in a lot worse shape than you are."

"I'm so sorry, Dr. Mik," Corey says as he starts to shut the door. "For everything."

THE TREK to Site Four only takes twenty minutes. Unlike the previous two days, the weather on the mountain is pleasant, with thin sunshine streaming through the clouds. Li opens the collection kit and spreads it out on a small tarp. "Root and leaf samples today, Dr. Mik?"

"Yes. Be careful with the roots. They're the most toxic when they're dried, but even fresh, they can give you one heck of a headache if a cutting touches your skin."

She pulls on a pair of latex gloves before picking up the sample scissors and sterilizing them. "I remember."

Kicking myself for not trusting her, I pop open one of the small vials and fill it with teaspoon of soil. "I should know better. You've never needed a reminder. About anything, really."

She offers me a shy smile. "I love this work. I won't screw it up."

It takes us three hours. Li carefully excises root samples

from six of the eighteen plants in this caldera, leaf cuttings from another six, and labels everything while I test the soil pH, collect rainwater from little pools all around the site, and download the temperature, humidity, wind, and rainfall data from the past four days.

The first week we were here, most of our time was consumed with setting up our equipment. The monitoring stations in the center of each grow site record fifty different pieces of data every hour of every day, but we're in such a remote area, there's no way to get a signal back to the lab. So all of our data has to be transferred manually. Tomorrow, we're supposed to spend the day installing a relay so once we leave, we can continue to collect data.

By the time we return to the trailer, it's well after 2:00 p.m., and my unease has risen to a truly unhealthy level. I hate that we couldn't get out to Site One today, and I just know I'm not going to be able to sleep tonight—or enjoy my date with Austin—if I can't find out whether someone's been spraying. I saw no evidence of anything untoward at Site Four, but One is the largest, with a full twenty-seven plants.

I took a puff from my daily inhaler once we got here, and my chest no longer feels tight. If I carried the full sample kit by myself, the normally forty-five minute hike would probably take me an hour. Still, I could make it there and back before sunset.

"Li, I'm going to Site One."

She looks up from the lab bench where she's cataloging her samples and frowns. "No, Dr. Mik. It's too dangerous. That climb..."

"I'll be careful. Take it slow. The other day was a fluke." It's hard not to let my frustration show. Asthma doesn't make me weak. Or vulnerable. "It'll be worse if I have to go another day wondering if someone's spraying up there. Trust me."

Li's warm brown eyes shine. "Do you really think—?"

This research project will help her make a name for herself in the academic community, and she wants that more than anything. To prove to her family that she chose the right career. Her parents—like mine—wanted her to be a medical doctor.

"I don't know." It's the easiest answer, though I don't believe it. Still, I'd rather not dash her hopes until after I climb the rocky path to Site One and see for myself. Let her be innocent and optimistic for another few hours at least. Kneeling next to my pack, I check for my inhaler, then add the sample kit, a couple of granola bars, and a bottle of water. It's been nice most of the day, but I still grab my poncho before clipping the GPS to my belt.

"I should be back in three hours. Lock the door, okay?" After I tighten the straps on the backpack, I force a smile. "Run the pesticide tests on all the samples we collected today while I'm gone, and as soon as I get back, we'll do a quick assay on the ones from Site One. Then we'll know for sure."

Before I slip out the door, I glance back to see her chewing on her lower lip, her face drawn with worry. "Be careful, Dr. Mik," she says quietly. "Don't push yourself too hard."

"I won't. I promise."

HALFWAY UP THE MOUNTAIN, a light mist starts to cool my cheeks. Not long after, the wind picks up, and what had been a pleasant tickle of precipitation turns into sharp, wet needles stinging my skin.

At the old wooden bridge, I stop and try to shield my face from the rain as I scan the sky. I don't like the look of those clouds, but as long as I'm quick, I'll make it back over the river before it's in any danger of flooding.

The climb gets slicker and more miserable with every step, and not even my poncho offers me much protection against the deluge. But I've come this far, and according to the GPS, I only have another tenth of a mile.

Head down. Keep moving. The trip back will be a heck of a lot faster. And easier.

My lungs are starting to protest, and the sky's turned from light gray to a sickly mix of green and slate by the time I reach the crevasse leading to Site One. At least I'm not climbing anymore. A bolt of lightning arcs through the looming clouds, and the thunder obliterates all other sounds only a second later.

Crap. This is bad. Ducking through the narrow entrance to the private oasis filled with orchids, I slide my pack off my shoulder, unzip it, and freeze.

Three men are spread out around the basin, each with a large, black plastic tub next to them and spades in their hands.

Poachers. Oh God. My lungs start to seize, and I pick up my pack and try to back away quietly, to get out of here and far enough away to be able to stop and retrieve my inhaler, but the panic tightening my chest spreads up to my throat, and I start coughing and wheezing. The closest man, tall, with forest green coveralls and a black raincoat, turns and stares right at me.

"Fuck! Arturo!" he shouts and sprints for me.

I won't be able to breathe in another minute, but the look in his eyes...I have to run. My legs give out after two steps, and I crash to the ground, clawing at the zipper on my pack until he hauls me up by the arms and shakes me.

"You should not be here, bitch!"

My whole world turns dark until a familiar voice reaches my ears through the roaring of my heartbeat. "Let go of her!"

As I'm about to lose the battle for consciousness, a hand braces the back of my neck and something presses to my lips.

"Breathe!" Corey says sharply, and a hit of Albuterol floods my mouth. I force myself to take as much of it in as I can, and the world in front of me comes back into soft focus.

I push the air from my lungs before Corey gives me another dose. "Fucking hell," he mutters when I blink up at him, my entire body shaking. Rain pelts my cheeks, and the thunder cracks so close, he curses again.

The two other men loom over us. "You said you were *positive* she wouldn't be here today," the big one snaps.

"I was! We never visit a site alone," Corey says, his brown eyes wild as his gaze pings between me and the man behind him. "I swear, Martín. I did everything you asked."

"You're an idiot," Martín says. "Now we have to clean up your mistake."

The young man I've worked with for two years flinches and tightens his hold on me. He's crouching on the wet, rocky ground, my torso braced against his bent knee. "Why, Dr. Mik? You should be in the lab with Li."

"Wh-what...are you doing?" I croak, my voice shaky from the meds and the looks on Martín and Arturo's faces. "These plants...are protected. The government—"

"Governments can be bought," Martín says, his eyes blazing with anger. "And these plants are worth a fortune."

The third man—Arturo—rummages through a bag a few feet away and comes back with a thick, plastic zip tie. I push against Corey, hoping to loosen his hold, but he's too strong, and Arturo grabs my hands, fastens the zip tie around my wrists tightly, and yanks me to my feet.

"Please don't hurt me," I whimper.

Martín pulls a gun from a holster at his hip. "We should kill her now." He nods towards the narrow entrance to the caldera. "Throw her off the side of the cliff. No one would question her falling to her death in this weather. Or we could knock her out and toss her in the river."

"No!" Corey shoves Martín back, and the thug stumbles, but doesn't go down. "You promised me no one would be hurt. I never would have helped you—"

"Your father owes the cartel more money than you can earn in a lifetime. You have no choice. But you said this grove would be deserted until tomorrow." Martín shakes his head and adjusts his grip on the pistol. "Two options, asshole. We kill her now, or we sell her with the orchids. Pretty sure the cartel could find a buyer for a woman as pretty as she is."

Oh God. No. They can't.

But they can. I'm no match for these men, wouldn't be even if my hands were free. Arturo still has an iron grip on my arms, and my heart is racing so fast, I'm terrified I'm going to succumb to another asthma attack any second. My gaze darts around the basin, to the narrow passage to freedom—or at least to a wider, more open space where I might be able to hide somewhere—but with the three of them surrounding me, and at least one of them armed, I'll never make it more than a step or two.

"You won't say anything, will you? Dr. Mik, you have to promise me," Corey begs, pulling me away from Arturo and turning me to face him.

"I promise." Anything to get out of this alive. How could Corey do this? To the orchids. To the chance for a real treatment for Parkinson's. To the team. To me? "I'll tell Li I couldn't reach the site. The storm was too bad. We'll just leave. Go back to the hotel like nothing ever happened."

As if Mother Nature wants to help me sell my story, another bright flash of lightning pierces the canopy. The thunder is even louder than before, and Corey hunches his shoulders.

"She's coming with us," Arturo says as he hefts one of the

large plastic totes with a massive orchid inside onto his shoulder.

Martín grabs a duffel bag full of tools and sneers at Corey as he passes us. "Bring her, fuckup, or you'll find yourself tossed over the cliff with her. Once we deal with her, we'll come back for the rest of the orchids."

The wind makes it hard to see as Corey drags me along behind them. "Why?" I ask, tears mixing with the rain pelting my cheeks.

"My dad...he owes so much money." His voice is choked with emotion, and he shakes his head as he pulls me through the narrow opening. The rocks scrape my left shoulder, tearing my poncho and the flannel shirt I have on underneath. "They threatened his life. And the orchids are worth so much..."

"Even if they kill me—" a sob wells in my throat, though I try to keep my voice low so only Corey can hear, "—you won't get away with this. The government will find out about the poaching, and they'll go after all three of you."

"No. They won't. Queenie? The Zebra Stripe hybrid? It's virtually indistinguishable from the Blushing Note visually. Last year, I flew down here and set up a greenhouse for the cartel. I would have come back in October to harvest the Blushing Notes and replace them with the hybrids, but then the fellowship came through and...well..."

They're taking me in the opposite direction of the lab, to the back side of the mountain, and as we pick our way over loose rocks on a path so narrow, Corey has to push me ahead of him, I get my first good look at a large plateau with a Jeep parked in the center.

Arturo and Martín load the tote and tools into the back, and Corey yanks me against his side. I'm shaking so hard, I can barely keep my knees from buckling.

Rainwater thunders down the mountain in a newly formed

waterfall, bringing twigs, rocks, and even whole tree branches with it, a massive, liquid landslide to our right, and to the left of the plateau, the cliff drops off sharply.

Corey stops a good twenty feet from the Jeep and hisses in my ear. "Punch me, Dr. Mik. Kick me. Just do *something* and *run*. Please. It's your only chance."

I'll never make it. Not as panicky as I am. Not over this unsteady ground.

All I can do is stare at Corey, pleading without words until he shakes me. "Do it. Now!"

If I don't try...I'm dead. So I bring my hands out in front of me and ram my elbow into Corey's gut. The strike is ineffective at best, but he plays it up, doubling over and crashing to his knees.

Spinning around, fighting off the lingering dizziness from the meds and my overwhelming terror, I take off a run back the way we came.

Behind me, Arturo and Martín shout, but with how loud the storm is, I can't hear what they're saying, and I fight my urge to look back, to see how close they are.

My boots slip on the rocks, and with my hands tied, my balance is off. I crash against the side of the cliff, but miraculously don't go down.

Keep going. Faster!

My legs start to burn, and the first wheezes and whispers of panic spread out from my chest.

Just. Breathe. If you don't, you're dead.

I repeat my new mantra over and over again, and for maybe a minute, it seems to work. But then rocks explode just in front of me, and a tiny shard slices my cheek. It isn't until it happens again that I realize what it is. They're shooting at me.

Blinding light sears my eyes, and a crack of thunder directly overhead makes me yelp. My left foot lands on a loose rock, and pain rockets from my ankle up my lower leg as I start to fall. Too afraid to think straight, I overcompensate and stumble across the narrow path.

No! I'm too close to the edge of the cliff, and I grab for something—anything—as I hit the ground and my head, shoulders, and chest dangle over the precipice. My arms are pinned under me, rocks digging into my hands, and I try to wriggle backwards, but I'm slipping by inches.

All I can see below me are spindly tree branches growing out of the nearly vertical cliff face, and a small, narrow ledge so far away, if I hit it, I'm sure I'll die.

And then a hand grabs my ankle. "Bitch," Arturo growls. "Guess I got what I wanted after all."

I don't understand what he means until he shoves me off the edge. Time shifts, moving so slowly, the tree branches come into perfect focus as I fall. I hit one, then another and another. I try to grab for them and snag my bound wrists for a split second until the branch breaks under my weight. The narrow outcropping rushes up to meet me, and my shoulder, hip, and head explode in pain.

My throat closes up, cutting off my scream, and I can't move. Can't think. Can't do anything but fight to breathe until the darkness takes me.

CHAPTER NINE

Mikayla

I'm choking. Can't get enough air. Every part of my body hurts. My head most of all. And my hip. Something sharp jabs into my skin, and after a few seconds, I realize I'm lying on my inhaler. I can feel it. Corey must have put it in my pocket after he dosed me back at the grow site.

Rolling over takes the last bit of energy I can muster. It's so cold. My clothes are soaked through, and the rain... Water pours down from the top of the cliff above. I can hear it, feel it splatter against my back. If I hadn't been lying on my side, I'd be dead already. Drowned by the runoff. The ledge is so narrow, barely six feet deep, and a stronger deluge pushes me closer to the edge, but I brace my feet against a rock jutting up from the uneven ground and manage to reclaim the few inches I lost.

Darkness surrounds me, and until a bolt of lightning brightens the sky in the distance, I don't process that I must have been down here at least two hours already. It was still light when Arturo threw me off the cliff. They haven't come back for me. Do they think I'm dead?

Inhaler. Focus on the inhaler.

It's my only chance to live through the night. I can feel my throat closing up, and it's like someone's winding ropes around my torso, tighter and tighter. The sharp pain in my hip intensifies as I wedge my bound hands into my pocket and fumble for the medicine.

The mouthpiece is cracked, and as I pull it free, a thin whimper escapes my lips. The piece of plastic is embedded in the top of my thigh, and it burns. I can feel the blood coating my fingers, but the rain washes it away quickly.

If I can stop this attack, I can take stock of the rest of me. Not until then.

My whole focus is on breathing out...just a little. My hands shake as I wrap my lips around the busted plastic, and my fingers almost slip off the inhaler twice before I get a good enough grip. The metallic taste fills my mouth, and I concentrate hard on drawing in just a little. Enough to take a second hit.

But when I try for another dose, nothing happens. It's empty.

No! Not now!

I'm so cold. My teeth chatter violently, and my entire body shivers, which only makes everything hurt more. I don't think I have the strength—or even the will—to move again. No one will ever find me here. Halfway down a cliff in the middle of nowhere? It's well after five now. Li's probably panicking and blaming herself. She won't come out here. Not in this storm. Not alone. At least she'll be safe. She and Isaiah.

Unless Corey tells Arturo and Martín about them. Unless they decide we all need to die.

My parents...my friends...they'll never know what

happened to me. And Austin. This was supposed to be our tomorrow. Our chance to talk about all the things he wouldn't say last night. To figure out if we had something worth fighting for.

Now we'll never know. I'll never feel his lips on mine again. His arm around me. I'd give anything to see him one more time. To be able to tell my parents I love them. To have a chance at living another day.

The only part of me that's warm? My eyes. Tears stream across my nose and down my left temple, hot trails that cool all too soon. I'm not shivering as much anymore. That's bad. My core temperature's dropping too low.

I won't last much longer, and maybe...the wind and the rain and the cold will be a blessing. Maybe I'll just fade away. Fall asleep and never wake up.

Austin

It's after eight, and I haven't heard from Mik. I've been pacing for an hour, even put a note on my door and went down to the bar, poked my head into the restaurant, and scanned all the tables. If she got bad news today, would she hide in her room? She was so worried about losing credibility, not being able to continue her research...maybe she needs to be alone.

But if the worst happened, she'll be leaving tomorrow, and I can't just let her go without seeing her one more time. Determined to knock on her door and beg her to talk to me—if she's in there—I climb the stairs, and as I reach the landing, I hear a woman's panicked voice.

"Isaiah! Open the door! Dr. Mik went out to Site One and

never came back! She's out there somewhere in the jungle. I need help!"

Racing down the hall as the door on the other side of Mik's room opens, I call out, "Wait!"

The young woman—she can't be older than mid-twenties—turns, and tears glisten on her cheeks. "You were with Dr. Mik last night," she says, pointing at me. A man stumbles through the open door, not much older, looking like death itself.

"Yeah, I was. Where is she? What happened?"

"You could be the one who...who...*did something* to her!" She darts behind the guy, and he stands up a little straighter, though the look on his face is nothing but complete and total confusion.

I glare at them for having the gall to think *I'd* do anything to Mikayla. But they don't know me and can't have any clue about the code I live by, so I snap to full attention. "I'm retired Air Force Major General Austin J. Pritchard. Former head of Joint Special Operations Command. JSOC. You ever hear of it?"

They both shake their heads.

"We're the ones who catch the bad guys. We oversee SEAL Team Six, Delta Force, and a whole lot more. You don't get much higher as one of the good guys. I haven't seen Mikayla since very early this morning. Tell me what happened."

The woman peeks out from behind her cohort, and her voice is so soft, I have to strain to hear her words. "Isaiah and Corey were sick today, so it was just me and Dr. Mik. After we went out to Site Four and took all of our samples for the day, we went back to the lab, but Dr. Mik was so worried about Site One, she decided to go by herself."

Shit. Hiking in the mountains alone?

The guy, Isaiah from the girl's gesturing, takes her by the shoulders. "When did she leave?"

"A little after two. She promised me she'd be back by five. I waited until six-thirty before I came back here. I wanted to go after her, but the second GPS unit wasn't working, and the storm was too bad. We have to call the police."

"The police aren't going to send a search party deep into the mountains in the middle of a storm," I say sharply, and both of them flinch. "If she's lost—or hurt—I can find her."

"How?" the woman asks. "You don't know where any of the sites are, or the lab, or—"

"Presumably, you can tell me. I'm trained for this. Or was. It's been a while since I've deployed on a search and rescue op, but I'm a hell of a lot more qualified than some city police officer."

The two of them stare at me. Ten seconds. Twenty. Thirty. I'm about to bark orders at them when Isaiah clears his throat. "Li, where's Corey?"

She shakes her head. "In his room, I guess. I came to see you first."

"That's your third?" I ask. "Where?"

Li points to the room across from Mik's, and I pound on the door. "Open up. Now!"

There's no answer, and I spin back around and level my gaze at Isaiah. "You two were sick?"

"Food poisoning," he says, his voice rough. "We went to this dive bar..."

"Then where is he?"

The door opens, and Corey leans against the frame. Dark circles brace his eyes, and his hair is wet. The rumpled t-shirt and pajama pants cling to his frame, like he just got out of the shower. "Who the fuck are you?"

I repeat my introduction, and the kid's bloodshot eyes widen when I give him my full title.

"Corey," Li says, "Dr. Mik went out to Site One on her own

and didn't come back. General? Major? Pritchard says he can find her."

"Shit. The weather report said we were in for a hell of a storm today." Corey's voice is strained, and I study him, trying to figure out why warning bells are going off in my head. But I'm so worried about Mikayla, I can't think straight.

Focus. Plan. Assess. Act.

"You're sure you can find her?" Isaiah asks. "She has asthma. If she had an attack hiking, she could be in real trouble."

"If you can get me the GPS coordinates for where she was going and show me the route she'd take to get there? Yes. I can."

Corey staggers towards the other two, with all the grace of a guy who's spent the entire day throwing up, and as I take a step closer to Isaiah's room, the stench—like a garbage can lined with shit left out in the sun too long—hits me like a sledgehammer. "I'm in two-three-six. You three figure out what the fuck you're going to do. I'm going to gear up so I can head out."

"I'm still going to call the police," Corey says and pulls a cell phone from the pocket of his pajama pants. "But you're really in the Air Force?"

"Was. Twenty-four years, six months, and nine days. Look, I get that you don't know me. But we're wasting time. I can make a few calls, probably find out where your Site One is in an hour or two. But that might be an hour or two Mik doesn't have."

They've got all of ten seconds before I call Ryker McCabe. Because his wife, Wren, is the best hacker I've ever worked with. She could break into the Smithsonian's computer system and probably into Mik's email faster than I can pack up my shit. "Fucking ridiculous," I mutter as I turn on my heel and stride for my room.

"Wait!" Corey calls just as I pull out my key. "I have a map and can get you the coordinates. But we should get Dr. Mik's key from the front desk. She has spare inhalers in her room. If she's hurt out there, she might need one." The kid sounds like he's about to lose his shit, and even though I could pick the lock on Mikayla's door faster than any of them could make it to the front desk and convince them to give them a key, I nod.

"Fine. You," I say as I point to Isaiah. He straightens with a groan. "You get the key. Li and Corey, you're going to show me where you last saw Mikayla and the route she'd take to get to the site."

LI SITS on the floor next to my bed with her arms around her knees. "I should have gone with her," she says while Corey pulls up a map on his laptop.

"If you had, both of you could be out there. And we wouldn't know," Corey replies and zooms in on a remote area a good forty minute drive from the hotel. "Site One is here, and Dr. Mik would have taken this trail."

I enter the coordinates in my GPS, along with those for the mobile lab unit. "Give me all the other sites as well. You keep supplies there?"

"Not really. A spare bottle of water. A protein bar."

Isaiah bursts through the door with two inhalers and a small plastic box of pills clutched in his hands. "Take these. The meds are anti-inflammatories."

"You have a car?" I ask. Shoving the inhalers and the box into my waterproof rucksack, I yank open my dresser drawer, grab my hunting knife, and strap it to my thigh. The second knife—my backup—is already sheathed to my belt.

My pack is kitted out with everything I'd need if I were stranded for up to three nights. Two Mylar heat blankets, a camping mat, waterproof fire starters, MREs, a full first aid kit, flares, and a solar-powered battery for the GPS and my phone. If only I'd listened to my dad and packed a sat phone, but those damn things are heavy.

Li hands me a set of keys. "It's the black Land Rover at the end of the first row of the parking lot."

Shouldering my pack, I usher the three of them out of my room and lock the door. "As soon as I can get a cell signal, I'll call the hotel and let you know she's safe."

"You say that like you're sure you'll find her," Li whispers.

"Failure is not an option." I zip up my windbreaker, then pat myself down, expecting to find half a dozen weapons and a tactical vest, but that's not my life anymore. Still, some habits don't die as easily as we hope.

Every time I blink, I see her face. Hear her laugh. And regret not sharing *anything* beyond the superficial with her last night. If I never see her again, I will curse my cowardice for the rest of my life. Because Mikayla? She's mine. I don't know how or why I know this, but I'm as sure of it as I am my own fucking name.

CHAPTER TEN

Austin

The closer I get to the mobile lab, the worse the weather turns. Thunderstorms in New England don't have anything on the ones in the mountains around here. If Mik is out in this, I hope to all that's holy she found shelter somewhere.

With the cloud cover, it's pitch dark all around me, outside of the headlights and semi-regular lightning strikes, which means slow going. The last thing I need is to drive off a cliff. GPS is a gift from the technology gods, but it's not foolproof.

My fingers ache from gripping the steering wheel so hard. Every scenario running through my mind is worse than the last. Mikayla injured somewhere after a bad spill. Suffering an asthma attack halfway back to the lab and being unable to get to her inhaler in time. Falling to her death—*No.*

I can't let myself go there.

I could drive halfway to Site One. It'd be dangerous, but this vehicle can handle it. If I did that, though, I could miss something. Some sign of Mik.

Or her body.

Forcing myself to continue all the way to the lab, I park and check inside, just in case she managed to make it back. No sign of her. The lights blaze—Li left them on so Mik could see them from a distance—but it's empty.

Tightening the straps on my pack, I steel myself for the climb. The trail—if you can call it that—is barely passable. Between the driving rain and the wind, it's half destroyed. My foot sinks into a six-inch-deep hole full of water ten minutes in, and I almost go down.

"Mikayla!" Shouting into the wind is useless, but I have to try. After close to an hour, I'm soaked to the bone, but Site One is just across the river and up a final steep climb.

The roar of the water is deafening, and the bridge...it's hanging on to the shore by sheer will. If I cross it, there's every chance it'll collapse under my weight. But I don't have a choice. Mikayla could be on the other side.

The wood cracks and strains with every step, but miraculously, it holds. Picking up the pace, I push myself through the last two tenths of a mile and squeeze through the narrow opening into the caldera.

The flashlight beam sweeps around the basin, and my God. It's so beautiful. Dozens of orchids cling to trees and large rocks, their roots gnarled and twisted like thick ropes. The entire space is smaller than a couple of baseball diamonds, but every single inch of it is green.

Clearing the caldera takes too long, and though the rain isn't as heavy as it was back at the lab, from the state of the ground, any evidence of Mik's presence—if she even made it here—is long gone.

A couple of the orchids look...odd though. Their roots are smaller. Shinier. And they're not as well entrenched as the others. Like someone's disturbed them recently. *Was* she here?

Did Mik do this trying to take samples? I pull out my phone, snapping a couple of photos.

Retreating to the rocky passage guarding the site, I have to duck under a curtain of hanging vines, and in my periphery, a scrap of orange fabric catches my eye. Mikayla's backpack. It was by her bed when I kissed her at her door a little after 1:00 a.m., and I'd commented on the color.

"For visibility," she'd said. *"The Mexican government promised us they'd patrol regularly up by the sites to deter the poachers."*

"Poachers? Mik, that sounds dangerous. And who'd want to poach orchids? You can buy them in every grocery store."

"Not this one. And if it goes extinct, all chances to use its roots to help treat Parkinson's go out the window."

She was here, and she left her backpack behind. It's open, everything inside soaked. A large sample with glass vials in individualized compartments, tools, a USB drive in a water-proof bag, a granola bar, and half a bottle of water. She'd never just leave this. No ID, no passport, no phone. The vials are empty, so something pulled her away from her work before she could start.

The icy pit in my stomach grows, and a large drop of rain slithering down my back only adds to my overwhelming sense of dread. "Mikayla! Answer me!"

She can't be far. Zipping up her pack, I secure it to mine with a couple of carabiners and push to my feet. The GPS shows a large, flat area on the other side of this spire, and I pick my way over the rocky trail, stopping every few steps to sweep the flashlight around the area and call her name.

When I emerge out onto the plateau, fear coils in my gut. Though the rain has half obscured the depressions, the tire tracks are still visible. Someone had a vehicle here. A big, heavy one. At least the size of the Land Rover. I follow the tracks for half a mile until they disappear, then return to the muddy expanse and search every fucking inch. Nothing.

Staring up at the dark sky, letting the rain pelt my cheeks, I beg whatever deity is up there to give me something. Anything. "Mikayla! Mik! Please answer me!"

"Some of the trails have steep drop-offs."

Corey's words echo in my ears, and I adjust my grip on the flashlight and retrace my steps on the way back to the grow site, searching for anything out of place. Small rock slides, anywhere the trees are sparse enough for someone to slip and fall over the edge. Every few feet, I aim the flashlight over the side of the cliff, peering down at the steep decline, calling her name.

And then the beam catches a glint of something. I almost miss it, but the rain is starting to let up now, and it's easier to see. There it is again. Twenty feet down. I grab the binoculars. "Fuck, Mikayla. No."

She's on her side, the small, rocky outcropping barely six feet wide. Spindly tree branches—some dead, some not—half-obscure her, but enough are broken that I can see her hands, shoulder, and part of her face.

I have to get down there—and find a way to get both of us back up.

I'm trained for this. To operate under the most intense conditions. But nothing prepares me for the fear that a woman I care for—a woman I think just might be the one for me—could be dead. My hands shake as I withdraw the rappelling line and secure one end of it around a large tree trunk. I don't have my belay controls, but the gloves I'm wearing will grip well enough —even in the rain.

Careful not to disturb too many rocks on my way down the cliff lest they fall directly onto Mikayla, I lower myself slowly, hand over hand, until my boots are solidly on the ground next to her. My bad shoulder aches, but I ignore the pain.

"Please be alive," I whisper as I kneel, strip off one of my gloves, and press my fingers to her neck.

A faint heartbeat. Thank fuck. But she's so cold. Her lips are tinged blue, and—goddammit. A zip tie is wrapped tightly around her wrists. Someone did this to her. The glint I saw? Her bracelet. The amethyst and tourmaline caught the light when nothing else would have.

I yank the hunting knife from the sheath on my thigh and snap the plastic in a single quick motion. "Mikayla, can you hear me, sweetheart?" I don't want to move her. The fall could have broken her neck, her back...any number of bones. But if I don't, she'll die of exposure. Between the wind and the rain, she's probably half-hypothermic already. Her fingers are badly pruned, which means she's been out here for hours.

I squeeze her hand, and she coughs weakly, then tries to draw in a wheezing breath. Relief sends me onto my ass, where I shed my ruck and paw through it for one of her inhalers. "Breathe out, Mik," I order as I gently part her lips and hold the mouthpiece in place.

Her eyelids flutter, and with my hand on her chest, I can feel the exhale. Dispensing a dose of the Albuterol, I wait, praying, until her lungs expand. She manages a second breath, then a third, each deeper than the last.

"Mik, it's Austin. I've got you now. Can you open your eyes? I need to know how badly you're hurt."

"Aus...tin?" Her voice is weak and slurred, but I've never been so grateful to hear anyone say my name.

"Thank God. I'm here, Mik. Tell me what hurts." Her lips aren't as blue as they were, but with the flashlight balanced on a rock just above her shoulder, I can't see any visible injuries other than a cut on her forehead close to her brow.

"Can't..." Mikayla forces her eyes open, but they aren't

focusing properly, and I lean closer so my face is bathed in light. "Numb."

If she broke her back—or worse, her neck—we're fucked. But as I race through a thousand possibilities for why she can't feel anything, she moves her legs, just enough. Then her right arm. Her left is pinned under her.

Field assessment was never my strong suit. I can shoot, fight, run tactical, but I was always shit at medical.

"Don't let them find me," she mumbles, her eyes closing.

"Who? Who did this to you? How long have you been out here?" I start at her feet, patting her down, gently squeezing her ankles, calves, knees, halfway up her thighs.

"Don't know." Her body trembles, and my heart leaps into my throat. No. Not trembling. She's shivering. She's numb because she's been out here in the rain and wind soaked to the bone.

"Mik, this is important." I slap her cheeks lightly to get her to open her eyes. "I need you to focus on me and answer my questions. As soon as I know your neck and back are okay, I can get you out of here."

She blinks hard a couple of times, and then nods. Shit. If her neck was broken, that was the *wrong* thing for her to do.

"What day is it?"

"Sunday."

"Where did we meet?"

The corners of her mouth curve into a weak smile, and shit, even out here, injured, half-drowned, she's beautiful and perfect and all I want is to be able to hold her. "Bar."

"Just a couple more, sweetheart." I take my finger and trace it along her jaw. "Can you feel this?"

"Uh huh."

Continuing down her body, I reach her right wrist. "What about now?"

"Uh huh."

Slipping my hand under her torn rain jacket, flannel shirt, and tank top, I find her waist. "Now?"

"Yes," she whispers. "Please...just get me out of here."

The desperation in her voice shatters my control, and I slide one arm under her knees and another behind her back with my fingers cradling her nape. She whimpers when I pull her to my chest and buries her face against my neck. I can't climb with her like this, but I couldn't let her lie there another second.

"It's a twenty-foot climb, Mik. Getting back up there is going to be hard. I need to know you trust me." Checking the back of her head for lumps under the guise of smoothing her hair, I'm relieved when I find only a little swelling. How she managed to fall without serious injury is a fucking miracle.

"You c-came for m-me," she says, her teeth starting to chatter. "I t-trust y-you."

Mik clings to me when I set her down, braced against the steep rock face, and I try to calm her. "Shhh, sweetheart. I'm not going anywhere. But in order to get us out of here, I need to find a way to tie you to me so you don't fall."

Her shivering is getting worse, and if I can't get her warm soon, she's going to be in real trouble. Pulling off my belt, I maneuver her until the canvas strap is under her ass, then buckle it as loosely as I can. I have a couple of bungee cords in my pack, and clip them almost like a harness, one around each of her thighs, and all four ends secured to the belt. "This'll hold you like a seat. But you'll need to hang on to me. Can you do that?"

"Th-think so."

Dropping into a crouch, I tie a figure eight knot to the belt, then turn so my back is to her, pulling the rope up and winding it around my torso and through the straps of my ruck. There's just enough slack for me to take the blight and use my last cara-biner to hold it fast.

"Put your arms around my neck. You have to hold on. Don't let go for anything. This is a shitty harness, but it's all I have."

"I can do it." The tremors in her voice don't give me a lot of confidence. She's fucking terrified. She's not the only one. I should have swapped my ruck around so I could feel her pressed against me, but I don't want to take the extra time. We have to get somewhere warm and dry so I can find out who hurt her. And then make them pay.

Mikayla

My head feels like it's about to roll off my shoulders, and the only thing keeping me conscious right now is holding on to Austin. The hard muscles under my palms, the grunts of exertion and pain as he climbs hand over hand up a thin rope to the top of the cliff. Where I fell. No. Where I was dropped.

I try to swallow my sob, but from his quick flinch, I don't think I was completely successful. He knows someone hurt me. I'm going to have to tell him what happened. How the kid I sponsored, the one who said I gave him a future he didn't deserve, was part of this.

I was so stupid, thinking I could come out here on my own. Thinking it would be safe. But in three weeks, we'd never seen another soul. And Corey...I never thought...

We slip a few feet, and Austin curses as I tighten my arms around his neck. How is he doing this? Carrying me up a mountain? Heck, how did he find me in the first place?

With a guttural shout, he pulls us up, again and again, his

feet making scraping sounds against the rocks, and my teeth chattering incessantly.

After what feels like forever, we're level with the trail, and Austin slides forward on his belly along the narrow path, twisting himself until he's stretched out safely, then pushes up on one elbow. It's dark, and I can only see a hint of his profile because my vision goes soft and hazy and my stomach pitches. I'm so cold.

Before he found me, I'd feared I'd crack a tooth. Until everything slowed, then stopped and I couldn't feel anything. Couldn't muster the energy to care. Now, I care very much, and all I want is to be warm. With him. In his arms.

And then I am. In his arms at least, huddled against the rocks. "Look at me, sweetheart." His firm tone helps me focus, and I force my eyes open. "We need to get out of these wet clothes, and you need a doctor. I parked the Land Rover at your lab, and it's a solid hour hike at least—"

"No." Shaking my head is a mistake, because everything goes fuzzy for a few seconds. "Poachers," I manage. "Stealing the orchids. That's who..." I shudder. "They know where the lab is. And the hotel."

It's hard to make out his expression in the dim light, but he cups my cheek and I lean into his touch. "Mik, we don't have a choice. I can't carry you all the way back to town, and you need a doctor."

"What if...? Austin, they had guns." I can't face Corey again, and if the other two...crap, I can't even pull their names out of my muddled thoughts...if they come after us, they could kill Austin. "If anything happened to you..."

"Sweetheart, if they come after us—hell, if I find them anytime, anywhere for the rest of their lives, they're going to wish they'd never been born. I've spent the past twenty some odd years of my life evading, fighting, and killing men trained to kill me." Austin traces my lips with his thumb, and I just want to be somewhere safe with him. "I won't let anything happen to you. But we have to get to the Land Rover."

He leans in, and his lips are warm. Demanding. Kissing him makes me believe everything's going to be okay. That maybe we'll get to have that tomorrow I so desperately want.

I whimper when he pulls away, but he smiles at me, though up close, I can see the concern in his hazel eyes. "You're safe with me, Mikayla. Always."

CHAPTER ELEVEN

Poachers. Fucking poachers. Those bastards zip tied her wrists and what? Pushed her over the edge of a cliff? Or did she just fall? Mikayla isn't in any shape to walk or answer questions, so I carry her, and she clings to me like her life depends on it, still shivering violently. I'd pull out one of the mylar heat blankets for her, but with the wind practically blowing sideways, it wouldn't do much good.

We don't make it more than a quarter mile down the mountain when the roar of the river drowns out the rain, the thunder, and the chattering of Mik's teeth in my ear.

"Austin? Wh-what's that sound?" She lifts her head from my shoulder, and when I shine the light over where the bridge should be, she swallows a sob. Alone, I might be able to find a way to cross and not drown, but with Mikayla, there's no chance. Only half of the bridge remains, and there's no way it'll hold us.

Swinging the light in a slow arc, I find a stand of three trees huddled together that should offer us a little protection from the wind. "We'll find another way back to the car," I say as I press a kiss to the top of her head and then sink down with my back against the thickest trunk.

"Scale of one to ten. How do you feel?" The GPS doesn't offer me much hope we'll be able to get anywhere safe tonight. Not if I have to carry her the whole way.

"Th-three." I check her pulse as she peers up at me, and fuck. Her pupils are dilated, her lips parted slightly, and her heartbeat isn't steady. She needs food, water, and to be somewhere warm and dry, and if I can't provide that soon, I'm afraid she won't survive the night.

I'd give my left nut for a better map—or cell signal—but since that's not going to happen, I have to improvise.

"I need you to focus for me, sweetheart." Shifting her closer in a desperate attempt to keep her even a single degree warmer, I show her the GPS screen. "You know this area a hell of a lot better than me. Have you seen any structures between the lab and Site One? Anything we can get to without crossing the river?"

"Nuh-uh." Mikayla's eyes close, and she curls against me, shaking so violently, I'm worried she's having a seizure. A low moan escapes her lips, and then she stills, all the tension leaving her body as she passes out.

"Mik!" *Fuck. No!* I need her to stay conscious. But not even light slaps to her cheek or rubbing her hands does any good. Though she's still breathing, her lips have taken on a bluish tinge again, and her skin—even under her tank top—is like ice.

Staring at the GPS, I zoom in and out, checking every square mile for something—anything—that might function as a shelter. We don't need much. Just somewhere I can protect us against the driving rain and wind.

There. About a mile away. A short, steep descent, but the

black square on the grid looks like a structure. Anything with at least three walls will work. Hell, even two. I have enough plastic sheeting and mylar blankets in my ruck to seal us off from the wind, and if there's a roof, we'll be protected from the rain.

Hoisting Mik in a modified fireman's carry so I can move faster, I follow the river for half a mile, then turn east. More than once, I slip on the steep, slick rocks, but I make it down two hundred feet in under half an hour.

Mikayla shudders from time to time, but thankfully, she doesn't protest being carried across my shoulders.

What I thought might be an old military structure turns out to be ruins of a small building—maybe a craftsman's shop—at least three or four hundred years old. I've studied every single known structure on the Maya Trail, and this one never came up in any of my research.

But if I never discovered it, it's unlikely anyone else knows about it either, which should keep us safe for the night. At least until the storm passes.

I set Mik down close to the entrance and clear the room. Plenty of brush in one corner, likely deposited by the wind, but I kick it aside and nothing skitters out from hiding. No wild animals, snakes, or poisonous spiders.

It'll work. Unpacking the camping mat, I roll it out along the back wall. The space isn't airtight by any means; the roof is missing in huge chunks—except for the back corner.

Carefully, I lay out everything I think we'll need. Sleeping bag, protein bars, two bottles of water, Mik's inhaler, anti-inflammatories, and the mylar blankets to help trap our body heat.

I can't stand being even a few feet away from her for another minute, so I cradle her to my chest and carry her back to the makeshift bed.

"Mik? I don't know if you can hear me, but you need to be warm, sweetheart. And that means getting out of these wet clothes."

I've been soaked for hours, but I've also been moving, and now that I'm not, I can feel the chills setting in. I strip off my own pants, t-shirt, sweatshirt, and socks. Everything except for my boxer briefs. I want her. I've wanted her since I first spoke to her, but I won't disrespect her, even if it means sleeping in wet boxers.

"No sex on the first date. Or second."

"I was raised in a very conservative family."

Her honor—her comfort—are second only to her life. After I get her shoes and socks off, I find swelling around her left ankle. Retrieving a small towel from my pack, I pat her foot and lower leg dry, then wrap the ankle securely with an ACE bandage.

Now? Things get challenging.

Draping one of the mylar blankets over her lower body, I carefully undo her belt, then the zipper on her pants, and maneuver them down her hips. All while trying to keep the blanket in place.

Her skin is soft, but so cold. Another blanket over her upper body, and I take a seat behind her and rest her against my chest. I can do this with my eyes closed. Strip off her ripped poncho, the flannel shirt, and fuck. Her tank top.

Her bra and panties are wet too, but they'll dry quickly once we're under the blankets.

I should check her for injuries. Bruises. Contusions. But not until she can consent. For now, it'll be enough to get her warm.

If I could hold her and build a fire at the same time, I would, but under two of the blankets and tucked into the sleeping bag, she'll be okay for five minutes. At least...I hope she will be. I'm second guessing everything at this point. All of my training. All of my missions. Everything.

I grab large handfuls of brush, pile them close to the entrance, and add a waterproof fire starter. The first sparks catch in just a few seconds, and I gather some of the larger branches to lay on top. The heat warms the small space quickly, and the open roof lets the smoke escape well enough.

When I slide into the sleeping bag at Mikayla's back, her skin is still so cold, but I guide her so she's lying half on top of me, her head resting on my good shoulder, and wrap my arms around her. "I need you to wake up, Mik. To talk to me and tell me you're okay."

Mikayla

A sweet, smoky scent teases my nose.

I can feel my nose.

My cheeks, nose, and lips were the first parts of me to fade into nothingness after I fell. Then my hands and feet. But I can feel them too. Little pinpricks of pain dance along my fingers and toes, and I flex them, then suddenly realize I'm lying on top of Austin. And we're both mostly naked.

"Mik?" he says, his voice deep and rumbling through his chest—the chest I'm draped over.

"Where are we?" Those three words take almost everything out of me, and I can't muster the strength to move beyond opening my eyes and blinking hard.

Flickering. Firelight. Dark, stone walls. Old. A dirty floor.

"Somewhere." The rustling of a sleeping bag accompanies his low chuckle. "Sorry, sweetheart. I can't tell you much more than that. This old building isn't on any map I've seen of this area. Hell, it was only a tiny blip on the GPS."

"We're safe here?" My whole body aches, all the bruises from my fall making themselves known, and I wince.

"As safe as I can make us." Austin brushes his hand over my hair, and the intimate gesture brings a lump to my throat. "How do you feel?"

"Awful." The word slips out before I realize its effect, and Austin stiffens.

"Tell me exactly what hurts and how bad, Mik." The command in his tone is unmistakable, and his arms tighten around me ever so slightly, as if he can keep me safe by holding me close.

"Austin—"

He shifts me onto my back, no longer holding me, and the sense of loss makes the pain in my hands and feet seem like nothing at all.

"What. Hurts?"

I can see it now. How he'd be a natural leader. How soldiers—airmen?—wouldn't dare disobey one of his orders. "My fingers and toes."

Carefully, keeping the sleeping bag pulled up almost to my neck, he eases my left hand from under the covers. "The pruning's gone. Flex your fingers for me?"

I do as he asks, even though my thoughts have finally cleared enough to understand what's going on. "I'm okay, Austin. This is normal—I think—after being so cold for so long. They're just tingling. Badly."

He sits up, the sight of his bare chest sending a flush creeping up my neck. He's built. I knew, of course. I'd caught a glimpse—crap, was that only last night?—when he'd answered the door without a shirt. And when he'd held me, those muscles were so strong and reassuring. But the reality of him is so much *more* than I'd dreamed of. And I absolutely did dream about him.

He notices me staring, even as he's rubbing my left hand between both of his to help warm me up, and he suddenly stops and grabs one of the thin, shiny blankets to cover himself. "I'm sorry, sweetheart. I needed to get you warm, and my clothes were almost as soaked as yours—"

"Don't apologize." I want to touch him, to trace those defined ridges, to ask him about the dozens of scars strewn haphazardly over his tanned skin.

"Mik..." His voice cracks, and he shakes his head. "I didn't look. Didn't see anything. I promise you..." Clutching the blanket so tightly his knuckles turn white, he looks away. "Turn around and I'll see if my clothes are dry enough. At least my shirt."

"Stop." I'm so tired. So scared. But not of him. Not of... seeing him. "You undressed me without looking?"

"Yes." He says it like he doesn't understand why I'm in awe of him in this moment. "Nothing happens to you—or in front of you—that you don't consent to, sweetheart. Nothing. Not while I'm here."

He *is* too good to be true. Except he's right in front of me, flesh and blood, muscles and heat, scars and sexy, deep voice. I wriggle enough to get my other arm out from under the sleeping bag, and though the air around us makes my skin prickle, and the sudden loss of warmth sends a brief flash of panic creeping up my spine, I need to be closer to him.

Wrapping my arms around Austin, I savor his warmth and the way he folds me into an embrace with his whole body. "Don't let go," I whisper, my lips close to his ear. "Please."

Austin eases me down with him, and I snuggle against his side as he rubs my back. "You're safe, Mik. I won't leave you."

My eyes burn, and the stress of the night threatens to drown me. "Everything's fuzzy. We couldn't get to the river?"

"We couldn't cross it. The bridge was half gone, and you were too cold—I couldn't risk it. At least here, we're warm and mostly dry."

Warm. Warm is good. Austin is safe. I'm safe.

Focus, Mik.

I blink hard as his handsome face goes soft and hazy for a moment. "What if we can't cross the river in the morning either?"

"By morning, I suspect your graduate students will have convinced someone to send out a search party. The loner—Corey?—he was insistent about calling the police. Hell, I'm pretty sure he called 911 before I even left the hotel."

"Corey..." My voice trembles, and I burrow deeper under the blankets.

"What's wrong?" Tension stiffens Austin's body, and he tries to get me to look at him, but I can't. "Mikayla?"

"I...um...I've known him the longest. Sponsored him for the fellowship. He...he came from an unstable home environment." I'm not lying. But I'm not telling Austin the truth either, and I can't let him see it. Corey betrayed my trust, but he also tried to save me. I won't just give him up without talking to him first. I can't. Even though I *know* I shouldn't keep this from Austin.

Silence stretches between us, filled with unanswered questions and need so strong, so desperate, it's drawing us together like magnets. I'm exhausted, but also panicked, on edge, and terrified. There's no way I'll be able to sleep, despite how tired I am.

Trailing my fingers over his chest, over the myriad of thin scars, I ask, "What happened here?"

"Not a story you want to hear." The caring, concerned tone his voice carried just a few minutes ago is gone, shuttered at my single question. But we're trapped here until the storm passes—or at least until it's light again, and I'm not letting him get away with this a second time.

"You're wrong." I tip my head up to meet his gaze, and though the room spins a little, it steadies quickly enough. "I want to know you, Austin. This...this was supposed to be our tomorrow. Our second date. The one where you said I could ask about that ugly story. About your shoulder injury. About these scars. About...a lot of things."

He stares up at the ceiling in the center of the room, the half-rotten shingles looking like they might not survive another night of this storm. But we're tucked in the back of this old building, and here...it's safe and warm and just the two of us.

"Tell me." I press a kiss to his chest, right over his heart. "Tell me or touch me. Because everything hurts, it's cold, and I need you. All of you."

CHAPTER TWELVE

Austin

Mikayla looks so small and frightened huddled against me, but God, having her in my arms, her soft skin and curves starting to warm...I don't know that I'll ever get enough of her. I play with her hair, the short strands now dry, slipping over my fingers as I give her a gentle scalp massage, being careful to avoid the swollen bump at the crown of her head.

"I left my post." Even now, eight months after I stood in Clarke's office for my dressing down, I hunch my shoulders at the memory. "My sister and one of my closest friends were in trouble back in January, and they needed me. But you just don't go AWOL in the military. Especially not when you're the commander of JSOC. You do what you're told. What your country needs you to do."

"But...your sister. Anyone should understand that," Mik says, her voice soft and tinged with exhaustion. Maybe she'll fall asleep and I won't have to tell her the rest. But she peers up at me, her eyes half-lidded, and though I could urge her to close them and probably get out of this...I want her to know. I *need* her to know.

"Not in my world. No. Each branch of the military is slightly different. In the Marines, it's 'God, Country, Corps.' In the Air Force, we say—they say—'integrity first, service before self, and excellence in all we do.' I'm trained to stay on post no matter what. I chose to disobey orders, and even worse, to engage in unauthorized combat on foreign soil. Other than killing a man in cold blood or committing outright treason, that's about the worst thing I could have done." Shifting onto my back to relieve some pressure on my shoulder, I stare up at the ceiling, focusing on a rotting beam halfway across the room. "My commanding officer could have had me court-martialed."

"No. He wouldn't have..."

Shit, she's so naive. Then again, so are most civilians. They don't understand the rigidity. The absolute need for it. The unwavering commitment to following orders at all cost. "He would have...if there'd been any evidence of me going to Venezuela to help Dani. Luckily, the group I went with—a K&R firm out of Seattle—has one of the best hackers on the planet working for them. She covered my tracks."

Mikayla traces her fingers over the scar from one of the bullets I took in Pakistan. "K&R?"

"Kidnap and ransom. Trev...he was in a Venezuelan prison. One you do *not* escape from. Not even when you're a former CIA agent who's deadlier than I am by half. Trev works for a security firm in Boston called Second Sight, and between them and Hidden Agenda—that's the K&R group—it took five of us on the ground and another five online to get them out."

"That's where you were hurt?" she asks. "Your shoulder?"

My scoff sounds so much louder than I intend in the small space. "No. I came out of that mission with nothing more than a few bruises. Dani and Trev were the only ones..."

My sister's face flashes behind my eyelids. She'll wear that scar along her cheekbone for the rest of her life. And Trevor... his scars aren't physical, but that might make them even worse.

"Austin?" Mik cups my cheek, and I cover her hand with mine. "You were somewhere else again. Somewhere...dark."

"Yeah." Touching my forehead to hers, I blow out a long, slow breath. "Dani and Trevor went through hell down there. I'm not sure they'll ever recover from it. Not fully. I should have..." Fuck. I don't know what I should have done. "Dani asked me to go with her. To Venezuela. But I couldn't, because I was on this fucking political song and dance tour across half a dozen countries. So Trev went. And his history with Venezuela...it's a lot worse than mine."

Mik settles closer to me. "So what happened to your shoulder?"

"When I came back, my CO—" I swallow hard, ill prepared to admit I was basically fired and sent halfway around the world as punishment for my actions, "—he ordered me to Pakistan."

"Oh." I *feel* her reply more than hear it, and I close my eyes. We need to sleep soon. Mikayla has to regain her strength before we hike back to the Land Rover.

Say it. Just...spit it out and move past it.

"Austin?" Mikayla whispers with her lips against my ear. "What happened to you?"

"I..." A barrage of gunfire echoes in my memories. I can smell the smoke. Feel the blowback from the grenade. Hear Griff's shouted warning, then his scream as that concrete wall collapsed, crushing his arm. "I can't."

The words escape hoarse and full of emotion, and I bury my face against Mikayla's neck. Fuck. She smells so good. Even here, dirty, bedraggled, left to die on a cliff in a storm. Like home. Like everything I never thought I wanted but now...don't want to be without.

"Five people died," I say against her soft skin. "Only one of my security detail survived. Lost his arm. His hearing. Most of it, anyway. He saved my life. But I still took three shots. The one to my shoulder..."

Mik threads her fingers into my hair and guides me back just enough to kiss me. Her lips are chapped from all those hours in the rain and wind, but there's no hesitation, no holding back, and I roll her on top of me, needing more. I almost lost her. Almost didn't find her in time. We could have missed out on our tomorrow. On all the tomorrows I want to have with her.

Her wince stops me, tames my dick jutting against her stomach, hard and eager for more than she's ready to give. Fuck. How can I be thinking about sex when she's injured? I didn't even examine her properly after I got her into the sleeping bag.

"What hurts?" I ask. She doesn't answer, and I cup her cheek and hold her gaze. "Mik. Tell me."

With a sigh, she shakes her head, then groans softly. "My head. Hip. Back. Shoulder. Ankle. I was thrown off a cliff, Austin. Everything hurts."

"*Thrown?*" The word explodes from my lips, and Mik squeezes her eyes shut. "Fuck. I'm sorry, sweetheart. But goddammit, if I ever find those shitstains, I'm going to turn them inside out."

It's clearly the wrong thing to say, because Mikayla's brown eyes fill with tears, and she swallows a sob. "I tried to run," she whimpers. "But the rocks were so slippery, and I'd just had an asthma attack. The meds...I get shaky."

"Mikayla..."

"No, let me finish." Her voice cracks, and she pulls her hands out from under the blankets, staring at the welts from the zip tie. "I could barely feel my fingers. When I tripped, I almost went over, but there were these branches. I tried to push myself back, but then he grabbed my ankle—"

"Who?" She's lost in her memories, panic edging her tone, and if I can't pull her out, she'll start wheezing any moment. I take her right hand and lay her fingers over the bracelet I bought her. "You're safe, Mik. With me. No one's going to hurt you here."

She fiddles with the beads, and I reach over for the first aid kit, digging out a roll of gauze and some ointment. "I'm going to wrap up your wrists so these welts don't get infected, okay?"

She nods, watching me as I tend to her. Her breathing is steadier now, and I try to get just a little bit more information out of her. Because when we get back to town and I know she's not seriously injured, I'm going after these assholes. "Can you tell me anything more about what happened? Who grabbed your ankle?"

She flinches, and I rub her fingers. "The bigger one. Ar-Arturo."

"How many of them were there?"

"Three. When I found them at the site, I tried to run, but I couldn't breathe." Her expression shutters, like she can't stand to remember, and I don't want to press her any more, but after a minute, she closes her eyes and whispers, "They wanted to kill me. Or s-sell m-me. Along with the orchids. I got away before...before they could get me into their truck, but I wasn't fast enough. And they were shooting at me..." Tears tumble down her cheeks, and I gently wipe them away with my thumbs. "I can't believe you found me."

"I'll always find you, sweetheart. Always." I press a chaste kiss to her forehead, then sit up with her in my arms. "Will you let me see your back and shoulder? The blankets will keep you mostly covered."

Mikayla shudders, but nods, and when I release her and scoot back, she lowers the blankets just enough, I can see her tight nipples straining against her sports bra. Her right shoulder is half a dozen different shades of purple, and I gently trace the edges of the bruising, then take her arm at the elbow. "I just want to see when it starts to hurt. Keep holding the blankets with your other hand."

She does as I ask, and thankfully, she seems to have full range of motion. Not like when I woke up in that godawful hospital in Pakistan. Her left side is worse, but again, she can move, albeit carefully.

A shiver runs through her, though the fire has warmed the air well enough. She's still cold. Probably will be until I can get some food into her. Shit. Why haven't I tried to get her to eat something?

"Austin?" Her uncertain tone pulls me out of my own head. Shit. She's more exposed than she's ever been with me, biting her lip like she's just made the biggest mistake of her life, and I'm sitting here having a whole conversation with myself rather than with her.

I follow her gaze to the blankets bunched around my hips and the very obvious tenting from my dick. Goddammit. I didn't even realize... This is inappropriate as fuck. She was just *thrown* off a mountain, and touching her is still making me hard.

I shift my legs to hide the evidence of my arousal, and she looks away. "Deep breaths, sweetheart. I'm going to see how far down your back the bruising goes. You still okay?"

"Uh-huh."

She's not, but I have to make sure there's no internal bleeding. Scooting behind her, I wrap one hand around her waist just below her breasts to hold the blankets.

"Relax. Drop your arms." Mik does as I ask, but from the

tension that springs to her shoulders, she's either in pain or incredibly uncomfortable with how exposed she is. "Did you land on your back?"

After another shuddering breath, she clears her throat. "I think so. Kind of, anyway. After I fell, everything went fuzzy."

"I'm just going to run my hand over your abdomen. If anything feels worse than a bruise, tell me." Under the blankets, I palpate gently, checking her ribs, her left and right sides, and though she tenses up more than once, her body language tells me she's more nervous than in pain. When I'm finished, I press a kiss to the curve of her neck. "All done. You're okay, and I won't ever let them touch you again."

Gooseflesh races down her arms, and I start gently kneading her shoulders around the bruises. A low moan escapes her lips, and shit. I'm so aroused, it's painful. Until I focus on the dark purple splotches right above her bra.

"Mik." I can't do this. Can't touch her without thinking about how close she came to dying. Wrapping both arms around her from behind, I plant a kiss to the back of her neck as she starts to cry. "I'm sorry. I'm so sorry..."

She tries to turn, but tangled in the blankets, something must hurt her, and she hisses out a breath. "Don't apologize," she says through her tears. "I just need you to make me feel safe again." The tremble in her voice breaks me, and I pull the sleeping bag up and over both of us, guiding her down and draping her over my chest so she can lay her head on my shoulder.

By degrees, Mik starts to relax, and when her breathing evens out and the tension has left her body, I close my eyes and let myself sleep with this woman I think I might be able to love.

Mikayla

Stretching, I try to ignore the twinges of pain arcing through my body. The first rays of light stream through the rotting roof, and while I'm warm, I'm also very much alone.

I wasn't. Not all night. Austin held me, whispered to me when I cried, and kept me safe, only leaving my side once to stoke the fire. I don't think he knew I was awake, but I watched him. Wearing nothing but a pair of boxer briefs, he gathered twigs and small branches from just outside the little building's entrance and arranged them carefully before spreading our clothes out to dry.

When he turned back to me, the firelight played over his abs, his scarred chest, his strong, muscular legs, and for a brief moment, something had stirred inside of me. Something I had no business feeling out here—in a crumbling building several centuries old, injured, terrified, and possibly still hunted.

"Austin?" I call as I push myself up on an elbow. The motion makes my back ache, but I feel better than I think I should after falling so far and being trapped on that ledge for so long. "Where are you?"

"Right here, sweetheart." He ducks back inside, wearing his boots and black pants, but no shirt. "Just had to, um...use the facilities."

I chuckle, which makes my side hurt. "We have 'facilities'?"

"We have a tree." Austin snags his shirt where it hangs on a stone jutting out from the wall, and tugs it on, his cheeks slightly red and his gaze pinned to the floor. "Don't try to get up, Mik. Your ankle was pretty swollen last night. I'll help you."

Now it's my turn to flush with embarrassment. This amazing, strong, protective man held me all night under the blankets and sleeping bag, skin-to-skin, and we've been on exactly one date. This isn't me. The last time I slept with a man, we'd been dating for a month. The time before that...two months.

And both of them hurt me.

Austin...he's different. Honorable to a fault. Respectful. Sweet. Protective. He grabs my tank top and flannel shirt and sinks down next to me.

"Do you think you can manage to put this on if I hold the sleeping bag up?" he asks, concern creasing his brow.

"Y-yes." I want to tell him that it's okay. That he doesn't need to keep me covered, but that's not a conversation I can have here. Not dirty and in pain with men who want to kill me still out there.

Dropping what used to be a white tank next to me, he curls his fingers around the top of the sleeping bag, brushing my collarbone as he does so. The contact sends sparks shooting lower. Down to my core.

Get yourself under control, Mik. Someone tried to kill you last night.

The thought keeps me from reaching for Austin, but I want to. So very much. I want him to kiss me again. To do...more. But not here. Not in these crumbling ruins in the middle of nowhere.

My back protests when I raise my arms, but I'm able to tug the shirt down to cover my body without too much of a struggle. "Okay. I'm, uh, decent. From the waist up anyway."

A muscle in his jaw ticks when he lowers the sleeping bag, and his breaths saw in and out of his chest like he's just gone for a run.

"Austin?"

With a muttered curse, he turns away to reach for my pants. "Ignore me, Mik. It's nothing."

"It's not nothing." I brush my fingers over his wrist, and he sucks in a sharp breath. His black pants are decidedly tight...*down there*, and he won't meet my gaze. "I...this isn't something I've ever said to a man before. But, I want you to touch me, Austin. Not here. Not now. But...when we're safe. When it doesn't hurt just to sit up. When I've—" my cheeks catch fire, "—showered."

Austin leans closer and cups the back of my neck. "You're beautiful, Mikayla. Every bit as beautiful as you were on our date two nights ago."

"You're not impressing me with your visual acuity," I say, surprised I'm relaxed enough to smile.

He traces his index finger along my jaw. "My eyes are just fine, sweetheart. You have a bit of dirt. Right here." Continuing down the curve of my neck, he reaches my collarbone. "And here."

The tension between us makes my heart beat faster, and if other biological needs weren't asserting themselves, I'd kiss him, or ask him to kiss me. Instead, I cover his hand with mine. "Help me with these," I say as I nod towards my pants. "Then help me outside so I can find that tree?"

CHAPTER THIRTEEN

Mikayla

My ankle doesn't want to hold my full weight, and Austin wraps his arm around my waist to help me out to a nearby tree. Thankfully, once I'm leaning against the rough bark with a clump of moss clutched in my fingers, he shoves his hands into his pockets and stares down at the ground. "You're going to need a crutch to make it back to the Land Rover. Will you be okay...?"

"Yes. Just don't go too far."

He cups the back of my head, and his hazel eyes hold such intensity, I want to look away, but I can't. "I won't leave you, sweetheart. I promise. You'll be able to see me the whole time."

Nodding, I watch him walk away, waiting until he's gone at least twenty feet before I drop my pants and awkwardly take care of my needs. By the time I'm done, he's standing by the dilapidated structure with two tree branches balanced against one crumbling wall.

"It's okay. I'm done," I call as I manage a few uneven,

painful steps closer to him. And then his arm is around my waist.

"Easy there," he murmurs. "It might only be a mild sprain, but you're going to be unsteady for a few days. Don't want you going down again."

"Do they teach all guys in the Air Force to be this...chivalrous?" I ask. We're back inside now, and he lowers me down to the camping mat, then sits next to me and digs in his pack for a minute, coming away with a bottle of water and two pouches labeled "Beef Stew."

"No, ma'am," he says with a smile. I open the water bottle while he tears into the pouches and fiddles with them for a minute before handing me one, along with...a spork? "Chivalry's my dad's department. I swear, my mom has never opened a door in her life unless he was nowhere around."

"Tell me about them?" The first sporkful of stew tastes like heaven, and I moan a little, my cheeks flushing hot at the look Austin shoots my way. "I didn't realize how hungry I was."

He chuckles, and it's such a sexy, toe-curling sound that I have to force myself to focus on eating. "Dad spent most of his life in the Air Force. Retired at sixty. Mom was a teacher until just a few years ago. Seventy-six years old, both of them, and they still go for walks around the neighborhood every single day."

His face practically lights up, and for a moment, I see him as I never have before. Relaxed. Almost...happy. But then he digs into his packet of stew, and it's like it reminds him where we are. His expression changes so quickly, I swear he flipped a switch.

"If the river's still too high to cross, we'll need to hike another two miles, at least. I'd carry you the whole way, but—"

"No, you won't. For Pete's sake, Austin. I know you're built like a super hero, but you carried me all the way here last night, and even though I was unconscious for a lot of it, I saw your face a few times. How hard it was. I'm not exactly...tiny."

"You're perfect," he says, almost automatically.

Now it's my turn to laugh. "Okay, Superman. You can stop with the compliments. I wasn't putting myself down. Just stating the obvious. I'm not supermodel thin, and I don't want to be."

"Not Superman." There's an edge to his voice. Rough and dark and dangerous. "That's Trevor."

"Huh?" For a brief moment, I wonder if I hit my head harder than I thought last night. "You're upset. What did I say?"

Austin crumples the stew pouch into a ball, tucks it into a plastic bag, and then runs a hand through his hair. "Sorry. I'm not. Not with you, anyway. A reflex, I guess. When we went to Venezuela, the guy who led the rescue mission—Ryker—he insisted everyone use code names in the field. Trev was Superman, Dani was Lois Lane."

"Who were you? Don't tell me you were Jimmy Olsen? That's just...wrong. You're nobody's sidekick."

He snorts, a hint of a smile curving the corners of his lips. "Perry White. Editor of the Daily Planet and the oldest guy in the movie. Except for Superman's parents. At least Ry didn't dub me Jor-El."

"Well, you need a better nickname than Perry," I say, nudging his shoulder. It feels good to joke, to relax, even though we're about to leave this crumbling sanctuary, and I'll have to hike several miles on an injured ankle, to a spot where men—including one of my students—might be waiting to kill us. But now that my mind's gone there, I can't muster the will to smile.

"When I was flying, my call sign was Danger."

I scrape up the last of the stew, then ball up my pouch and let him pack it up with all the other trash—first aid supplies mostly, and a tiny energy drink bottle Austin drained almost as soon as he woke up. "There's a story behind that I want to hear."

"When we're safe." He's all business now, withdrawing a roll of duct tape from his pack, along with a large knife, and going to work on the two branches he found earlier. "This isn't going to be the most comfortable thing. But it'll be good enough when I'm done."

I watch, amazed, as he cuts notches in the wood, fits a thick, slightly curved short branch between a *V* at the end of the longer branch, and tapes them all together. Then, he cuts off several pieces of the camping mat we're sitting on and secures them to the curved branch, giving the makeshift crutch some padding. After he tests it out to make sure it holds his weight, he nods once, then helps me up and shows me how best to use it.

Walking still hurts, but taking a lot of the weight off my injured ankle turns the sharp pain into more of an annoying twinge. "You're right. You're not Superman. Indiana Jones maybe. Or...MacGyver."

"Just basic field training." Helping me over to what looks almost like an old table made out of thick, weathered pieces of stone, he eases me down. "Sit, and keep that foot up while I pack the rest of our stuff. Any time we stop, elevate your ankle, and if the wrap starts to feel tight, if you can feel your pulse around it, you have to tell me immediately. Understand?"

He's back in full Air Force Major General mode, and though a small part of me bristles against the orders, this is the man he needs to be right now. This is the Austin who'll keep me safe no matter what. I nod and maneuver my leg up onto the stone. But before he turns away, I reach for his hand and link our fingers. "You saved my life, Austin. You don't have to worry. I'm not going to do anything to put myself in danger ever again if I can help it."

His eyes darken, and he slides his fingers into my hair and presses a brief, hard kiss to my lips. "Good. Because when we get back to the States, I'm going with you to Edgewater. I want a second date with you, Mikayla. And a third. As many as you'll give me."

"I...I want that too."

Relief flashes in his eyes, and he turns his focus to his back-pack. No man has ever made me feel like he does, and a tiny spark of hope catches deep inside. Along with the idea that we just might get that tomorrow we both so desperately want.

Austin

The hike back up the mountain takes hours, and more than once, I sweep Mikayla into my arms and carry her for a few hundred feet just to give her a break. Her expression twists and tightens with every step, though she's trying damn hard to hide it.

We've only spoken the few times we've stopped for water or when I've insisted she tell me her pain level. She says she's fine, that it's not much above a three, but I'd bet my hunting knife she's really a five or six.

The river's no longer roaring, though it's still close to over-flowing its banks. The bridge is gone, but I think I can get us across safely. Mik's not going to like it, though. I drop my ruck and pull out the rope.

"What are you doing?" She asks, leaning against a tree twenty feet from the water.

"Something risky," I mutter, then look up to meet her gaze.

Fuck. She's exhausted, and if she continues to put weight on that ankle much longer, she's not going to be able to keep going. "I'm rigging up a guide rope between that tree behind you and the one across the river."

"That's...you're going to have to... No. Austin, no." She wedges the crutch under her arm again and straightens. "We'll find another way."

"Any other way across is going to take us at least two more hours. You need a doctor." Passing the rope around the trunk, I fasten it off in a quick bowline knot, then give it a hard tug to make sure it holds. "I've been in rougher waters, sweetheart. And I've got the rope. I'm not going to drown."

"Promise me." She digs her fingers into my sides, and I wrap my free arm around her and pull her close.

"I promise." Kissing the furrow between her brows, I let her go, shoulder my pack—and hers—and tie the other end of the rope around my waist.

The water's warmer than I expect, but after being soaked through last night and caught up in the middle of a windstorm, it's still a shock. The river bed is slippery as fuck, and I almost go down twice, but the water doesn't rise higher than my chest. Good. I'll be able to get Mikayla across and keep her mostly dry.

When I reach the other side, I roll onto the bank and stare up at the clouds gathering on the horizon. There's another storm coming. I drop my pack, tie the rope off around the second tree and wade back into the water.

The look on Mikayla's face when I return to her side makes my heart beat a little too fast. Her brown eyes blaze with emotion, and she shakes her head. "I don't know if I can do that," she says, gesturing to the river.

"You don't have to. Hold the crutch in your right hand. Lift your left arm and spread your legs a little. You're going on my shoulders."

"What?" Her voice rises half an octave, and she shakes her head. "No. You're not...you can't."

"It's the only way I can keep you mostly dry. It's going to feel weird, but you'll be completely safe. I carried you the same way last night for most of the hike. Please, Mik. Those clouds on the horizon look pretty angry. If we get caught in another storm..."

"Okay." She raises her arm, and I duck my shoulder between her legs as I grab her wrist. She yelps when I straighten and hook my right arm under her left thigh. Bringing her torso across my shoulders, I grip her wrist tightly.

"Keep hold of the crutch, and don't wriggle too much if you can help it. I'll try to keep you as dry as I can." Carrying her in this position leaves me with one hand free, and I grab the rope as I splash into the water.

To Mikayla's credit, she stays almost perfectly still, even when I stumble and have to catch myself. "Almost there," I grunt as I start to pull myself up onto the river bank.

Once she's leaning against the tree on the other side, I wade across once more to untie the rope. We may only be a little over two kilometers from the lab, but I'm not taking any chances. Five separate trips across the water isn't my idea of a good time, nor is hiking the rest of the way in soggy boots. But I've been in too many situations where I wished for rope and had none to leave any part of it behind.

"Ready?" I ask when I have the rope safely stowed in my ruck.

"Not really. I don't want to go back to the lab. Or anywhere close. But we don't have a choice."

I rub my hands together to warm them as best I can, then cup the back of her neck and pull her in for a kiss. "You're not alone, Mik. And there's nothing I won't do to keep you safe." Unclipping the small folding knife from its sheath on my belt, I press it into her palm. "It's not much, but take this."

Her eyes widen, and her fingers aren't steady as she examines the blade. "I don't know how…"

"Press here." She does, and the knife snaps open. The speed of it startles her, but she doesn't drop it. "And then to close it, hold here and fold it carefully. Good. It's not a great weapon. But it's better than nothing."

After she opens and closes the knife two more times, she nods and slides it into her pocket. "Okay. Let's go."

CHAPTER FOURTEEN

Mikayla

It takes us the better part of an hour to reach the trailer, and before we round the last bend, Austin pulls me down into a crouch and holds his finger to his lips. I don't hear anything but the birds and the rustling leaves, until I turn my head slightly and pick out a low rumble underneath the ambient noise.

Whatever it is stops, but then a vehicle door slams, and I start to shake. It could just be my students. Right?

Austin's posture says he doesn't think so, and he presses closer to the trees hiding us, angling his head slightly. I can't move as well as he does, so I wait, my heart pounding against my ribs, and try to keep taking slow, deep breaths.

After a few seconds, Austin's fingers curl around the handle of the large knife he has sheathed on his right leg, and the look on his face? It's deadly serious. He motions for me to get behind him, and as I maneuver myself on hands and knees, I hear one of them—Arturo, I think.

"Get in the truck. And hurry. When this thing goes up, it's going to be big. We need to be back to the main road by then."

"How long do we have?" Martín's voice sends ice flooding my veins.

"Five minutes. Seven tops until the accelerant catches."

Crap. They're going to burn it down. All our work...

"These fuckers aren't getting away," Austin hisses in my ear. "Here are the keys. As soon as I distract them, take my ruck, go to the Land Rover, and get the hell out of here."

They'll kill him. I can't lose Austin. I won't. "They have guns. Please don't do this. Let's just wait until they leave. Maybe we could even save the lab..."

"Mik, it's too dangerous." He presses the keys into my hand, then cups my cheek. "Go down the hill and wait for me right before the main road. If you see their truck, floor it all the way back to the hotel and call the *Policia*. Understand?"

"No. Austin—"

"I can handle these two assholes. They tried to kill you and they are *not* getting away."

He's so confident, but we've been hiking for hours, and he has to be exhausted.

"Go as soon as they're distracted," Austin says, then plants a hard, swift kiss on my lips. "I'll meet you."

My eyes burn as he takes off, staying low, the knife still in his hand. After a dozen steps, he breaks into an all-out run, and I heft his pack and start limping towards the Land Rover. My ankle throbs with every step, the extra weight not doing me any favors.

Austin reaches the black truck rolling slowly over the rough terrain and jumps onto the back bumper, clutching one of the roll bars and riding the Jeep partway down the hill.

I keep to the far side of my vehicle, hiding behind it as I try to get the key into the passenger side lock with my hands shaking. It takes me several tries, but finally, the door pops open and I shove his backpack onto the seat.

How long has it been? Three minutes? I have time. I can at least grab my laptop or one of the sample cases. Bursting through the door, I yelp and stumble as I hear a gunshot from halfway down the hill. My crutch bangs into something small and light, sending it tumbling across the cheap carpeted floor. *What the heck?*

It's a road flare. Lit. Smoke fills the space, and I cough until I hear muffled cries. Oh God. Squinting, I can barely make out Li's face. She's on the floor, bound, gagged, and struggling. Isaiah's a few feet away, and to my left, Corey lies on his side, blood streaming from his temple.

The sparks from the flare hit a dark stain on the carpet, and with a *whoosh*, flames rush all the way to the back corner of the trailer, so bright and hot it's like looking into the face of the sun.

***

Austin

If I needed to feel like a badass, hanging onto the back of a Jeep as it rolls slowly down the side of a mountain? It's not exactly doing it for me. Maybe if the vehicle were moving faster than ten miles an hour, things would be different. I don't risk a glance behind me at Mikayla. Her vehicle should start any second.

Digging my knife into the Jeep's soft top, I rip a four-foot hole in the canvas and drop down into the rear seat. "*Buenas tardes,* assholes." A shot whizzes past my left arm as I sink the blade into the soft flesh behind the passenger's collar bone. His scream brings me more satisfaction than I should admit, and I grab for his gun, twisting it out of his hand, but I can't relish in the victory because the driver jams his elbow back and catches me in the jaw.

Fuck. It's been too long. I've lost my edge. My vision blurs for a second, but I still manage to lurch forward and get my hand around the wheel. Wrenching it hard to one side, I lose my balance as the Jeep lurches, landing on my ass behind the passenger seat and firing at the driver.

My shot goes wide, hitting him in the forearm, and he says something I don't understand because metal screeches as the front bumper crumples against a large tree.

The scent of blood fills the Jeep, and I scramble up and back out through the hole in the roof. The driver's head hit the windshield—seatbelts, fuckers, learn to love 'em—and the other guy...he's struggling to push himself up and get to the roof to follow me.

"Austin! Help me!"

Mikayla. From the faintness of her cry, she's still back up at the lab, and fuck me. If these two idiots were telling the truth, the whole thing's going to blow in the next five minutes.

The driver won't be an issue. But the passenger? Backing away, I aim three shots at the roof and pray it's enough.

Sprinting two hundred yards up the hill, I panic when I see the thick, black smoke pouring from the trailer. Mikayla's limping out the door with someone *leaning* on her.

Li. Her student. If the other two are in there...

"Mik! Start the goddamn car and get clear!" I'm still eighty yards away. Sixty. Forty.

"Isaiah and Corey," she croaks, her breathing labored and her face stained with soot.

"Get in the car and start driving. Now. Down the hill!" Fuck. I don't even know if I can get to them. Flames lick along the bottom of the door, and I jump, landing in a crouch. Halfway across the room, Isaiah's struggling to rip through the duct tape wrapped around his ankles. Corey's unconscious. And unbound. The harsh scent of alcohol burns my nose. This whole place is going up any minute.

I slash at the tape, and Isaiah gets to his hands and knees. "Go. Get out of here!"

Just as I turn to Corey, the entire back wall bursts into flame like someone hit it with a Molotov cocktail. My pants catch fire, and part of the roof caves in, falling across Corey's legs.

If we don't get out of here in the next ten seconds, we're both dead. I can already feel my lungs seizing, and the smoke, thick and black and acrid, is just inches above our heads.

Yanking him up and over my shoulders, I lurch for the door, jump down the steps, and roll with Corey on top of me, over and over to dampen the flames.

He's not moving, but I stagger to my feet and, sighting the Land Rover halfway down the hill, drag him towards it. If only I could catch my breath. Or feel my face.

The lab erupts in a giant fireball and the entire trailer collapses with a roar as the rain pelts my back. I can't keep going much farther. But I can see Mikayla get out of the car before my vision starts to dim.

And then I'm on the ground, staring up at the stormy sky as she screams my name.

"Austin!" Her rough, rasping voice helps keep me from passing out, and her fingers trail over my cheeks. "Oh God. You could have died..."

Groaning triggers a coughing fit, and she helps me sit up and passes me a bottle of water. After two sips, I croak, "Corey," and Mik tears up.

"He's alive," Isaiah says. Li sobs into his shirt as he rubs her back. "But the guys who took us hit him really hard."

Poachers. Jeep. Shit. Pushing to my feet, I scan all around us. "Where are they?"

"I don't know." Mik's voice cracks, and I wrap my arm around her waist and help her limp over to the Land Rover. "As soon as I started driving away from the lab, they took off." Tears tumble down her cheeks, carving trails in the soot and mixing with the rain. "They could have killed...all of us." She hiccups, shaking her head, and I pull her close.

"I know, sweetheart. But I'm okay. You're okay. And we're going to get everyone to the hospital." But that doesn't console her. She's starting to shake now, the beginnings of shock, likely, and I have to calm her down. "Breathe for me, Mik. Long and slow. Can you do that?"

She nods, and once I help her into the passenger seat, I stumble around to the back of the Land Rover and open the lift gate. "We need to keep Corey as still as possible. Isaiah, can you sit back here with him?"

"I don't...Li..."

"I'll be okay," the young woman says and swipes her tears away. Isaiah helps me maneuver Corey into the back, then climbs in with him, sitting next to the unconscious man and holding his head still. Corey's chest stutters with each breath, and his right leg, hip, and arm are covered with burned patches of skin. I check his pulse. Rapid and weak. He's in full shock— or heading there pretty damn quick.

Grabbing my rucksack, I pull out a bottle of water and then shove the pack under Corey's legs. I fix Isaiah with a hard stare and force as much command into my tone as I have left in me at this point. "Take off your shirt and tear it into strips." To the kid's credit, he doesn't ask any questions, just pulls the blue tee off and starts ripping. "Pour some water onto the strips and lay them over the burns. If he stops breathing, tell me immediately. Got it?"

The young man nods.

We're all dragging ass, but I climb into the driver's seat and turn to Mik. "Tell me you're all right, sweetheart."

"I'm okay." She clutches her inhaler like it's life itself, and her mouth opens and shuts twice before she can force her next words out. "Drive. Please. I don't ever want to see this place again."

I throw the Land Rover into gear and floor it towards the main road. The ride is rough as shit, but what we all need right now is medical treatment. As quickly as possible. Once we make it onto the roughly paved road, I reach for Mik's hand, thread our fingers, and hold on tight.

As long as those assholes who hurt her are still walking free, I don't know that I'll ever be able to let her go.

CHAPTER FIFTEEN

Mikayla

The past twenty minutes are a blur of terrible images I'll never forget. Seeing my students, my kids, tied up, gagged, terrified. Smelling the alcohol in the air. The blood. The flames racing towards Li's bound feet. I didn't think. Dropped the crutch, grabbed the small knife Austin gave me, and fell next to her, hacking at the duct tape.

The fire extinguisher wasn't where we always kept it. The smoke was so thick, and it burned my throat. Even now, my lungs are close to seizing, and I clutch my inhaler in my free hand, ready in case I can't fight an attack off any longer.

We're all coughing, and the scent filling the Land Rover— burnt skin, the alcohol soaked into Li and Isaiah's clothes, and blood—is too much. I roll down the window, forcing myself to breathe as slowly as I can.

Austin shifts his hand to my thigh.

"I'll be all right," I manage. "Just..."

"Don't talk unless you need to. We'll have time for that

later. According to the GPS, the nearest hospital is still a little more than twelve kilometers away."

The concern in his voice makes my heart hurt. I have to tell him about Corey. But he's in full protector mode right now, and if he finds out one of my students tried to kill me, it won't matter that Arturo and Martín decided to murder Corey along with the others.

"If I ever find those shitstains, I'm going to turn them inside out."

The look on his face when he'd said those words... He's not a man who jokes about violence. Not with what he's seen. Though he's only told me a little, his eyes practically scream the horrors of his past.

I watch the mountainous trees turn to flatland grasses, and we speed up. The air's less humid here, and we've left the rain behind, making it easier to breathe. Stealing a quick glance at this man who saved me—who saved all of us—my eyes water, and I blink hard to stop myself from crying.

"Mik? You okay?" he asks, so softly I don't think the others can hear. Not with Li still coughing from time to time and Isaiah talking to Corey, urging him to wake up.

"Fine," I answer automatically. It's the furthest thing from the truth. I don't know if I'll ever be fine again. But I don't have a lot of practice talking about my feelings, and if I try now, I'll lose it completely.

"I don't believe you, sweetheart." He brings my hand to his lips and presses a kiss to my knuckles. "But you can be fine for now." Checking the rear view mirror, he calls, "Isaiah? How's he doing?"

"Not good," he says. "I think we need to hurry."

"Doing my best." Austin takes the next curve so fast, I grab onto the handle over the door, and the landscape shifts again, houses replacing the brush and dense trees of the Mexican countryside.

Less than five minutes later, the Land Rover screeches to a halt in front of a squat building in the middle of a run-down strip mall. "This is the hospital?" I ask.

"It's this, or another half an hour to San Cristóbal de las Casas. He might not make it that long," Austin says as he jumps out of the car and races around to the passenger side to help me down. "Li, go inside and tell them you need a gurney out here right now."

With his arm around my waist, he half-carries me to the back of the Land Rover, and my stomach flips. I don't want to see Corey. What they did to him. As hurt and betrayed as I was, as much as I hate what he did, I would never want him dead. And he did try to save me. If I hadn't fallen, maybe I would have been able to get away.

Corey's so still, only weak, shallow breaths stirring his chest, and his face is covered in blood and soot, the gash above his right eye so deep, I think...oh God. Is that bone?

A pair of orderlies dressed in blue scrubs come running out with the gurney, and Austin barks orders at them in rapid-fire Spanish. I only know a little of the language, but I catch the words fire, help, and police before Corey is wheeled inside, and the rest of us follow.

The interior looks relatively modern, and the harsh scent of antiseptic fills the air. An older nurse, weariness etched on her face, waves us over to the desk as Austin says something about a doctor in a tone that leaves little room for argument.

"Okay, okay," the nurse says, holding up her hands in the universal gesture of *calm down*. "Sit. *Lo ayudaremos.*"

They check us very briefly for smoke inhalation, and then forms and questions and too much waiting follow, until finally, another nurse comes through a set of double doors. "Mikayla Salim? You follow me?"

"I'm going with her," Austin says, and relief floods me, making my fingers and toes tingle. I don't want to be alone. Or anywhere he's not right now.

"No, sir. Exam. You wait here." She continues in Spanish, too quickly for me to grasp what she's saying, but Austin's body language is clear.

"I want him with me."

"No, *la póliza...*"

"I don't care about your goddamn policy. She's mine, and until I know she's safe, she's not going anywhere without me."

His possessive, growling tone should probably make the "strong, independent woman" in me angry, but it doesn't. It makes me feel safe. Protected. Cared for. And I need that more than anything.

The nurse relents and shows us to an exam room, where she tells us that both doctors are working on Corey, and someone will be with us soon. After she hands us both gowns to change into, she breezes out of the room, and I sink down onto the single bed.

"Mik? Do you want help with this?" Austin gestures to the blue material. "I can turn around. Or close my eyes."

"I'll manage. Help me off with my flannel shirt and then, maybe...just look away." In truth, a part of me doesn't care if he sees everything. I trust him. But now that we're safe—or at least not about to die—I want more. To be alone with him. Truly alone. After we've showered. Have clean clothes. Food. Sleep. I want to go on our second date, figure out how deep our connection goes.

Austin eases the flannel off my shoulders, and I try not to let him see that every movement brings a new twinge, a fresh bruise or cut making itself known. Stripping off my tank is even more painful, and when the gown covers my torso, I turn my back to him. "Tie it for me?"

His fingers skim my neck, then my back just above my bra, and my body tingles all over, tiny sparks of electricity everywhere he touches.

"All done." His lips brush my ear, and I lean against his chest, his arms gently wrapping around me, offering without another word what I need most. To feel...protected.

I still need to take off my pants and my boots, but for a few minutes, I savor our closeness, how he doesn't pressure me to say anything, to talk about what happened at the lab, about Corey, about the men who tried to kill us and almost succeeded.

When I pull away, he unlaces my boots, then helps me up and holds onto my waist, his eyes closed, as I unbutton my pants and let them fall to the floor. The gown covers me almost down to my knees, and I curl up on the bed while Austin folds my clothes and sets them on the little table next to us.

"You're not changing?" I ask when he slides a hip onto the bed next to me. "Your pants are burned. Your legs..."

"The rest of me's fine." He leans down, rips the black pants all the way up to his knees, and tears the excess material away. Both of his legs are dotted with angry splotches of reddened skin, but I don't see any actual blisters, and I'm amazed he got so lucky.

For another hour, we wait, Austin stretched out on the bed with me tucked against his side, and I nod off from time to time, but whenever I open my eyes, he's awake, watching the door, his body relaxed, but somehow still hyper focused.

"Doing okay?" he asks when I shift so I can meet his gaze.

I can't keep this secret from him. Not for another minute. What was I thinking? That Austin would bring me back to the hotel I'd magically forgive Corey? Or forget? What he did...all the orchids he helped them harvest, replace with others that are "harmless." That won't help millions of people living with Parkinson's. Or any number of other neurological diseases Dr. Branch thinks could benefit from his experiments.

"Austin, I have to tell you—"

The door opens before I can finish my sentence, and the nurse enters, followed by one of the doctors. "Were you treating Corey Larkin?" I ask. "He's in Mexico working for me on a research project, so I'm kind of responsible for him. How is he?"

The doctor runs a hand through his messy black hair. "He suffered a severe head trauma, as well as second-degree burns to his legs. Two broken ribs, and a dislocated shoulder as well. He is stable, and in a few hours, he will be transferred to the hospital in Tuxtla Gutiérrez. He is in a medically-induced coma because of the swelling in his brain, and will be for at least another few days. After that, we will know more."

"He needs protection," Austin says. "We've been here almost two hours, and I asked for the police when we arrived. Want to tell me what the holdup is?"

The nurse steps forward with a kindly smile. "They are with the other young woman now. I insisted the doctor examine you first."

Whatever he sees in the nurse's face and body language must satisfy him, because Austin relaxes slightly, though he still hasn't let go of me.

Our earlier insistence on staying together must have made its way to the doctor, because he doesn't even try to get Austin to leave, just asks him to turn around when he examines me. After a handful of butterfly bandages to the gash on my hip, he has the nurse help me dress and fit me with an ankle brace while he examines Austin.

"You both were lucky," the doctor says as he pulls off his

gloves and turns to the nurse. "Señor Pritchard needs some salve for his burns, then you can prepare the discharge paperwork."

Lucky. Yes. We were. Though one of the poachers caught Austin in the face with an elbow, it didn't break his nose, and the various cuts and bruises he suffered while saving me—and fighting them—aren't serious.

Less than five minutes later, there's a quick knock on the door, and two police officers enter. "I am Detective Chavez, and this is Officer Lopez. May we sit?"

Austin nods, and they sink into hard plastic chairs across from us. "We have finished taking statements from Li Chen and Isaiah Williams," Chavez says. "They are on their way to the Hotel Veracruz, where we will take you when we have finished this interview."

"What?"

Panic sets in, until Austin leans over and whispers in my ear, "Safer that way, sweetheart. In case the assholes decide they need to try again."

Oh, crap on a cracker. How could I have been so stupid?

I knew *I* didn't want to go back to the hotel. Couldn't. I didn't even think about Li and Isaiah. But after losing the lab, now I'm more worried than ever. "My things," I say. "I have USB drives in my hotel room with data I can't replace."

Chavez offers me a kindly smile. "I have sent two officers to pack up your rooms. Everything will be delivered to your new hotel by morning, if not sooner."

"Th-thank you." I reach for Austin's hand, needing something to hold on to, some way to stay present and grounded so we can get through this next bit. Because they're going to ask me what happened, and the last thing I want to do is remember.

"We will have questions, of course. But please tell us how

this all started." Chavez leans back in his chair while the younger officer sets a voice recorder on the little table next to us and then takes out a notebook and a pen.

"I'm here studying the Blushing Note orchid. It's endangered, but it's also very valuable. Both for medical research and for collectors. Each plant can sell for as much as fifteen thousand dollars to private traders—and that was before a handful of researchers in the US and the UK discovered a possible treatment for Parkinson's that uses the pollen and dried root matter from the Blushing Note."

Chavez and his officer look at me like I've lost my mind, and I straighten as much as my bruised back will allow. "If you don't believe me, you can contact Dr. Howard Lowenstein at the Smithsonian Environmental Research Center." I rattle off the number with a huff, but my little burst of indignation saps my energy, so I sink back against Austin and let him prop me up. I'm so tired, I just want to sleep, but I know this is important.

"My apologies," Chavez says. "Please continue."

"A few days ago—crap. Sunday, I think. We noticed some anomalies in the photos from one of the study sites—Site One. There's a bug that likes to attack orchids—a spider mite. It doesn't kill them, just mars the petals and leaves so they can't be sold as collectors' items. When we arrived two weeks ago, the orchids at all five sites had spider mite damage. But the photos we took just a few days ago didn't show any of the damage we'd seen before. So either someone sprayed them with the world's best pesticide or those weren't the same plants we'd photographed when we arrived."

"You believe someone was stealing the plants and *replacing* them?" Chavez asks.

"Someone *was.*" Nerves twist into an icy ball in the pit of my stomach, and I wrap my arms around myself, pulling away from Austin as much as I can.

"Mik? What's wrong?" he asks.

"I'm sorry." The words escape on a whisper, and I can't look at him. "We were going to go to Site One on Monday after-noon—all four of us—but Corey and Isaiah had food poisoning. Li and I had readings we needed to get from Site Four, and after we finished those, I decided to hike up to Site One myself. When I got there..." I swallow hard. I can't keep this secret any longer, and he's going to hate me.

"Go on," Chavez says.

"Three men were harvesting orchids from the site. I tried to get away before they saw me, but I had an asthma attack. I was about to pass out. One of them got to my inhaler and helped me. I didn't know...not until I could breathe again...but it was Corey. He was with them. Helping them."

"What?" Austin springs to his feet and stands directly in front of me, fingers gripping my shoulders. "Mik...what the fuck? Why didn't you tell me?"

"I...he tried to help me. After the other two—Arturo and Martín, I don't know their last names—zip tied my wrists and were trying to decide what to do with me, Corey...he told me to run. He tried to distract Arturo and Martín to give me a chance to get away."

Tears burn my eyes, and I shrink away from his touch.

"Mikayla—"

"Let me finish, please? I can't...I need to get this out so maybe I can stop replaying every minute of that night over and over again in my head." I'm actively crying now, and Austin drops his hands and sinks back down onto the bed, this time at least a foot away from me. The loss of his warmth, of his arm around me, his support? It hurts. So much more than my memories, and I sniffle and swipe at my eyes. Detective Chavez is watching me intently, and I focus my gaze on his tie.

"I sponsored Corey for the Smithsonian internship. His grades weren't perfect, but he's *smart*. From his essay though, I knew if someone didn't step in and give him a chance, he'd drop out of school. His home life is a mess, and that's how they got to him."

Chavez narrows his eyes at me. "Can you explain, Señorita Salim?"

"Dr. Salim. Or Mikayla." The automatic response, one I'm used to giving any time someone tries to patronize me, slips out before I can stop it, but Chavez waves his hand.

"My apologies. Dr. Salim. Why do you think Larkin's home life was to blame?"

Lowering my gaze to the floor, I have to force the words out. "He told me so. Right before he tried to help me get away, he said he knew how valuable the Blushing Note was. His dad was in so deep with one of the cartels that's active in Los Angeles—where he grew up—and so he contacted them. Said he could get all the money his dad owed and more."

I recount the whole story, stopping only when I need water. How Corey used our research to cross-breed the Blushing Note. How the poachers replaced all of the plants they stole.

Austin doesn't say a word until they ask him for his statement, and as he explains how he found me, how he got me off that ledge, carried me to the dilapidated building in the middle of nowhere, and then got us back to the lab, Chavez whistles.

"That is quite impressive, señor. Not many men would be able to accomplish such a feat."

Bristling, Austin snaps, "You're right. I'm one of the few who could. I'm also a retired Major General in the United States Air Force and I've spent the past two months hiking and climbing my way here from the start of the Maya Trail. So before you go accusing me of anything, you might want to make a couple of calls and verify those facts."

"I am sorry," Chavez says. "I meant no disrespect. It is my job to ask these questions."

With a sigh, Austin unclenches his fists and rubs his hands over his thighs. "If it gets these guys arrested, it'll all be worth it," he mutters.

It takes another hour for us to finish our statements, and then Chavez offers us a ride to the hotel they've booked for us. "Can we have a minute?" Austin asks.

"We will be right outside."

The door closes quietly, and then we're alone. Austin turns towards me, and the look on his face makes me want to cry. "Why didn't you say anything, Mikayla? I thought you trusted me."

"I do." An errant tear races down my cheek, and I swipe it away, then straighten. Sort of. I'm so tired and sore, it's probably an ineffective gesture. "When my cousin was eleven, her parents tried to *sell* her for drug money. She ran away, and eventually, my parents were able to get custody of her. The stories she'd tell me... I recognize the signs, Austin. The body language. The look someone gets in their eyes when they're living in constant fear." Shaking my head, I swallow hard. "Corey's father sold drugs right out of their tiny apartment. He's been beaten up, threatened, had to bail his dad out of jail... over and over and over again. It's a miracle he made it as far in school as he did. Had to depend on scholarships and a heck of a lot of hard work. It...*does* something to you, when the people you're supposed to be able to trust more than anyone else in the world betray you."

Austin flinches like I just slapped him and stumbles back. His entire demeanor shifts, the anger fading into a deep, emotional pain. I've seen that look in his eyes. Every time he's closed down and shut me out. He knows what it's like to be betrayed.

Taking a chance, I reach out and wrap my fingers around his wrist. When he doesn't shake me off, I pull him closer. "I should have told you. I'm sorry. I don't think Corey's a bad guy. I think he was just...trapped."

Something shifts in Austin's eyes, and the hazel depths turn dark and stormy. "People do terrible things when their backs are against the wall." Before I register the movement, he wraps me in a gentle embrace, and I bury my face against his neck. Even after everything, after the fire, the blood, the night spent in ruins easily two centuries old, underneath the sweat and the smoke, he smells like pure male strength. Like home. Like everything I've ever dreamed of in a man.

His fingers slide into my hair, and the intimate gesture sends me over the edge, my tears spilling down my cheeks as I fight to keep breathing.

I almost lost something I never knew I was looking for. Something real. Something I'm now desperate to hold onto. "I'm sorry. So sorry..." I manage between sobs.

"Shhh, sweetheart. You don't have anything to apologize for. Just promise me one thing." He eases back slightly so he can hold my gaze. "No more secrets, okay?"

I nod, and in that moment, my entire world rights. It doesn't matter that the poachers have my driver's license, passport, and credit cards. That they're still free...somewhere. That I almost died twenty-four hours ago. All that matters is what's right in front of me.

"No more secrets."

CHAPTER SIXTEEN

Detective Chavez and his partner drive us to a hotel a few kilometers away from where we'd been staying and accompany us to the front desk.

"For tonight," Chavez tells the clerk as he pulls a business card from his pocket, "You can send the bill to me. Two rooms—"

"One," Mikayla and I say at the same time. Thank God I don't have to convince her to let me stay with her. I'll sleep on the couch. Hell, in front of the fucking door. I'm not leaving her side while those assholes are free.

"One room then," Chavez says and scribbles something on the back of his business card and passes it to the clerk. "Please put them on the same floor as Li Chen and Isaiah Williams. A uniformed officer will be patrolling that floor tonight." Turning to me, he offers me his hand. "Major General Pritchard, Dr. Salim. It is late. We will call you in the morning with what we have been able to learn about these two men."

"Our things, Detective?" I ask. We're both filthy and bloody, and more than anything, Mikayla needs to feel like herself again.

"When the Hotel Centro learned the students were kidnapped from their loading dock, they became very...uncooperative. We may not have your things until morning, but we have officers at the hotel now, and we will not allow anyone to enter your rooms."

Mik doesn't respond, and from the look on her face...she's so worn out, so mentally and physically drained, I need to get her into bed before she topples over.

"Just do what you can. We've been in these clothes for two full days."

Chavez gives me a curt nod, and his officer leads us to a fourth-floor suite and bids us goodnight.

I clear the living area, bedroom, bathroom, and two closets while Mik stands just inside the door, totally silent. "It's all good, sweetheart. Come with me." Leading her into the bath, I turn on the hot water in the shower, then lift her up onto the counter.

Steam fills the room as I kneel in front of her and unlace her boots. Once I have the brace off and set it down next to her, I push to my feet and shove my hands into my pockets. It's either that or touch her, hold her, and I don't think she's ready for that. "There's a robe on the back of the door. Can you manage with that ankle?"

"Y-yes. I'll be okay," she whispers. Her cheeks flush, and she stares at her knees, her khaki pants torn and stained, like she's seeing them for the first time. "I don't...we don't have any clothes."

"I'll call down and see if the hotel has anything available. If not, we'll live in the robes tonight. First thing in the morning,

I'll get us a flight to Maryland." Brushing my knuckles along her cheek, I wait for her to look up at me. "We're safe now, sweetheart. As safe as I can make us. If you want me to stand guard at the door all night, I will. Otherwise, I'll take the couch."

She watches me as I leave, and dammit. I wish I could say something—*do* something—to reassure her. With no clue how to fix what the past few days have broken in her, I call the front desk, then rummage in the closet and find a spare set of sheets, a blanket, and a pillow to make up the couch.

Every muscle in my body aches, and I'm tempted to lie down right now, but I wasn't kidding. I'll sit up all night, stand guard, if that's what she needs. Plus, I smell like the ass end of a burned-out garbage truck.

The water turns off, and I set my hunting knife on the table next to the couch, then dig through my ruck for my phone. Battery's mostly dead, but once it's plugged in, I fire off a quick text to Trevor.

What would it take to get a flight from San Cristóbal de las Casas to Maryland? One that doesn't go through channels? Four passengers. I'm fine. Don't worry Dani.

He replies in under a minute.

Explain. Right fucking now.

I should have known. He won't let this go and while I have no doubt he's already on the phone to Dax or Ryker making arrangements, he'll let me twist in the wind until I give him a halfway acceptable answer.

Met someone in trouble. That's all I can say tonight. Need you to trust me. If we have to fly commercial, we'll be stuck here for days waiting on passport replacement. Going dark for the night, but text me in the morning.

I'll catch all kinds of shit for this when we get back to the

States. Hell, if he waits much after sunrise to demand answers, it'll be a fucking miracle.

Five minutes later, my phone vibrates on the table. "Trevor, you better not expect me to answer you," I mutter as I check the screen.

A Cessna Citation Sovereign, N354TV, will arrive at the San Cristóbal airport tomorrow at 13:00. It takes off for Baltimore no later than 17:00. Be on it. And you're going to explain everything. In person. No more than twenty-four hours after you land. Even if I have to drive down there myself. Got it?

I haven't felt like laughing in two days. But I chuckle as I thumb out a reply.

Crystal, Superman. I owe you.

The little dots on screen dance for a few seconds, and one final message pops up.

No. My ledger's going to be red for the rest of my life. But that's a discussion for another time.

Mikayla

A shower has never felt so good. For the first time in...I don't even know how long—I'm warm, and I don't smell of mud and sweat and soot and blood.

After I dry myself off and belt the robe tightly, I shove my clothes into the trash. My wrists are still red and a little raw from the zip tie, and every step—even after I put the ankle brace back on—hurts, but I'm alive, and Austin's on the other side of that door.

I almost found the words to ask him to shower with me. They were there. Pinging around in my brain. But though I'm almost forty years old, I can't just forget how my parents raised me. No swearing. No casual sex. No revealing clothing.

If this were a normal relationship, I'd know what to do. Despite my parents' wishes, I'm not a virgin. I've slept with three guys since college. Each one of them, I thought I might be on my way to loving. That's always been my rule. If I care for the man, if I think I might love him one day, then I'll take that plunge.

With Austin, there's no question in my mind. I care for him. More than I've cared for anyone in a long time. But do I love him? Or are all these confusing feelings a result of almost dying?

A small toiletry kit in the bathroom affords me the chance to brush my teeth, and when I limp out to the main room, Austin's staring out a one-inch gap in the drapes.

"Hey," I say quietly. "Bathroom's yours."

When he turns, his gaze softens, and the corners of his lips twitch into what might almost be a smile. "You look...stunning."

"I'm exhausted and wearing a white bathrobe. Are you sure you don't need a CT scan? I'm really starting to worry about your eyesight."

He chuckles, the tension leaving his shoulders, and for the first time since this whole mess started, I think...maybe things will be okay.

"I don't need a doctor, sweetheart. Just a shower. The concierge sent up t-shirts and shorts. I guess they keep some on hand for guests who don't realize this place has a full gym. Yours are in the bag on the bed. The door's double-locked, and I wedged a chair in front of it. No one's getting in here tonight." On his way to the bathroom with a folded set of clothes under his arm, he pauses and takes my hand. "My wallet's on the desk. If you're hungry, order up some room service."

"I don't think anything would stay down. But what about

you?" I ask. "That granola bar at the hospital couldn't have been enough for you."

"I'm a guy. I can always eat. But I'd be just as happy falling asleep on that couch there and not seeing another soul until morning. I'll be out in just a few minutes."

I want him to kiss me, but he doesn't. Probably because he still smells like sweat and smoke and death. Or maybe it's because we're safe, and he's as unsure as I am.

As soon as the shower turns on, I open the bag and pull out the gray t-shirt and shorts emblazoned with the hotel's logo. The shirt isn't exactly loose, the shorts not overly tight, and I have no bra or panties, but it's still so wonderful to be wearing something clean, I don't care.

The king-sized bed feels empty with all this space next to me, and I prop myself up against the pillows and wait until Austin emerges from the bathroom, his dark brown hair damp and tousled, and his face clean—other than the three-day growth of stubble. With all the soot and dirt, I hadn't even noticed.

"What's wrong?" he asks as he sinks down onto the couch and rubs a hand towel over his hair. "I figured you'd be passed out by now."

"I...you don't need to sleep over there." I chew on my lower lip, clutching the blankets just under my breasts. "I'd feel better if you weren't so far away."

Austin's at my side in three steps, but he doesn't get under the covers, just sits next to my hip. "Mik, you have no idea how badly I want to sleep with you. Even if it's just sleep...for now." He grins, and my cheeks flush red hot. "But are you sure?"

"Yes." I don't know where this boldness comes from, but I'm going with it. In my professional life, I kick butt regularly. With men? I fumble around like they're hot potatoes. Covered in bees.

He nods, his expression turning serious, and skirts the bed. "If you're uncomfortable—"

"Austin." I pull back the blankets and pat the mattress next to me. "You've been nothing but a perfect gentleman from the moment I met you. Stop."

"Being a gentleman?" He chuckles as he lies down next to me, his eyes fixed on the ceiling, and when he pulls the sheet over him, it tents more than a little. "I want you, sweetheart. I can't tell you how difficult it was to keep my...err..."

"Hard on?" I supply.

"That's one term for it." His laugh is so relaxed here in this room where no one can find us. "But I was going to say 'keep my dick under control.'"

I look down, wishing I'd stayed in the robe. My nipples are tight and hard under the t-shirt, and warmth blooms in my core.

"When we get back to the States, I hope you'll be willing to go on a proper date with me. And after that...maybe we can talk about the next step." Austin urges me onto my side next to him and wraps his arm around my waist. His lips find my ear, and goosebumps race down my arms as he scores his teeth over the sensitive skin. "I've never met anyone as strong as you, Mikayla. I want to see where this goes. Because I think it could be somewhere amazing."

"It already is."

His whole body vibrates as a low, possessive sound rumbles through his chest. "When I came down to Mexico, I wanted to get away from everyone and everything. Pretend for just a little while that I wasn't a fucked up asshole who..."

"Hey." I wriggle until I'm facing him and cup his cheek. "Whatever it is, you can tell me."

"Tomorrow." He shakes his head, buries his face in my neck, and inhales deeply. "After we've slept. Had more of a meal than an MRE and that hospital-issued granola bar."

"We're here now. Together."

"And we'll be together tomorrow too," he says. "Just...be patient with me for another day. It's not a good story, and the idea of telling you here, when everything's so raw? I can't. For you or for me."

The strain in his voice worries me. This isn't the strong, confident hero I've started to fall for. This is a man with secrets. With a past. With ghosts more terrible than I can imagine haunting him. Though after the past two days, my imagination is a lot more...vivid than it ever used to be.

"I'll be here, Austin." I kiss him, savoring the feel of his full lips, the way he wraps his body around mine, even the hard length of him pressing against me. "I'll be right here."

Austin

The nightmare's always the same. I know the room. Even six years later, every detail is seared into my memory.

I'm alone in the dark. Bound to a chair, duct tape gagging me, something tied over my eyes so tightly, no light penetrates.

I can't feel my hands, but every single cut Gil's made over the past two days burns with its own terrible fire. My chest. Abs. Back. All the way down my leg. He laughs from somewhere behind me.

Not alone. Fuck.

Gil claps a hand on my shoulder, digging his fingers into one of the deeper cuts. "Smile for the camera, brother."

Hostage video. I have to do *something*. Trevor will see this, and I can't let him come rescue me. Gil's lost it. Whatever his birth father did to him, said to him...the boy I grew up with is gone. The man he is now? Doesn't give a fuck about anyone unless his daddy says so.

Gil's footsteps recede, there's a beep, and then he returns to my side.

"You shouldn't have sent him, Trevor. I know all of his secrets. I grew up knowing them. Just like yours. You can't stop me. *La justicia está de mi lado!*"

Something hits my thigh, and for a split second, I don't register what it is. But then the pain lances through my leg, and I can't stifle my strangled scream as I thrash against the ropes holding me to the chair.

When we were kids, Gil excelled at knot tying. I think that was his favorite badge in the Scouts. And the one time I let him test his knots on me—not long after I'd graduated from the Air Force Academy, there was no escape. I had to promise him fifty bucks to let me go. He's better than anyone.

"Pull all of your American agents out of Venezuela by the end of the week, or I'll send Perfect Pritchard back to you in pieces," Gil says, his voice an odd mix of fury and glee as I shake my head as hard as I can, the only signal I can give Trevor. Or anyone. A beep sounds once more, and then he grabs my hair and pulls my head back, exposing my throat.

The knife he presses to my Adam's apple is sticky with the blood from my thigh. "All you had to do was walk away, Austin. Walk away and let me do my own thing. But no. You came after me. Regretting that now, aren't you?"

I can't answer him. Not through the duct tape. But no. I don't regret a fucking thing. Gil's a traitor to his country, to the CIA, and to his own family. The one that took him in. Adopted him. Loved him. Worst of all, he turned on his own sister.

The pressure from the blade disappears, and a second later, pain explodes across the back of my skull. All sounds fade into a dull roar, and I wish I could tell Trevor not to come. That I'm already dead. Gil's going to kill me. Soon.

"Austin?" Cool hands run down my arms, and her fingers are so delicate and gentle, I start to pull myself back from the depths of my nightmare. "Wake up, Danger."

I groan her name and pull her against me, relishing her curves, the way she molds her body to mine. The faint light seeping in around the privacy curtains halos her face, making her look like an angel. My angel. "Shit. What time is it?"

"A little after eight."

"Was I...saying anything?" I don't want to have this conversation until we're back in the United States, but from her tone... she's not going to cut me much slack.

"'Gil.'" Mikayla snuggles closer, laying her head on the pillow so we're facing one another.

Change the subject.

Except I promised her. That after we slept, we'd talk. "Mik, my brother..."

Before I can admit my truth, my phone vibrates on the nightstand, and I roll over and check the screen.

"Detective Chavez. What can I do for you?"

Mikayla wriggles closer so she can listen in, and I put the phone on speaker.

"Corey Larkin is still in a medically-induced coma, but we searched his hotel room, and under the mattress, we found a slip of paper with the full names of the two individuals who attacked Dr. Salim. We have not located them yet, but we will."

"What does that mean for us? Is there any reason we need to stay in Mexico? We'd like to return to the United States this afternoon if possible."

"We may have more questions," the detective says, "but as long as you make yourselves available as needed, there is no reason you cannot go home. I can reach you at this number?"

"Yes."

"And Dr. Salim?"

Mikayla clears her throat. "My phone was destroyed. But I'll get a new one when I get home." She rattles off the number, and the detective thanks us and wishes us well.

I toss the phone back on the nightstand and link our fingers. "Want to go home, sweetheart?"

"Yes. Absolutely."

CHAPTER SEVENTEEN

Austin

One of the local *Policia* knocks on our door only a few minutes after Detective Chavez ends the call. "Your luggage, señor."

I came to Mexico with only my rucksack, but before I left to find Mikayla, I'd dumped half of it onto the bed to lighten my load. Whoever packed up my room shoved everything into a Hotel Centro duffel bag. I hope they got it all.

But beyond that, there's only a single, rolling suitcase.

"You pack light, sweetheart," I say when Mik shuffles out of the bathroom, moving too slowly, too carefully for my liking. She's in pain, and I hate that I can't do anything for her.

Her smile holds a bit of strain, but still, it's more relaxed than I've seen since our date. "My wardrobe out in the field is pretty basic. Khakis, tank tops, flannel. I didn't expect to *meet* anyone." A flush spreads up her neck to her cheeks, and she sinks down onto the bed and unzips the suitcase I set there for her. "Not that I dress much differently at home."

"Mik." I crouch in front of her, my hands on either side of

her thighs. Her bare thighs. Other than the various bruises, her skin is perfect. Soft. Smooth. She doesn't pull away, despite only wearing shorts and a tight t-shirt, and I love how much more comfortable she is with me now. "You don't have to impress me with clothes or make-up or...anything. I hope you know that."

"You've seen me at my worst," she says softly. "And for some reason, you're still here. That's pretty strong scientific evidence."

"I'm still here because I care for you." The words break something loose inside me, and dammit. I have to start letting her in—despite how much I wish I could keep my pain locked away. "The past few years have been difficult. I don't think I even realized *how* difficult until I left my post. But when I came down to Mexico and suddenly had all of this time...alone? I'm fucked in the head, Mik. On an epic scale. And I'm terrified that once you know just how epic, you're going to run away and I'll never see you again."

My admission stirs a storm of emotion in her brown eyes, making the copper flecks shine brighter, and she leans forward and kisses me. It's gentle, almost sweet, but full of understanding, of need, of the reassurance I'm desperate for—that she'll give us a chance when we're back in the real world. The one where no one wants her dead, and we can just be. Two people with a connection forged during the most intense circumstances, who just maybe...can help one another heal.

Her stomach growls, putting an end to the tender moment. Mik's cheeks flush a shade darker, and she presses her hand to her belly and offers me a sheepish smile. Pushing to my feet, I head for the phone to order us the biggest breakfast this hotel has to offer.

NINETY MINUTES LATER, Mik pokes her head out of the steam-filled bathroom. "Um, Austin? I could use a little help."

Zipping up my ruck, I turn and lose my words entirely. She's wearing a pair of slim black pants and gray socks, but though she brought a maroon tank top in with her, she has a towel clutched to her chest instead. "What do you need?"

Her face is redder than I've ever seen it, and she turns around, revealing her unhooked bra. "I can't..." Her voice fades as she stares down at the floor.

I stop with my hands inches from her back. The bruises look so much worse today, and shit. She's going to be miserable sitting on a plane for five hours. "I have some arnica in my bag. Will you let me put some on you before I do up your bra?"

"Arnica?" She peers back at me, uncertainty playing over her features.

"Yeah. Friends turned me on to it. Works wonders on bruises. Take a seat on the bed."

Mik sinks down onto the mattress, and—fuck me—lowers the towel. She's still holding her bra in place, but this is the most comfortable she's ever been with me.

Don't screw it up.

Sitting behind her, I warm a bit of the arnica in my palms and then start at her shoulders.

With every inch of her skin I touch, she relaxes by a degree, until I'm massaging only a couple of inches above her waistband. Back up again until I secure the clasp of her bra, then wrap my arms around her from behind. "Your back should start to feel better soon."

"It already does." Twisting in my embrace, she cups my cheek. I was finally able to shave today, and her thumb skates over the smooth skin. "Too good to be true."

"I'm not. There's so much I still need to tell you, Mik." The thought of losing her now, after all we've been through, after hiking for hours in the pouring rain searching for her, after strapping her to my back and scaling a cliff, after carrying her, unconscious, through the jungle... If she runs from me once she knows the truth, I'll never trust anyone ever again.

Her eyes flash with emotion, and she drops her hand, scooting back on the bed a few inches and facing me without embarrassment. I fight not to let my gaze drop to her breasts. I may respect the fuck out of her, but I'm still a man—last time I checked.

"Austin, have you ever knowingly hurt a woman?"

I straighten my spine, years of military training lending strength to my words. "No, ma'am. Never."

"Have you ever cheated? Lied for your own benefit? Or been anything other than completely and totally respectful to me?" Warm fingers circle my wrist, and she brings my hand to her breast.

I barely manage to stifle my groan. She's a perfect handful. Her nipple pebbles under my palm and goosebumps race down her arms. Keeping perfectly still, unwilling to do anything she's not completely ready for, I hold her gaze. "No. At least not...intentionally."

"That's what I thought. Don't try to tell me you're someone I *know* you aren't," she says with a huff. "You're a good man, Austin. And if we'd had that second date when we'd planned, we'd probably be naked in this bed right now."

My dick goes from zero to granite as that last sentence sinks in. "Mik...God. You have no idea how much I want you."

She chuckles, and though I refuse to let my gaze leave her eyes, she makes it a point to stare directly at my hard on. "*No idea?* I'm not *that* naive." Leaning in for a quick, passionate kiss, she pushes up and then shuffles back to the bathroom.

Fuck. This amazing woman might actually accept me as

broken as I am—with all my darkness, all my flaws, all my nightmares and pain.

My phone buzzes, and I roll my eyes as Trevor's name pops up on the screen. I'm surprised he waited this long. "Yeah?"

"Should have known you wouldn't reach out on your own," Trev mutters. "You going to make that flight?"

"Yes. We'll be at the airport right around 1:00 p.m. But... there's something else I need to ask you for."

"Name it."

Despite his matter-of-fact tone, I know I'm about to push my luck. "I need a protective detail for three people."

"Three?" He snorts. "What the fuck are you doing down there, Austin? Rescuing a small village?"

"Just one botanist and two twenty-something research assistants." I run a hand through my hair, hoping he won't make me explain here, with Mik in the next room.

"Twenty-four-seven?"

"Yes. The botanist...I can handle nights, but a couple of external surveillance cameras wouldn't be a bad idea. For everyone. I don't know how far this particular cartel is willing to go to keep them quiet."

Trev chuckles. "You can *handle nights?* We're going to have a long talk when you get back, man. And I assume you're going to let me and Dani meet her. Or...I guess I shouldn't assume...him?"

"Her," I say sharply. "And maybe. If things work out. Don't push me. Not on this."

"Austin, I get it. You don't think it was damn near impossible for me to admit my feelings for Dani? I'm not pushing you. I'm..." He sighs, and there's a long silence followed by a whispered curse. "I'm trying to say I understand. And if there's one thing I've learned since Venezuela," his voice cracks, and I sink down onto the bed, "it's that holding all this shit in doesn't do you a damn bit of good. Only makes life harder. Don't make the same mistakes I did. Don't shut your family out. And if whatever's going on with this botanist is serious, don't shut her out either."

Someone knocks on Trevor's door, and he calls out, "Come on in, Dax," before lowering his voice again. "When you land, Ronan will be there with a car. Stay safe, brother."

Brother.

The word rattles around my brain as Mik emerges from the bathroom and I tuck the cell phone into my pocket. Every time I see her face, she takes my breath away. Now, with her hair swept back and a hint of blush on her cheeks, it's like she's rediscovered some of her confidence. The tank top molds to her breasts, and though she's still limping, her steps are smoother, her shoulders a little straighter, and when she reaches my side, she wraps her arms around my waist. "Who were you talking to?"

"Trevor. He and his boss, Dax, were the ones who arranged the flight for us." Staring down at her, I almost can't believe she's real. That I met her in a bar in the middle of Mexico, and now...there's something between us so intense, I don't ever want to let her go.

"Are you ready to go home?" I skim my knuckle over her cheek, and her eyelids flutter as she settles against me.

"Are you sure it's safe?" Uncertainty clouds her gaze. "They took my driver's license. What if they show up at my house?"

"It'll be the last thing they ever do. Dax's firm—Second Sight—they're the best in the world. I asked Trev to set up surveillance for you, Li, and Isaiah. No one's going to get to you on my watch."

"And you're..." She shakes her head. "Crap on a cracker, I'm so bad at this."

"At what?" Pulling her over to the bed, I ease her down and take her hand.

"This is all new to me, Austin," she says with a little wobble to her voice. "Sharing my...my life with someone."

"Your—?"

"I don't want you to leave," she says, her words tumbling over one another like she can't get them out fast enough. "It's only been a few days, but I *know* you. This—" Mik nods at our joined hands, "—this connection? None of the normal rules apply here. At least, I hope they don't."

"My life hasn't been normal since...all the shit that happened with Gil." I have to start letting her in. No matter how much it hurts. For Trev to warn me, to tell me to open up? He's one of the only people in this world I trust. Or was. Until I met her.

Mik frowns, concern etching faint lines around her eyes. "I know we have to get going. But...once we're back in the United States? You're going to tell me, right? At least some of it?"

"I'm going to try."

She leans in and kisses me deeply, passionately, and her contented sigh when she pulls away? This woman truly believes we have a future. Together. I won't do a damn thing to screw that up.

***

Mikayla

I haven't stopped gawking since Austin helped me up the stairs of the private Cessna. It's luxurious in a way I always thought was reserved for *James Bond* movies or...at the very least, the super rich.

"Major General Pritchard?" one of the flight attendants

says as Austin and I take seats across from one another, a polished wood table between us. "Dax Holloway wanted me to tell you that whatever else you need—both in flight and once we land in Maryland—is yours."

"Whatever else you need?" I whisper when the man heads for the jump seat to buckle himself in. "Austin, how much did this cost?"

"No fucking clue." He runs a hand through his hair, then glances around the luxurious cabin. Isaiah and Li are sitting two rows behind us, staring out the windows as we start to taxi. "I didn't ask. Pretty sure Dax hasn't worried about money in a long time, though. Not with some of the clients Second Sight's handled over the years. And Ryker? He's loaded."

I'm confused now. "What does Ryker have to do with Dax's financial health?"

Austin shakes his head and chuckles. "Those two are so tight, you couldn't drive a nail between 'em with a sledgehammer. They teamed up last year—merged Hidden Agenda, Ry's K&R firm with Second Sight—and now, they're expanding. If Dax needed anything, under any circumstance, Ry would make sure he had it."

"And you worked with them both in Venezuela?" I ask. I want to *know* this man. Really know him. And meet his friends.

"Not exactly." The plane levels off, and Austin glances at the flight attendant before he turns back to me. "I used to run the United States Joint Special Operations Command, Mik."

"I know. I've seen your Wikipedia page, remember?" My lips curve into a smile. I'm still shocked I had the gall to look him up that first night.

"We—they—oversee the most elite of the military. Delta Force, SEAL Team 6, the Air Force's 24th Special Tactics Squadron, the 75th Ranger Regiment, and a whole lot of other units I can't talk about.

"If this—if we go the way I hope we go, you're going to meet Dax before too long. Trevor, Ryker, Wren, Graham, West, Inara..."

His face softens a little when he says their names, so they're obviously important to him.

"Maybe even Ripper."

"Ripper? What kind of name is Ripper?" My query is supposed to be teasing, but Austin's face hardens, his hazel eyes turning dark and stormy in a heartbeat.

"The one he wanted. The man spent six fucking years being tortured, brainwashed, and forced to do the unimaginable. No one knew he was even alive until fifteen months ago. Dax, Ry, and Trevor—along with a few others—went to rescue him. He'd been using a different name—one his captor forced on him—but Ripper was his call sign when he was in the Special Forces, and so that's what he goes by now."

"Oh, crap. I'm sorry. I didn't mean..."

"It's okay, sweetheart. You couldn't have known."

"Where was he?"

"Afghanistan." Austin's still tense, and I rest my hand, palm up, on the table between us. He stares at it for a minute, then links our fingers. "Finding him...it should have been my job. Hell, knowing he was even alive in the first place *was* my job. But JSOC had two assholes in our ranks who kept it quiet so they could sell arms to the guy torturing Rip."

"Oh, God."

"There was a hell of a lot of bureaucracy to cut through. You bring a single member of the Armed Forces into any operation, and paperwork bullshit goes up a hundred fold. But the long and short of it is...technically, Ripper could have been sent away for war crimes. For treason. I couldn't let that happen. He's the most honorable man I know—along with Dax and Ry. Hell, he'd been completely brainwashed, his whole identity destroyed, and he *still* managed to find small ways to resist the bastard who had him. And those ways helped Dax, Ry, and their team put an end to that scourge on humanity."

From the way he talks about these men, I don't have to ask if they're close. They clearly are. And Austin trusts them with his life.

"Trevor came to me, asked me for my help when the guys—*my guys*—were after Ripper. I pulled a few strings, buried some intel—because it was the right thing—the honorable thing—to do, and that whole crew...they're kind of like my extended family now."

When he squeezes my hand and does that amazing thing with his thumb along the inside of my wrist, I feel like nothing will ever hurt me again. I know it's an illusion. That Austin can't really stop anything and anyone who might ever want to hurt me—but he stopped Arturo and Martín, and for now, that's enough.

"Well, when I meet Dax, remind me to thank him for this. I've never been on a nicer plane."

Austin's brows shoot up. "When?"

"Yes. When."

CHAPTER EIGHTEEN

Mikayla

Before we even unbuckle our seatbelts in Baltimore, the cabin door opens, and a dark-haired man, on the wiry side, enters and nods in our direction.

"Pritchard. Ya' look a bit thinner than the last time I saw ya'," he says with just a hint of an Irish brogue.

"Hiking more than five hundred miles through Mexico will do that to a guy," Austin mutters as he wraps his arm around my waist. "Ronan, this is Dr. Mikayla Salim."

"Hi. Mik is fine." Austin's body language gives me the impression he's not thrilled with Ronan's presence, and when a second man, this one a little bulkier with dark blond hair and blue eyes ducks through the door, Austin narrows his eyes.

"Are we having a party?" he asks, his voice tight.

"This is Clive. Works at Second Sight? Cut me some slack, mate. Did ya' really think I'd bring someone on board I didn't trust?" Ronan scowls, then nods to Li and Isaiah, who stand off to the side, both looking like they want to shrink into oblivion. "Clive is goin' to handle settin' up the outside surveillance."

Clive shakes my hand, then Austin's. "You're a bit of a legend around the office."

With a snort, Austin rolls his eyes. "I'm no legend. That's Dax. And Ry. Maybe Trev."

Ronan leans closer and lowers his voice. "Call him, mate. You disappearin' did a number on him."

"I'm working on it." Austin guides me to the stairs and practically carries me down to the tarmac. "Ronan was on the mission in Venezuela," he says quietly. "But I think this is the most I've heard him talk at once...ever."

"And he and Clive work for Dax."

Nodding, Austin waits for the two of them to retrieve all the luggage and join us—along with Isaiah and Li—close to two black SUVs.

"Hey Perry White. Catch," Ronan says as he unlocks the closest vehicle to load up the bags, then tosses Austin a set of keys. "That one's yours. We're takin' these two home, then I'm droppin' Clive off at his cousin's place. Oh, and there's somethin' in the console for ya'."

Austin nods. "Thanks. You'll be on days with Mik if I can't be?"

Staring back and forth between Ronan and Austin, I ask, "What?"

As he opens the passenger door for me, Austin lowers his voice. "I can't be with you twenty-four hours a day, Mik. Not and try to find out who these assholes were, how they got to Corey in the first place, and whether or not you're still in danger. When I'm not with you, Ronan will be."

"You got me a bodyguard." The words escape on a whisper, and though I'm scared the cartel will somehow follow me back home, I believed Austin when he said we'd be safe. But now I wonder...does *he* even believe it?

Ronan clears his throat. "Mik, ya' won't need to worry. We protect our own, and Clive has contacts here. He vetted the locals assigned to your two grad students. All we need now is for Pritchard here to tell us what we're protectin' ya' from."

"A Mexican cartel involved in the illegal sale and trade of endangered orchids," Austin says. "We don't know much more than that. They operate out of Chiapas, and they're not exactly happy with any of us for disrupting their operations. Once I get Mik home, I'll call Wren and see if she can find out anything more."

"Roger that," Ronan says. "Text Clive the address so he can take care of the cameras. We'll take care of these two first, then head your way. After that, you're on your own until mornin'. But I'll find the closest hotel to Dr. Salim's place."

"Dr. Mik?" Li has her arm around Isaiah's waist, and her brown eyes blaze with confidence. "Isaiah and I don't need separate people. I'll be staying at his place from now on."

"Our place," Isaiah gently corrects.

Despite the constant stream of worried commentary running through my head, I grin at them. "So, when we get back to work, does this mean you'll stop arriving at the lab in two cars, exactly ten minutes apart?"

Li covers her face with her hands. "Were we really that predictable?"

"Every single day." I pull Li into a hug. She stiffens for a brief moment, but then hugs me back. "I'm just glad you two are okay."

"Why didn't we see it?" Isaiah asks.

Behind us, Austin, Clive, and Ronan are talking in hushed tones, but I ignore them for now. My students need me, and I haven't been a very good leader the past few days, and I was so wrapped up in my own pain and fear, I forgot they're still... kids. Twenty-six and full of idealism, hope, and the belief that people are basically *good*.

"I don't know. As soon as Corey wakes up, I hope he'll have some answers."

While we waited to be seen at the hospital, Li told me how Arturo and Martín kidnapped them. Corey had called their room and told them to come down to the loading dock. That I was back. When Li and Isaiah came running, Corey was already unconscious and bleeding in the back of the Jeep. Arturo held a gun to Li's head while Martín bound and gagged them both with duct tape. Neither of them had known Corey's part until Arturo and Martín taunted them during the drive to the lab.

Li touches my arm, "Are you okay, Dr. Mik?"

"I'm fine." Forcing a smile, I ignore how my back feels like it's one large bruise and my neck and shoulders have turned to granite. "I think...it's Tuesday, right?" We all laugh, but I suspect that's because no one's completely sure. "No work this week. Don't even think about coming in. We all need to heal up a bit. Mentally and physically. I'll call Dr. Lowenstein tomorrow and tell him what happened."

Isaiah takes Li's hand, and it's so amazing to see the two of them comfortable showing affection around me that my lips curve into a smile. "Are you sure?" he asks. "If there's work to be done, you shouldn't have to do it by yourself."

"I'm sure. Go home and enjoy some time together." Glancing back at Austin, something inside me heats, sending goosebumps racing down my arms. "I promise. I'm going to take my own advice."

Li and Isaiah exchange a single, meaningful look before they head for the second SUV with Clive already behind the wheel. Ronan leans close to Austin and whispers something in his ear before clapping him on the back and striding away.

"Ready, Mik?" Austin asks as he lifts me up into the impossibly high passenger seat. At five-foot-five, I'm not exactly short, but this car is a beast, and I'm grateful for the help. "I want pizza, a bath, and my bed. I don't think I've *ever* been more ready to go home than I am right now."

Austin clips his phone to the air vent, then looks at me expectantly. "I need your address, sweetheart."

"Oh." Why didn't I think of that? I rattle off the street number and name, and he leans across the car to brush a kiss to my cheek.

"Nothing's going to happen to you, Mik. Not while I'm around. I promise."

When he talks like that, I believe him. Or...at least, I want to.

Austin

After we stop for a pizza, where Mikayla surprises me by asking for a fully loaded pie—and insisting on paying for it—we turn onto a quiet residential street in northwestern Edgewater.

"It's the white house with the little porch," she says, clutching the pizza box like it's a suit of armor.

Sleek and modern, the house sits back from the road with native plants arranged artfully in front. Windows reflect the sunset, giving the entire building a warm, golden glow. Two stories, all perfectly white paint. "How long have you lived here?"

"Almost three years." Mik relaxes a little when I park the SUV. "My mother and father loaned me the money for the down payment." Her cheeks take on a deeper hue, and she stares down at her death grip on the pizza box. "Too many student loans."

She refuses my help to the door, balancing the pizza in one hand as she digs in her pocket for her keys with the other. "Mik, hang on before you go inside."

Her brows furrow, and she glances down at the box like it's the Holy Grail.

"I just want to clear it," I say when I come up behind her and unsnap the holster on my belt. I didn't ask for the Beretta M9, but despite his surly attitude, Ronan's whip smart and damn quick on the uptake. "Stay right behind me."

"What are you... Oh my God. You have a gun?" she hisses.

"Not taking a chance with your safety. Set the pizza down on the entry table and stay close." The bottom floor is almost completely open, the dining room, living room, and kitchen all easy to clear. And then we reach the stairs. I don't want her putting all that extra strain on her ankle, so I reach for her hand and give it a squeeze. "Wait here, sweetheart, and don't move from this spot." I kiss the top of her head before I head up, finding the exact opposite of open space on the second floor. Three bedrooms, two baths, and a handful of closets, all perfectly organized. Not a single item out of place, and the whole house smells like her.

Only her.

When I reach her side again, she's chewing on her lower lip and tugging on the short strands of her black hair.

"All clear, sweetheart. Why don't you sit down and put that foot up. I'll get the bags."

She lets out an adorable huff, but shuffles slowly over to the entry table for the pizza and carries it with her to the coffee table. Sinking down onto a cream-colored leather sofa, she flops back and closes her eyes. "Fine. But we're going to talk about where you got that gun."

I chuckle on my way out to the SUV. She's angry with me—or frustrated at least—but there's still affection in her tone, and most importantly, she's safe. As safe as I can make her.

Five minutes later, the door's locked, luggage upstairs, and I grab two glasses of water, plates, and napkins from her kitchen before I join her on the couch.

"Sorry I don't have beer," she says as she lifts the lid on the pizza box. "Or anything stronger."

"Sweetheart, all I need is you."

"Liar." She nudges my shoulder with hers.

I set the plate down and turn to her. "Mik, I'll never lie to you. Most of what I've done for the past twenty plus years falls under Top Secret clearance. You might ask me questions I *can't* answer. But I won't lie to you. Ever."

"That sounds like a line."

My laugh feels good, and some of the tension in my shoulders eases. "Is it working?"

"Maybe. Though you do realize I'm going to sleep with you tonight anyway, right?"

Oh, fuck.

There's nothing I want more than to be with her. I'm half tempted to carry her upstairs this second, but she turns her focus to her plate, and moans through her first bite. "I missed pizza."

"The first time we met, I had you pegged as a vegetarian."

Now it's her turn to laugh, and it does something to my gut I'm not prepared for. Stirs an emotion I didn't think I could feel and don't want to acknowledge. Not yet. Because if I'm right...

"Austin? Where'd you go?" she asks, smiling up at me.

"You're even more beautiful when you laugh, Mik." Skimming a knuckle down her cheek, I lean in for a decidedly pepperoni-flavored kiss. "But I missed something. What were you saying?"

"Just that my parents raised me to eat everything. Well, almost everything. No sushi. I draw the line at raw fish." Her nose wrinkles, and she dives back in for another bite, then licks her lips, and damn. The next hour or two—or however long she wants to wait to go upstairs—are going to be the longest of my life.

Forcing myself back to the present, I snag myself a second slice. "No raw fish. Got it. So what's the nicest restaurant in Edgewater? That's not sushi." I settle back with my plate and stretch my legs out under the coffee table.

Narrowing her eyes at me, Mik replies, "The Wharf Rider. Why?"

"Because I'd like to take you there for dinner tomorrow night. If that's okay with you." Her eyes widen, and I offer her a smile. "I still owe you a proper date."

"Austin, I don't need...proper." She exhales slowly and sets her plate down. "You have a *gun*. You felt the need to—what's the term? Clear my house?—before you let me come in. If 'proper' is going to put us in danger or mean you have to be armed and constantly on watch, then we should just stay here. Get takeout. I'd offer to cook, but my skills are pretty limited. Mac and cheese, soup out of a can, and some traditional Syrian dishes that don't always...go over well."

She's so open and unabashedly pragmatic. As if nothing affects her now that we're in her home, in a place she feels safe. "I don't know if we're in danger. If *you're* in danger. Anytime we go out, anywhere, whether it's to the grocery store, for food, or to refill your prescriptions, Ronan will be close by. I won't have to be 'on watch' the whole time. But I'm also not going to take any chances."

With a sigh, she deflates and stares down at her pizza. "I wish we could be...normal."

"Normal?" Nudging her chin up so I can hold her gaze, I take a deep breath. "Mik, five years ago—almost six now—my brother decided to commit treason. He was on the CIA and JSOC's most wanted list, and he knew it. So he set a trap in Venezuela, captured me, and tortured me for almost a week. The CIA sent Trevor, and he had to put a bullet in Gil's head. So normal? It flew right out the window a long time ago."

"Oh my God." Mik sets her plate down and scoots closer to me. "Austin."

"You wanted to know the darkness inside me. I killed my brother. I wasn't the one to pull the trigger, but he died because of me." No longer hungry, I dump my remaining slice back in the box and reach for the glass of water.

Mik rests her hand on my thigh, and shit. I can't decide if I want to hold her or run away. Both, at the same time. "Will you tell me the whole story? Beginning to end?"

There's so much. All of my failings. Every time Gil came to me and asked me to help him find his birth father. Every time he told me he just didn't feel complete. That he wanted to know where he came from. Every time he walked away angrier than the last. "Don't ask me that."

"Why not? Because you're afraid?" Mik's close enough now, I can feel her warmth. The tension in her body. And her understanding. "You don't have to be afraid with me."

Clearing my throat, I take her hands. "This past week...it's been the best and worst of my life."

Mik arches a brow. "You're not the one who was thrown off a mountain. I think I cornered the market on bad weeks."

There's my Mikayla. So direct, I almost laugh. "True. You win. But, Mik...what happens if I tell you everything and you... decide it's too much. That I'm too broken?"

"Everyone's broken, Austin. No one's life is perfect. Granted, most of us don't cause or contribute to the death of a family member." She shakes her head and curls an arm around my waist, resting her head on my shoulder. "I want to know all of it. I'm not going to run away. Or suddenly decide you're not the man I know you are. But this isn't the place. Help me clean up, then let's go upstairs."

She keeps saying I'm too good to be true. But she's wrong. Mikayla Salim is the one who's so perfect, I fear one day, she's simply going to disappear.

CHAPTER NINETEEN

Mikayla

"I killed my brother. I wasn't the one to pull the trigger, but he died because of me."

Austin's words rattle around in my head as we put the pizza away. As we're about to head upstairs, there's a knock on the door, and in under five seconds, I'm hiding on the stairs while an armed and very lethal looking former Air Force officer checks my peephole.

"It's all right, Mik. Just Clive and Ronan."

He opens the door as I come around the corner and mutters, "A little heads-up might have been nice."

"I texted," Ronan says with a shrug. "Check yer phone once in a while." Turning to me, he inclines his head. "Apologies, Mik. Didn't want to be creeping around yer backyard without letting ya' know we were there."

"What exactly do you need to do?" This wall needs me to prop it up. At least that's what I tell myself somewhere deep inside. I'm physically exhausted, and so very tired of being "on alert" all the darn time.

"We'll be installing these." Clive pulls a small, black device from his duffel bag. It's no bigger than a pack of gum, and when he drops it into my palm, I stare back at him, confused. "What is this?"

Ronan grins and shows me his phone screen. With a live feed of...me. Well, the underside of my chin. With a frown, I thrust the device towards Clive.

"Ugh. No woman wants to see the herself from that angle. Doesn't matter how secure she is in her appearance," I say. "But where's the power cord?"

"There's solar-powered battery in there with twenty-four hours of backup juice," Clive says. "So unless someone covers it up completely, it'll keep recording. Sends signals back to the main receiver unit." He pulls out a larger box—this one with a plug—and passes it to Austin. "This needs to go somewhere inside, preferably hidden and not in the dead center of the house."

"This is like...movie-level stuff," I say with a vague gesture at the equipment. "How...? This stuff isn't reserved for like...the CIA?"

Ronan sends a meaningful look Austin's way, and he curls an arm around my waist and waits until I meet his gaze. "Sweetheart, the CIA doesn't even have shit like this. Wren— she works for Second Sight, but she moved to Seattle to be with Ryker—she's a tech genius."

"She *made* this?"

"Her and Royce," Ronan says.

My head is swimming. Too many names I don't know. "Who's Royce? I feel like I need a cheat sheet. Flashcards."

The men all chuckle, and Austin plants a kiss to the top of my head. "You're not the only one, Mik. When I went out to

Seattle to give Ripper his Medal of Valor, shit. Trevor got almost everyone Dax, Ry, and Rip know together. They were afraid I was coming to arrest Rip and wanted to present a united front. Either that, or they were planning on killing me and burying me somewhere no one would have ever found me."

The way he talks, he holds real affection for these men and women, but his words don't reassure me.

"I came back to Fort Bragg and pulled every single one of their files. Just so I could put names and faces together."

"Pritchard," Ronan says, his voice taking on a hard edge. "Do we—?"

"Seriously?" Austin lets me go and draws up to his full height. His face is a mask of anger. "You think I'd do a damn thing to fuck things up for any of them? I went through back channels and then I buried every single file so deep, Wren and Ripper are probably the only two smart enough to find them. If you don't trust me by now, why are you even here?"

Ronan holds up his hand. "Look, mate. Ya' don't work for Second Sight for long without bein' cautious as fuck."

"Sorry. It's been a long ass day. I'll set up the receiver. Anything I need to do besides plug it in?"

Blowing out a deep breath, Ronan shakes his head. "No. We'll get out of yer hair. If Wren's software finds anythin', she'll call. Oh, and Mik?" The young Irishman digs into his messenger bag and pulls out a box. "Austin said yer phone was destroyed. This is all programmed with yer old number—as well as mine, Second Sight's, and Pritchard's. Also, fully charged."

I gape at him. "You bought me a new phone? I could have—"

"If ya' feel that strongly about it, ya' can talk to Dax about payin' him back. But if we're goin' to protect ya', we need to have a way to contact ya'. You'll see and hear us movin' around outside for about thirty minutes. We'll text ya' when we leave."

Austin locks my door after the two men leave and rests his back against the dark wood. "Ronan and I have never gotten along."

"Why not?" I let him wrap his arm around my waist and help me up the stairs.

"When we had to go to Venezuela, Dax didn't have a lot of resources he could send. Ford—that's his business partner—had just gotten married. Hell, so had Dax. And Ry. And Ripper." Austin lets out a heavy sigh. "Ronan didn't want Dani there, and anyone who messes with my sister goes on my shit list."

"Oh."

"He warmed up to her. She's an unstoppable force. No one messes with Dani Monroe."

"Wait. Dani Monroe. I know that name. Crap on a cracker." All of a sudden, so much of what he's said makes sense. "The fall of the Venezuelan government. She broke the story. Her name was all over the papers for like a week. I saw her on the news. *That's* your sister?"

Pride transforms Austin's features, wiping away the exhaustion in a single breath. "Yep."

"And Trevor. He was the former CIA agent." Now that I can put some of the names into context, the pieces fall into place. "I don't remember all of the details, but he was arrested for murder, right? That's why he was sent to prison in Venezuela?"

"He didn't *murder* anyone. He was protecting Dani and things went sideways."

"Austin?" I pull away, then point him to my home office. "First, you can plug the receiver in there. Second? You don't have to justify anything to me."

From his knees where he's hiding the receiver behind a pile of reference books, Austin glances up at me. "Yes. I do."

Unwilling to have this conversation without touching him—or at least being close to one another—I shuffle into the bedroom, sink down onto the bed, and take off my boots. I don't want to see these things again. Ever. The ankle brace is next. There's only a little lingering discomfort, and as long as I don't have to hike anywhere, I think I'll be fine without it.

Austin hovers in the doorway, his hands clasped behind him like he isn't sure what to do next. He's not the only one.

"So, this is awkward," I say.

His laugh breaks the tension in the room, and he comes to sit next to me, but doesn't touch me. "Your move, sweetheart. If you're too sore, we could just go to sleep."

"No." I turn and rest my hand over his heart. "I want to know you, Austin. I'm just not sure what we do now…"

"Didn't you say something about wanting a bath?" He nudges my shoulder gently. "What if we just…?"

The sound that escapes me is something between a whimper and a moan, and I cover my face with my hands to hide my embarrassment. I don't know how to deal with any of this. The intense *need* for Austin, the way my core clenches every time I'm near him, and my incredible lack of experience in what's supposed to happen in the bedroom.

"Let me take care of things, Mik," Austin says with a kiss to the shell of my ear. "Just relax. I'll be back in a few minutes."

As soon as I feel him stand up, I bury my face in my pillow. How can he be attracted to me when I can't even manage to admit I want to have sex with him?

While he rummages around in my bathroom, I head for my closet to find my favorite robe and emerge with it draped over my arm to find Austin leaning against the door frame. "Come with me?"

My nervous fingers steady when I put my hand in his, and he leads me into the bathroom, which is only lit by a handful of candles. Bubbles fill the two-person soaking tub—one of the main reasons I bought the house—and it's utterly silent except for a few last drops escaping the faucet.

"I thought, maybe you'd be more comfortable if we kept the lights down low," he says, his voice rough.

"It's perfect." I *want* to be brave. Brazen. Unashamed of my curves, of the slightly rounded belly I'll never be able to exercise away, of this body I really do love, despite my asthma. But Austin's built. Chiseled. From the quick look I got of him in the dim light as he stoked the fire to keep us warm, there isn't an ounce of spare body fat on him.

I tip my head to meet his gaze. "Every time I don't know what to do, you just...figure it out."

His hands slide around my back, under my tank top, and I shiver. I love the way he touches me. When I'm no longer bruised all over, I think I'll love it even more. Deft fingers unhook my bra, and then he steps back. "I can wait outside until you're in the water..."

"No." I return his hands to my waist. "I don't want to hide from you, Austin. I was raised to be modest. That means I don't have...moves. But I'm not afraid of you seeing me. Help me off with my tank."

Carefully, he eases the top over my head, and my bra comes with it. My heart hammers against my ribs as he holds my gaze.

"You can touch me." Smiling through my nerves, I add, "Looking is also allowed."

Before he lowers his gaze, he cups the back of my neck and captures my lips. The motion presses my breasts to his shirt, and the friction makes my entire core vibrate with need. Gently stroking his hands down my shoulders, my arms, all the way to my waist, he unzips my pants and lets them fall to the floor.

"No fair," I whisper when I come up for air. "You have some catching up to do."

"Don't worry, sweetheart. You're allowed to look too." He peels off his shirt, and up close, the candlelight flickering across his scars, over the well-defined muscles, the broad expanse of tanned skin... I want to touch him. All over.

"Pants too."

"Oh, we'll get there." Even in the dim light, I can see the storm in his eyes. And the bulge in his pants. "But this isn't going to be a quickie, sweetheart. We're going to talk first. About...everything. Because once we do this, once we take this step, I don't want any regrets between us."

"See?" I say quietly. "Too good to be true."

Austin

She's so fucking beautiful I can't tear my gaze away. Perfect skin, a body I'm aching to touch, and the look on her face...it's like she's waiting for me to unwrap her like a Christmas present. Molding my hands to her waist, I take things slow, skimming my palms up her sides.

Mikayla shivers when I cup her breasts, and fuck. Her nipples harden into tight nubs, and as I drag my thumbs over them, a little moan escapes her parted lips. Dipping my head, I kiss her as I pinch, lightly at first, then harder.

"Austin," she whimpers. "I need more."

"And you'll have it." Releasing her, I snag her panties and ease them down her hips, then turn her around and urge her towards the steaming water. "But sweetheart, you have a terrible poker face. I can see how much pain you're in. I found some Epsom salts and added them to the water. We're going to soak first."

Mik pouts, but she sinks down and sighs, the first truly contented sound I've heard from her since we landed. She stares up at me, the bubbles hiding her body from view, and her expression...she's so open and honest in everything she does. And right now, her gaze tells me exactly what she wants.

I can't get my boots and socks off fast enough, and when I shed my pants, Mikayla's lips part, and she breathes a little *"oh"* sound. I'm hard as a fucking steel rod, and a part of me thrills at the unabashed desire in her eyes.

Desire that only increases when I drop my boxer briefs. The caveman side of me wants to stand here, let her get her fill, but behind all that need, all that lust in her gaze, there's also fear. Fear that mirrors my own. Fear that we won't be able to find common ground. Fear that my past will come between us, despite her assurances she doesn't care.

The hot water does more than hide my obvious arousal. Scented with lavender and lilac, it envelopes both of us in warmth, and I motion for Mik to relax against me. "Can I hold you?"

"You don't have to ask," she replies as she turns and lets me wrap my arms around her waist. My dick nestles between her ass cheeks, and she shudders. "I...I like this."

"Me too." Nibbling on her ear, I relish in her little mewl. "But you've asked me more times than I'd like to tell you what happened with Gil."

"More times than you'd *like?*" she asks, tossing a challenging gaze over her shoulder.

"Yes. Because I should have told you the very first time you asked." I nuzzle her neck, my eyes closed, enjoying the feel of her as she relaxes against me once more. "I didn't mean to keep things from you, Mik. But this isn't a good story. I don't want to tell it. In fact, I've *never* told it. To anyone."

She snuggles closer and covers my hands with hers. "So tell it to me."

"GIL WAS DANI'S BROTHER." Even saying his name makes my shoulders tense. "My parents adopted them when Gil was fourteen and Dani was barely nine. And for a while, we were a family."

"For a while?" Mik's voice is soft and tinged with exhaustion, and a part of me hopes she'll decide she wants to soak until the water cools, then go to sleep. As much as I need her, as I need to bury myself inside her, I don't know how to let her in.

"Yeah. Gil...changed. So much. But none of us realized it. He and Trevor joined the CIA, and I lost touch with Gil for a while. Trevor did too—the CIA is famous for separating friends, colleagues who get too close. Helps prevent...issues."

"Issues?" she asks.

"Like sending Trevor to *retrieve* his best friend. To *contain* him and bring him to a black site where he'd disappear forever."

"Oh my God."

"This is my world, Mik. *Was* my world. It's exciting and dangerous and great and terrible all at the same time."

"A world in which best friends have to kill one another? A world where brothers *torture* brothers?" she asks.

"Yes." I reach for Mik's shower gel and drizzle a little over my hands before I start massaging her shoulders. "That's one of the reasons I left."

"Just one?" She moans as I find a particularly hard knot and go to work on it. "Oh, I could get used to this."

So could I. Used to having Mikayla in my arms. Used to

being wrapped around her, naked. Used to having her trust me implicitly.

"Keep talking," she says softly. "Gil changed?"

"He tracked down his birth father. The man was *big* in the Venezuelan terrorist network, the *Loma Collectivo*. He ran it for years. And when Gil found him, his father managed to convince him to turn on everything he'd ever known."

"Oh, Austin." Mikayla wriggles so she can meet my gaze in the flickering light, and what I see in her eyes makes me want to stop and lose myself in her. "What did he do?"

"He set a trap. For me. Made a call on an unencrypted line that gave us the information we needed to prove he was working for the *Loma Collectivo*. And then he sent me an email."

"Why?"

I snort softly and bury my nose in her hair. "To get me to come for him."

"He meant to torture you?" The horror in her voice mirrors my memories, and I nod.

"He had me for six days. Started small." I shift our positions so she's facing me, her legs draped over mine in the hot water. Taking her hand, I place her fingers over the thin, long-healed scars. "Shallow cuts. Painful, but not dangerous. Not fatal."

"Crap." Mik inches closer, and when she kisses one of the pale slashes, something in me shatters. "Austin, I'm so sorry."

"Can't change the past, sweetheart. And...all of this...it brought me to you. If all of Gil's torture, all those hours, days, fearing I'd be the reason Gil *and* Trevor died...if they led me here, to you... Maybe they were all worth it."

CHAPTER TWENTY

Mikayla

The water starts to cool, and Austin climbs out and wraps a towel around his waist before retrieving a second one for me. I can't be sure, but I think he finally told me everything. The deep, haunted look in his eyes has faded slightly, an undercurrent of something akin to peace taking its place.

It's surreal, standing next to this man, mostly naked, brushing our teeth like we've done this for months or even years, but it also feels right. Normal.

Until suddenly, we're done and I'm staring at the bed like it's both everything I've ever wanted and everything I fear at the same time. What if...what if I'm *bad* at this? I don't exactly have a lot of experience to go on here.

"Do you want to sleep?" Austin asks, wrapping his arms around me from behind and pressing a kiss to my shoulder. "If you do...it's okay. Nothing needs to happen tonight."

I turn in his embrace, cup his neck, and pull him down for a kiss. Slowly, we inch towards the bed as our lips meet again and again, tremors of nerves and heat and intense *need* rocking my core. Emboldened by his hard length pressing against my stomach, I flick my tongue out, searching for his, and Austin groans as he lets me in.

Rough, calloused fingers slide under the towel to cup my ass, and there's only a moment of fear, of uncertainty, before he lifts me and I wrap my legs around his waist.

"You say stop at any time..." he manages, but I shake my head.

"I want this, Austin. I want you." Another kiss, this one so desperate, I feel it down to my toes, and I slide my fingers into his hair. He nips the corner of my mouth, then shifts my weight so he can pull back the sheet and blankets.

"Lights on or off, sweetheart?"

With no doubt in my mind—or my tone, I answer, "On."

After he lays me down in the center of the bed, he turns to his pack, rummaging inside to retrieve a strip of condoms.

I use the moment to wriggle free from the towel, and the look on his face when he sees me...no one's ever looked at me with such intensity before. *Seen* me like he does. And then he's standing naked next to my bed, fully erect, and my God. It takes me three tries to form words, and when I do...

"You're... You won't fit. All that..." I wave my hand at him, still gaping, equal parts terrified and more turned on than I've ever been. He moved so quickly getting into the tub, I didn't fully appreciate...him. The way all those muscles taper into a narrow waist, the *v* that leads down to short, dark curls and all that hard length.

"I'll fit, sweetheart. Promise." With a reassuring smile, Austin climbs into bed with me, then eases me against his side. "But you're going to come at least once before we get to that part."

Long, languid kisses have my insides melting into goo, and

his hands. Oh, God. His hands. Fingers playing over my breasts, little pinches to my nipples that send zings of pleasure straight to my core, gentle caresses along my hip, my inner thighs.

And his words.

"You're perfect. So perfect. So soft and strong at the same time." Every time he does something new, kisses me in a place no one's ever kissed before, he flicks his gaze to mine, asking for permission, watching my expression.

"No one's ever...made me feel like this before," I say, almost panting as his fingers stroke closer and closer to my clit. To where I desperately need him to be.

"Like what?" he asks before scoring his teeth over my nipple.

My eyes start to burn, because it's all too much. Too good to be true. Even though I know he's very, *very* real and every bit as good as he seems. "Like nothing else in the whole world matters but me."

Austin pushes up on an elbow and skims the back of his hand along my cheek. "Nothing else does. Only you, Mikayla. And if no one's ever made you feel like that before, I renew my offer to hunt down your exes and tell them what idiots they were."

"I'd much rather you stay here," I say, "and finish what you've started."

"Your wish is my command." With a grin, he finally gives me the pressure, the touch, the pleasure I've been aching for and strokes his finger over my clit. The sound I make...it's pure need, and he slides down my body until he's lying between my thighs. "I want to taste you, sweetheart. Can I?"

No one's ever done that to me—with me—before, but I trust him completely, and with arousal clouding my mind, I don't even think before I mumble, "Uh huh."

"Austin!" I cry out when his tongue starts to dance over the sensitive bundle of nerves, and a finger slides deep inside me.

He freezes, meeting my gaze with fear in his eyes. "Did I—?"

"More," I demand, not caring that his mouth is...*there* or that my neighbors might hear us. Every part of me, every cell in my body needs him right where he is.

He doesn't reply, but I think, through half-lidded eyes, I see him grin as he returns his focus to...whatever the heck he's doing to me.

His free hand molds to my hip, a feral, rumbling sound in his throat, and my entire body implodes with my scream, endless waves of pleasure so intense, so overwhelming, I can't see, can't think, can't do anything but ride them and hope I don't drown.

Austin

"You're so damn sexy when you come," I whisper in her ear as I carefully pull Mik into my arms, trying to avoid the various bruises on her back.

"Huh?" Her eyes don't quite focus as she peers up at me, a lazy, bemused smile curving her lips. "You said something..."

"*You* said a lot of things. Or precisely, one thing over and over."

"Please tell me I didn't make a total fool of myself?" Her cheeks flush, and she bites her lip, her brows drawing together as she waits for my answer.

"Not one bit. You just kept asking for more." I still taste of her, and when she curls her fingers around my neck and pulls me closer, the surprise registers in her eyes for a split second before she deepens the kiss, wriggling against me in a way that makes me groan.

"Mik, are you—fuck—are you sure?" I ask. "We can wait…"

"I'm sure." Her voice is deeper now, sexier, the aftershocks of her release sending goosebumps racing down her arms. "I want this, Austin. *That* was amazing. But there's this place inside me that *needs* more."

"Kiss me again." It's more plea than command, because when we kiss, everything that makes Mikayla *her* is so clear to me. Her fears fall away, and with them, mine vanish too. I'm so hard it's painful, and there's nothing I want more than to bury myself in her, but if she's not ready, if there's even a single second of doubt in her kiss, we'll wait.

There isn't. All I feel is her desire, her need, her arousal. Tight nipples pebble against my chest, and delicate fingers trail down my abs, over one scar after another, until she lightly strokes my shaft, and *fuck*.

"Tell me what to do."

"You're…doing just…fine," I manage. Though I'm not. Like any red-blooded American male, I rub one out in the shower from time to time, but it's been almost two years since I had a partner. If she keeps this up much longer, I'm going to come all over her hand.

"Condom," I mutter as I reach for the foil packet. Rolling it on is painful, and I hiss out a breath, willing my body to obey my commands long enough for me to get inside her.

Mik lies back against the pillows, looking up at me with a mix of desire and apprehension playing over her features, but before I can ask one more time if she's ready, she spreads her legs. "Inside me, Austin. Just…go slow."

Bracing one hand on the headboard, I guide myself to her entrance. "Relax, sweetheart." I don't have to remind her, because the second my crown slips between her folds, it's like all the parts of her that were unsettled, all her fears, all her uncertainty just melts away.

By inches, I slide deeper, waiting for her body to adjust, our gazes locked on one another. This woman sees all of my broken pieces, all my pain, and she doesn't brush it away. She accepts it. Accepts *me*. Nothing has ever been sexier.

"I...fuck, Mik. There's so much I want to say to you." Fully seated now, I kiss her, then slowly, gently, start to move my hips. Her moan is everything, and she clutches at my back, drawing me closer with every thrust.

I want to see her eyes, want her to see mine, but I'm terrified if I break off the kiss, I'll say something she's not ready for. Something I didn't think *I* was ready for until this moment.

Instead, I kiss her for all I'm worth, rocking into her, relishing in the tiny mewls and moans, the way her breasts scrape against my chest, and the pleasure I swear I can *feel* coiling in her belly.

I'm so fucking close I can't hold on much longer. Sliding one hand between us, I find her clit, and with the barest hint of pressure, send her flying once more. Her release is too much, and as she clenches around me, I let go as I break off the kiss and shout her name.

AFTER I DISPOSE of the condom and clean up a little, I run a washcloth under warm water and return to the bed where Mik's curled on her side, watching me. She holds out her hand, but I want to do this—need to do this—after what we just shared. "Let me take care of you a little, sweetheart." Swiping the cloth over her body, I memorize every line and curve, marveling at her trust, her strength, her understanding.

"Do you...sleep naked?" she asks, a hint of uncertainty in her voice.

"Not usually." I snag a clean pair of boxer briefs from my bag and tug them on. "But I will if you want me to."

Mik shakes her head gently and scoots to the edge of the bed. "I've tried...a few times. But then, I can't fall asleep. I just keep thinking...what if there's a fire? I'd be running out the door with no clothes on." Her little laugh warms something inside of me and chips away a little more of the wall life built around my heart.

She pads over to her dresser and once she's donned an old Berkeley t-shirt, panties, and a silky pair of shorts, she slips under the sheet and snuggles up to me. "This is real, right?"

"Us?" I ask, smoothing a hand over her hair.

"Yes." Her voice has dropped to a whisper, and she drapes her arm around my waist and holds on tight. "This doesn't happen in real life."

"Well, don't look now, sweetheart," I stretch up to flip off the light, "but we're here. In your bed. And what we just did? That felt pretty damn real to me."

"What happens now?" Mik yawns and settles closer to me.

"Now, we sleep. You're exhausted."

She nudges me with a knee. "You know that's not what I meant."

"Tomorrow, maybe we'll see what it feels like to do something...normal."

"Normal? I'm not sure we *do* normal. But okay. I'll try anything. Once." Her laugh settles me in a way no other sound can, and I close my eyes as she adds, "Anything but sushi."

CHAPTER TWENTY-ONE

Austin

After twenty plus years on active duty, even with the last six spent behind a desk, it's impossible for me to sleep in, and I'm up by 6:00 a.m. All Mik has in her fridge are a few jars of condiments, and I don't even see coffee beans.

An hour later, I have a grocery order on the way, and hunch over my tablet, checking my email for the first time in weeks. Shit. Two messages from Griff.

Pritchard,

When you said you were going off the grid, I didn't think you meant completely. Couldn't have given me a heads up? And what's with sending me to Boston to meet with a blind guy? In case you didn't know, I'm mostly deaf, not blind. Don't try to tell me I can still live a full life. Not until you're walking around without your fucking arm too.

Don't contact me again.

-Griff

The only way I control my urge to throw the tablet across the room is to remind myself this is Mik's house. There's no way I'm going to disrespect her like that. Given how he signed off, I'm amazed he sent a second email a few hours after the first. Until I open it.

Austin,

I owe you an apology. I didn't ask how he found me, but Dax Holloway knocked on the door of my hotel room a couple of hours after I stormed out of his office. The dude is...intense. Asked me questions for-fucking-ever, then told me to show up at Second Sight in three days without the massive stick up my ass.

I guess I'm going. Not like I have anything better to do.
-Griff

Unsurprising. The few times I've been in the same room with Dax, his presence...it's heavy. Serious. I outrank the man by miles, but Special Forces guys always carry themselves the same way. With an attitude that says, "Don't fuck with me, or they'll never find your body."

SEALs are even worse.

Knowing the man will be awake, even this early, I call Dax. "So, found yourself some trouble down in Mexico?" he says without even a greeting.

"Like you never 'found yourself' any in your life?"

"Didn't say that. Found plenty of it. Want to fill me in?" His Southern drawl lends a gentleness to his words, but he's not asking. Not really. Not when he sent guys to protect us. And paid for the plane to fly us home.

"I will. But I'd rather do it somewhere more..."

"Private?" His rough laugh always seems to surprise him. Then again, from what Trev told me, Dax hadn't laughed for years. Not until he and Ryker patched things up. "Fine. But I gotta know at least some of it. What you're plannin' to do about it. How long you need Ronan. Whether we need to bring in Wren."

"I'm definitely going to want Wren's particular talents. Still don't know who these assholes are or whether they're going to come after Mikayla now that we're back in the States. Until we find out, I can't tell you how long she'll need protection." Lowering my voice, I add, "We're new. She could tell me to take a hike tomorrow, and if that happens..."

"Pritchard, you went and fell in love with her, didn't you? Fuckin' A. I'll make you a deal. I won't say a word to Trevor, if you promise me you'll tell him in person. Then call me and describe the look on his face in precise detail."

Chuckling, I settle back on the couch and run a hand through my hair. "Deal. But Dax? That's not the only reason I called."

"You mean your former associate with a chip on his shoulder the size of Fenway Park? Yeah. He was here. Wren and Royce are working with Evianna's people on some cuttin' edge shit. We got him set up with the same voice-to-text software I use, but flipped the algorithm for him."

"I don't know what to say, Dax. I fucked up his whole life."

"No, you didn't. I read the ops report. He made a choice," Dax says, his voice taking on a tone you only get from years as an elite soldier.

"That's not how he tells it."

Dax snorts. "You were just an easy target for him to blame. He'll come around. Give him a little time. And for fuck's sake, respond to the guy's emails."

"I will. Thanks. I owe you—"

"Stop right there. Family doesn't owe family. We're square."

BY THE TIME Mik comes downstairs, I have the food put away, coffee brewing, and bacon sizzling in a pan.

"Austin? What are you doing?" she asks, peering at the clock on the microwave. "It's only a little after eight. Did you...*leave?*"

"No, sweetheart. No." I turn the stove down and wrap an arm around her waist. The fear in her eyes is like a knife straight to my heart. "Grocery delivery. I ordered online."

"Oh. Good." She's still shaky, so I guide her over to the far side of the kitchen island and pull out a tall chair for her. "Sorry. I just...I hate not knowing if I'm...if we're safe."

"You're not the only one." As I check on the bacon, I frown. "How do you take your coffee? I ordered whole milk, half-and-half, and almond milk, but—"

She gapes a little when I open the fridge. "Did you buy out the entire store?"

Shit. "No." My shoulders stiffen, and I kick myself for going overboard.

And then she's behind me, her arms wrapping around my waist. "Relax, Danger. I'm not mad. Just...surprised."

"I can't talk to Wren—she's Second Sight's computer genius—until at least ten. She's in Seattle. And I didn't want to call Detective Chavez until you were awake."

"What does that have to do with you buying three types of creamer?" Mik reaches around me and grabs the half-and-half, splashes a small bit into a mug, and pours herself coffee. My cup is next to the stove, and she tops that off too before she sits back down again and watches me expectantly.

"Between the cameras all around the property, and Ronan doing drive-bys every hour, nothing's happening to you here. But the minute we—you—leave this house, the risk goes up." I'd give anything to be able to reassure her, but I can't. Not yet.

"Okay." Mik nods, accepting my words easily. Too easily.

We're going to have a serious talk once I finish making breakfast. But she has other ideas. "A week ago, you could have called me naive," she says. "And heck, I probably still am. But I believe you, Austin. Most of all, I trust you."

Her confidence in me is so staggering, I almost drop the plates. "I've never met anyone like you, Mik."

"Well, I'd hope not. If my parents hid a twin from me for my entire life, they have some explaining to do."

I almost choke on my coffee. "I love—your sense of humor." Fuck me. I almost said something I can't take back, and from the way her fork clatters to the countertop, she knows it.

Neither of us say another word as we eat, and as I'm loading the dishwasher, my phone vibrates on the counter. The number starts with fifty-two, Mexico's country code. This better be Chavez with an update.

"Pritchard," I say. "You're on speaker."

"Major General Pritchard, is Dr. Salim with you?" Chavez asks.

Mik clears her throat. "I'm here."

"Give us some good news, detective." Setting the phone on the counter, I let Mik lean against me and bury my nose in her hair. She smells like lilacs, lavender, and sex, and I don't think I'll ever get enough of her.

Chavez sighs over the line. "I wish I could. Señor Larkin is no longer at the hospital in Tuxtla Gutiérrez. At seventeen hundred hours, I was told he was being brought out of his coma. When I called the hospital twenty minutes ago, they had no record of him. But there is more, and I must apologize to both of you. I have been assigned to another case."

I know the tone in his voice. Resignation. The sound of your superiors giving you orders you don't agree with, and having no choice but to obey. "Chavez, is this line secure?"

"As secure as one can be on short notice."

"What about the two assholes who hurt Dr. Salim?"

"I issued arrest warrants for Arturo Lopez and Martín Salvador last night, but as of this morning, I can find no evidence they were ever put into the system." Chavez clears his throat. "Mexico is a wonderful country. We have untouched natural beauty, and some of the most genuine, kind, and honorable people I have ever met. But we also have corruption. The cartels own so many."

I wish I didn't know just how terrible life under a corrupt government can be. Gil. Trevor. My own time in Venezuela. No. Not now. Those memories have no place here. Not anymore.

Shoving them down as far and as fast as I can, I let training take over. Assess. Plan. Act. Pretty sure that's McCabe's mantra, but it's a good one.

Muting the call for a brief moment, I turn to Mik. "I'm going to take him off speaker, but you can listen in. Trust me?"

She nods, and I switch the call and unmute. "Detective Chavez, I would advise you to cease all investigation of Arturo Lopez and Martín Salvador immediately. Do not look for Corey Larkin, and forget meeting Dr. Salim. For your own safety."

"I am not afraid, señor. This is why I joined the *Policia*. To fight corruption. To protect my people."

"Keep doing so. But leave this case alone. 'Live to fight another day' if you will. You are a good man, Chavez. You kept us safe when we needed it most. If you ever need *outside* assistance, this number will reach me. Do you understand?"

"Yes, I think I do. You have a friend in Mexico, Major General Pritchard."

"And you have one in the United States."

The call ends, and I sink down onto the stool and meet

Mik's gaze. She understands, and the fear in her eyes mirrors what I feel. "Sweetheart, things just got a lot more complicated."

CHAPTER TWENTY-TWO

Mikayla

Austin's tense, moving stiffly to retrieve his tablet from the coffee table and set it on the counter in front of me.

"What's the plan?" I ask. I'm torn between needing to know and wanting to crawl back in bed and hide away from the world with him for a day...a week...however long it takes for the cartel to forget about me.

Thumbing out a text message, Austin nods towards the tablet. "Now we do this my way."

"Your way?" His entire demeanor's changed. Gone is the caring, thoughtful man I've started to think of as my...what? Boyfriend? In his place, a hard, all-business intelligence officer with a plan he's not sharing. At least not yet.

"Be right back." Despite his new attitude, he pauses to press a swift kiss to my lips before taking my stairs two at a time. He's back in under a minute with a small, black bag from which he pulls two boxes and a cable, then hooks everything up to the tablet.

"Who's Red?" I ask when he taps a contact from his list.

"Wren. You'll see."

The woman who answers the video call has a mop of red curls that brush her shoulders, and though she smiles, it's tight-lipped. "We secure on your end?"

"Yep."

"Stars and Bars knows better than that," a rough, deep voice says from behind her. The man who leans over the back of a sofa has to be the biggest guy I've ever seen. Bald, half his face scarred, and tattoos covering both arms. "You back in the land of the living, Pritchard?"

"Ryker."

"Shoo," Wren says as she tips her head up to look at him. "Austin called *me*, not you. Go knock down a wall or something."

"Knock down a wall?" Austin asks.

"We're remodeling. Well, Ry is. I'm—"

"Supervising," Ry calls out.

This time when she smiles, it's like someone told the sun to come out and play. At least from the look on her face. But in the next breath, she sobers and scoots forward on the couch. "What do you need?"

"Wren, this is Mikayla. Dr. Mikayla Salim. We need you to work some of your magic."

<hr>

HALF AN HOUR LATER, Wren knows everything. Well, mostly everything. Not what happened upstairs last night. Not how I feel about Austin. Or how I suspect he feels about me. Or...maybe she does, because when she signs off, she says, "Give me a couple of hours, tops. You'll be together, right?"

"Yes," Austin replies as he drapes his arm around my shoulders. "We're not going anywhere today if I can help it."

"Well, just make sure you answer the dang phone, okay? No funny business." With a wink, she ends the call, and I groan.

"Not going anywhere? You practically told her we were going to spend the day having sex."

"Would that be such a bad thing?" He cups the back of my neck and leans in. This kiss isn't quick, it's anything but, and if he weren't standing so close, I think I'd melt right off the chair into a puddle of goo. At least that's how my insides feel.

"No, but we can't simply hide away from the world forever. I have to call my boss and tell him what happened. And...oh God. Dr. Branch."

"Who?" Austin's eyes narrow and he reaches for his tablet.

"Dr. Brian Branch with Johns Hopkins. The phytotoxin from the Blushing Note's pollen and root system are a key component in a new Parkinson's treatment he's developing. He co-signed the grant application that sent us to Mexico in the first place. He's going to be devastated."

Snapping a Bluetooth keyboard into the tablet, he sends Wren a message to add Branch to her research, then glances up at me. "I need your boss's name too."

"Brian's not involved in any of this. Neither is Lowenstein. Heck, Howard was diagnosed with Parkinson's six months ago. There's no way he'd put this research in jeopardy." I shake my head. "I know you're just trying to protect me, Austin. But not everyone's out to get me. Some people are just...basically good."

"Some are." He threads his fingers through my hair, and though I try to pull away, he urges me closer. "But we thought Corey was a good guy too. And maybe a part of him was. He helped me find you. Too little too late for my liking, but he could have given me the wrong coordinates, done...any number of things to stop or delay me until it was too late." His body's gone rigid again, and a muscle in his jaw ticks as fear swims in his hazel eyes. "I won't take a chance that someone else in your life contributed to this shitshow. Until Wren gets us some answers, *everyone's* a suspect."

"Even Li? Isaiah? They almost *died*, Austin."

"So did Corey. Almost dying? Doesn't mean shit. Not where these assholes are concerned. They didn't have a problem killing you, shooting at me, or burning your students alive. There's something *big* going on here, Mik. Bigger than any of us. Big enough whoever's behind it doesn't mind a hell of a lot of collateral damage. So yes. Everyone's a suspect."

Ducking out of his hold, I stalk toward the stairs, doing my best to ignore the lingering pain in my ankle. "Then you might as well add yourself to the list. Heck. Add me too while you're at it. Maybe I jumped off that cliff." Anger and terror make for a bad mix, and my stomach roils, sending nausea crawling up the back of my throat as I turn with my hand on the banister. "You're being an overprotective jerk. I need a shower. Alone."

"Mik," he calls, but I ignore him as I flee up the stairs and lock myself in the bathroom. I refuse to believe that Howard or Brian have any part in this, let alone Li and Isaiah. I just wish I had some idea who could have set this whole thing up and why.

BY THE TIME I come downstairs again, two hours have passed. I took my time. A long shower to rinse the scent of Austin—of us together—from my body, careful application of what little makeup I wear, and then, unpacking my suitcase and starting laundry all gave me enough time to calm down and find a little perspective.

I'm alive. Currently safe. At home, where I'm comfortable

and, if I'm honest, have the upper hand. If I asked Austin to leave, he would. Granted, he'd probably sit in the SUV within sight of the house for however long it takes to find out who's after me and why, but I wouldn't have to see him.

The problem? I want to see him. I want more than that. Earlier? He barely caught himself in time and almost told me he loved me. And I might be falling in love with him too.

I find him sitting on the couch hunched over his tablet, the television playing a twenty-four-hour news channel on low, and an empty coffee cup next to the keyboard.

"Can I get you a refill?" I ask, pouring myself another cup from what's obviously a fresh pot. "Along with an apology?"

"For calling me an overprotective jerk?" He leans back, stretching his legs out. "I probably deserved it. But Mik, it's my job to keep you safe."

"Your job? Please tell me I'm not just...a job—"

Austin's across the room before I finish my sentence, eases the mug from my hand, and holds me close. "You are *not* a job, Mikayla. You're everything. I don't want to lose you to these assholes. Or because I chewed on my own boot leather one too many times." He nuzzles my neck, trailing kisses from my ear to my collar bone. "I've never felt this way about anyone."

His assurances soothe some of the incessant destructive thoughts rattling around in my head, and I relax in his embrace. "But...this isn't *normal,* is it? Feeling this much this fast?"

Nudging my chin up with the crook of his finger, he locks his gaze on mine. "When my parents adopted Dani," he swallows hard, "and Gil, it was hard for them for a while. Dani in particular. She was this skinny kid, and they'd been in Texas for the first nine years of her life. Bounced around from foster home to foster home. Some of them...were truly horrible. But Dani? She was fierce as fuck."

"I want to meet her."

"You will, sweetheart. Soon." We head for the couch, and once we're sitting close enough our thighs touch, he rubs the back of his neck and shakes his head with a small smile. "One day, Dani came home mad as hell. She never cried. Just got mad and kicked a ball so hard, it broke a window."

It's a good thing I hadn't taken a sip of coffee yet. Even so, I almost spill it all over myself. "Now I *really* want to meet her."

"She was so scared. Ran and hid behind the shed. But Mom always knew where she was. We all did, really. If she wasn't behind the shed, she was at the summit of East Rock. After she and Trev started getting close, it was *always* the summit of East Rock." Austin chuckles again. "Those two were meant for one another from the start. Anyway, Mom found Dani, and I eavesdropped on them."

"Austin!"

"I was fifteen. That's all fifteen-year-old kids do. Break the rules."

"Fair enough."

"What Mom said to Dani that night stuck with me for... well, my whole life. Dani asked why she couldn't be normal. Mom's reply? 'Normal is only a dryer setting. Well, fine. It's also a city in Alabama. And Kentucky. A person can't *be* normal. Every single one of us is unique and special. Don't let me hear you ever try to be normal. Be special." He's doing that thing again. Where he caresses my cheek and skims his fingers along the shell of my ear. It's so intimate, so tender, that I'm left defenseless and utterly in love. "You're special, Mik. What we have is special. Is it normal? No. But that doesn't make it any less real."

Draping my arms over his shoulders, I press my lips to his, and we fit together like we were always meant to be.

Maybe we were.

Austin

A little after two, Mik's phone rings, startling both of us in the middle of a superhero movie with enough muscles on screen, I think I should be jealous. Except that Mik's curled against me and from time to time, runs her hand over my abs or my thigh. We missed at least ten minutes of the beginning because she started kissing me and neither one of us wanted to stop long enough to find the remote.

"It's my boss." Her fingers only tremble for a second or two, but it's enough. That and the expression on her face. "Howard? How are you?"

I lean close to her, and Mik rests her head on my shoulder with the phone between us.

"A little confused. A case of samples just showed up, but they're not labeled like all of the other shipments. Your name's on the manifest, along with the Department of Agriculture seal, but they're not even in the standard packaging." The man sounds exactly like his photo—the one I found on the Smithsonian's website when Mik was upstairs. Older. Late sixties. A well-lined face, short white hair, decidedly on the thin side.

"How many cases have come in total?" Mik asks. "There should be..." Her eyelids flutter for a moment as she's thinking, "seven."

"There were. Today's is number eight. Everything all right down there?"

Reaching for my hand, Mik links our fingers and holds on tight. "No. Not exactly. I'm...in Edgewater, Howard. And there's a lot I need to tell you."

"Dr. Salim, I think you'd better explain. Right away. And in person."

"No," I mouth. I don't want her going anywhere near the lab until we hear from Wren.

"Let me put you on hold for a minute, okay? I'll be right back," Mik says, then mutes the call and turns to me. "This is my boss. He hired me. He went to bat for me with the board when they wanted to cut our funding. Right before we figured out how we could use the Blushing Note's phytotoxin."

"It's still you out in the open."

"The lab—really, the entire Smithsonian—it's a fortress. So much research goes on there, it has to be. Keycard entry to the building, a ten-digit code to get into my lab, and we have a full security staff. You can come with me. Heck, Ronan too. I won't be in danger there any more than I'm in danger here."

"I don't like it." If anything happens to her, I'll never forgive myself, and the urge to be an overprotective jerk again rears its head. If not for the look on her face. Mik's every bit as headstrong as I am, and probably twice as smart. "But I suppose I can't stop you."

Her smile rights my world, and she says, "Nope," before she unmutes the call. "Howard, it'll take me an hour or so to get there. Do me a favor? Don't tell anyone else I'm back, okay?"

"Mikayla, this had better be good. Otherwise, the World Horticultural Society and Johns Hopkins are going to demand we return money we've already spent. And your professional reputation? I don't know that it'll survive."

"I understand," Mik says quietly. "I'll see you soon."

Fuck. I thought all I had to worry about was her physical safety. But the way she talked about her research when we first met? So much of Mik, of *who* she is, comes from the kind of work she does. The damage of losing it might be more than we could survive.

CHAPTER TWENTY-THREE

Austin

"I'm at the end of the block," Ronan says in my ear. That bag he left for me? It had a lot more than just the Beretta inside. Two comms units, two small GPS trackers—thank God not the subdermal ones we used in Venezuela—and most of the contents of a standard go-bag. Pre-paid credit card, burner phone, five hundred dollars in cash, and a fake ID in case we need to get the hell out of here and go on the run. Mik's ID will take another few hours—at least according to Dax's last message.

Mik descends the stairs carefully, dressed in a pair of black slacks and a dark green tank.

"Did you hide the GPS—?"

"In my bra, yes." In a move I can only imagine she designed to torture me, Mik cups her left breast, gently adjusting herself and sending desire shooting straight to my dick. "It's the diameter of a pencil eraser and thinner than a dime. This thing really works?"

"Yep. Thirty-six hour battery life and unless you're in a

lead-lined room or at least fifty feet underground, the signal's always readable." I show her my phone, with twin dots flashing on a map of Edgewater, right over her house. Taking a small, black box from my pocket, I open it and offer her the earbud. "I'm not leaving your side, Mik, but if you want to be able to hear Ronan, you can wear this."

"No. I'm drawing the line right here. No offense to Ronan. He seems like a very nice guy. But all of this extra precaution is ridiculous. *Nothing* is going to happen. My world doesn't require stuff like this, and I don't want that to change." Copper streaks blaze in her eyes, and there's no arguing with her expression or the edge to her voice. She has the GPS and she has me.

"If you change your mind, I'll keep it with me," I say, then adjust my white button-down shirt so it hides the holster at my hip. "Ronan, we're heading out now."

"Roger that," he replies, and though it goes against everything my dad ever taught me, I head out of Mik's house first to scan the street. At least I can get the car door for her.

The drive to the Smithsonian takes less than fifteen minutes, and Ronan weaves in and out of traffic, passing us occasionally, then reappearing a block later five cars back. The man's solid, and he's gotten even better since Venezuela.

The parking lot isn't secure, but the building's entrance has a card reader as well as a security booth with a tall, beefy man inside. He ambles out to greet us, and Mik smiles. "Hey, Thom."

"Dr. Salim. I didn't think you were due back for another week," he says as he checks his clipboard.

"I wasn't. We were hit with some pretty bad storms, so we had to get out of there fast." Mik takes my hand and smiles. "This is my...um..."

"Boyfriend," I supply.

Her cheeks turn bright red, and that smile...every time I think she can't possibly look any more beautiful, be any more perfect, I'm wrong. "My boyfriend, Austin Pritchard. Can you set him up with a visitor's badge for the day?"

Thom looks me up and down, a hint of a fatherly glare in his eyes. "Been working this desk for two years, Dr. Salim. You've never brought a visitor with you."

"Austin's special," she says. "I know I'm supposed to get him on the list twenty-four hours ahead of time, but I just got back last night and I didn't think I'd need to come in at all today. Can you bend the rules just this once?"

With a chuckle, Thom nods. "Just this once. Can I make a copy of your driver's license, Mr. Pritchard?"

I hand it over, and while Thom busies himself in his booth, I stare around the large, open lobby with floor-to-ceiling windows between narrow white pillars. We're in full view of the parking lot, and will be until we reach the elevator. Not an ideal situation, but I count four security cameras, and when I lean forward to accept my license and visitor's badge from Thom, I catch sight of a faint red glow from the underside of his desk. Just the right size to be a silent alarm.

"Thanks, Thom," Mik says as she scans her card at a metal turnstile and then gestures for me to do the same with my temporary badge. "Next week, when I'm back to a more normal schedule, I'll bring you some of those scones you like from Cookie's Diner."

"I'll hold you to that, you know." With a little wave, the guard heads back to his booth.

Once we're in the elevator, Mik peers up at me. "See? I told you it was safe. No one's getting in here without ID or an escort. The lab is even more secure. That visitor's badge? Won't do you any good past the elevator."

She's so earnest. But the one thing she's not? Naive. Not

anymore. I can see it in her eyes, and dammit. I'd give anything to put that hope, that light back in them. "Sweetheart, this place is a hell of a lot safer than I expected. You were right." She smiles up at me with a look that screams *I told you so*, and I'd roll my eyes if I didn't think it'd earn me a trip to the doghouse. Because I fully intend to be in her bed tonight. And every night for as long as she'll have me. "I'll feel better after Wren gets back to us."

At least, I hope I will.

Mikayla

Being back at the Smithsonian is deeply satisfying and worrisome at the same time. This is my home—almost as much as my actual house—and for three years, some of my happiest moments have been spent here.

I show Austin my little office, the lab where we analyze all of our samples, and the greenhouse. "You can't enter the lab without protective gear. The phytotoxin the Blushing Note releases can cause bradycardia, even in small amounts."

"Bradycardia? Is that like heart palpitations from watching the *Brady Bunch*?" he asks with a wicked smile. "I had a major crush on Marcia when I was a kid."

Slapping a hand to his chest, I level him with my most serious stare. "You do not joke about bradycardia. Your heart rate plummets, you get dizzy, weak, and you can pass out and die because your blood doesn't circulate like normal, so not enough oxygen to your cells—or your brain."

"Fuck, Mik. Why do *you* go in there?"

"Because it's my job. And because I know how to properly treat the samples. I wear a full face shield, gloves, and only work under a fume hood. We keep Atropine on hand just in case, but even that's not guaranteed to be a hundred percent effective. The room's kept at negative pressure, so nothing escapes, and we have a giant filtration system on the roof."

Peering through the thick glass window, I frown. "There's the sample box Howard told me about. We never use plain brown cardboard. And there are no warning labels that I can see. Wait here. I'm going inside."

Austin snags an arm around my waist. "I'll suit up. Wear whatever you need me to wear. But I'm going in with you. And I'm opening that box."

"Austin."

"I mean it. *Nothing* about this feels right to me. You told me all of the shipments were packaged up under your supervision. No one ever deviated from proper procedure. Until now. What if there's a bomb in there?" He's in full protector mode again, his shoulders straight and rigid, like he's right back in the Air Force commanding his—battalion? troops? squad?—whatever a group of Air Force men and women are called.

Making a mental note to ask him later, I relent. "We scan for explosive material. Everything that comes into this building goes through an X-ray. But you're right. There could be other dangers in there. So you can come. But this is one time you do exactly what *I* say. Got it?"

"Yes, ma'am." He gives me a curt nod and follows me into the decontamination chamber directly outside the lab.

Once we've suited up in thin, plastic bodysuits, masks, booties, gloves, and face shields, I enter the code for the lab. The light's green, so no contaminants have been detected in the air, but Austin's right. This is highly irregular, and I *know* I didn't authorize this shipment.

"Just in case," I say, wrapping my gloved fingers around his wrist, "the Atropine is in the top left cabinet. It's an auto-injector. Jab the needle into the outside of the thigh and depress the plunger. Got it?

"Got it." He moves the box under the vent hood, and I hand him a small scalpel so he can break the seal. So far, everything's normal.

"If there's any particulate matter loose in there, the light over the hood will turn yellow. If it's a known toxin, it'll turn red. If so, back away."

"Understood," he says as he slides the blade over the taped seams. Carefully, like he's handling nuclear waste, he pulls the lid from the box and sets it upside down under the hood. "Looks...relatively normal to me. Sample boxes, like the ones you had in your backpack when I found you."

"Okay. Step back." Slowly, I reach in and pull out one of six cases. Each has twelve samples inside. Leaves and roots from the Blushing Note orchids, dirt, grass, and moss from the surrounding area. One by one, I remove them, and when they're all spread out on the metal surface, I frown. Not that Austin can see it under my mask.

"Wait. What's in that compartment?" he asks, pointing to the fourth case.

The plastic cover isn't completely clear, but whatever's inside is definitely not organic. It's metal. Defined edges. Almost oblong. I reach for the lid, but Austin stops me, his gloved fingers curling around my wrist.

"Let me."

"No. Not this time. I need to be the one to break the seal." Picking up the scalpel, I pierce the tape sealing the single compartment's cover.

As soon as I open it, the light over the fume hood turns red. Austin tenses, but I hold up my hand. "It's okay. We're protected. That hood is rated for anthrax-level contaminants.

The Blushing Note phytotoxin isn't quite that lethal. Close, but not quite. And the particles are bigger. We'll be fine."

"I don't like this."

"Tough. This is my job, Austin. Let me do it." I nudge him out of the way, and to my surprise, he steps back.

"It's...a USB drive." I take a pair of forceps and pick it up, holding it as close to the vents as I can. A gray dust mars the shiny surface. Setting the drive down, I reach for a small vial half-full of blue reagent and a cotton swab. In a move I've done hundreds, if not thousands of times, I drag the cotton tip over the drive, collecting some of the dust, then flip the cap on the vial and drop the swab inside.

A little shake, and the solution turns green. But it's not the right color green. "That's odd."

"What?" Austin's on edge again, and I shoot him a look that hopefully says *calm down, now.*

"This tests for presence of the Blushing Note phytotoxin. But it should be a much lighter green. Closer to lime than emerald." Opening two more of the sample compartments, I examine their contents. With a freshly sterilized pair of forceps, I pick up a leaf cutting. "I need to run some more tests, but I don't think this is the Blushing Note. Crap on a cracker. Corey said he created a hybrid. A plant that was almost identical, but hardier. One that could grow outside of the narrow altitude band the Blushing Note is restricted to. What if this is it?"

"I don't understand. Why would it matter?" he asks.

"Because we didn't sample any of the hybrid plants. There's only one person who could have possibly sent this." Turning to Austin, I wait for him to make the connection.

When he does, his eyes harden, the hazel orbs darkening and his brows drawing together. "Corey. Which means this USB drive is from him too."

CHAPTER TWENTY-FOUR

Austin

Mik's boss, Dr. Lowenstein, eyes me with suspicion as we sit across from him. She introduced me with my former title, but he's not convinced.

"You do understand, Mr. Pritchard, that this is highly irregular? Dr. Salim's research has the potential to change Parkinson's treatment forever." Lowenstein crosses his arms and leans back in his chair.

"And you understand I have Top Secret clearance and used to be in charge of military operations so clandestine, if I even whispered their names, neither one of us would ever be heard from again?" I'm not in the mood to be intimidated, or to waste time. I want Mik back home where I know she's safe, and goddammit, I want Wren to call with news.

"Stop this stupid posturing. Both of you. Howard, Austin saved my life down in Mexico, and I trust him." She turns to me. "And you. Calm down. We know who sent the samples, and now that we've decontaminated that drive, we'll figure out what's on it soon enough."

Stifling my grumble of protest, I say, "This *is* my calm face, Mik."

She smashes her lips together, her eyes turning dark with need and a flush creeping up her neck. "Uh huh."

Oh, the things I'm going to do to her tonight. If she lets me. The momentary thought is all I allow myself because just then, Ronan's voice comes through my earbud. "Wren sent me to Ripper. Something about being too close to breaking into the Federal Ministerial Police servers to stop now. He's tracing the shipment, but says it'll probably take him an hour."

Ripper's estimates are always twice as long as they need to be, and I check my watch. We'll at least know where that shipment came from by the time we leave here. I clear my throat, the only acknowledgement I can give Ronan at the moment, and return my focus to Mikayla. Her voice cracks when she recounts her hike to Site One, and I reach over and take her hand.

The grateful look she gives me is tempered by pain, and by the time she gets to the fire in the mobile lab unit, she's holding on for dear life. Lowenstein looks like he's seen a ghost, and I shift my focus to him, watching every change in expression. Analyzing. Thinking. Shuffling puzzle pieces around in my head.

"I told Li and Isaiah to take the rest of the week off, and I don't want anyone in the greenhouse, the lab, or my office," she says finally. "Not until we figure out where Corey went and who's behind the poaching."

"My God, Mikayla. I can't believe any of this," Lowenstein says, then shakes his head. "I don't doubt you. Not for a moment. But why would anyone steal all Blushing Notes?

Even if it was only for profit, why try to kill you and the students?"

"That's what we're trying to find out." I sit up a little straighter and arch a brow at Lowenstein. "Have there been any inquiries into Mik's research lately? Anyone with an unusually strong interest in her work? You must have a marketing or public relations department. Any chance we can speak to them?"

"They're already gone for the day," Lowenstein says. "It's after five. But I can send them an email and have them meet you tomorrow." He rests his elbows on his desk and steeples his fingers as he focuses on Mik. "Are you in danger?"

"That's what we're trying to figure out." Her voice is stronger now, and she pulls her hand from mine. "Please don't share anything we've talked about today with anyone. Not the details. If anyone asks why I'm back early, just say the storms got too bad for us to finish out the week."

"And what about the shipment that came in?" he asks.

Mik steals a quick glance at me, and I give her a barely perceptible nod. We agreed on a course of action, but it's going to require her to keep some secrets, and she's so open, so trusting of those she works with, I know it's going to be hard for her.

"All of the sample cases were empty. The Chiapas police apparently boxed up all the cases in my hotel room and put them in the mail. That's why none of the standard protocols were followed." She stares down at her hands, and if Lowenstein is at all trained in reading body language, he'll know she's not telling the truth.

The older man nods and when he scrubs his hands over his face, there's a tremble in his fingers. Parkinson's, Mik said. He needs this cure, and though I can't get a read on him—at least not one I'm confident in—I don't *think* he's involved. "Call the PR department in the morning," he says. "Let them know I said they should give you any information you need."

Rising, Mik threads her fingers with mine. "Thanks, Howard. As soon as we have any more information, we'll let you know."

Ten minutes later, we're in the SUV. "Ronan, we're headed back to Mik's house. As soon as I confirm the interior's clear, you can head out for the night."

"About damn time," he mutters. "It's hot as fuck out here. I need a beer and a shower."

Chuckling as the air conditioning hits us full blast, I turn to Mik. "You okay, sweetheart?"

"Not really." With a sigh, she closes her eyes and rests her head against the seat. "I hated lying to Howard. And tomorrow? When I analyze those samples? I don't know what I expect to find—or *want* to find. I just hope soaking the USB drive in bleach to kill the phytotoxin didn't destroy any message Corey wanted me—or someone—to have."

The sadness lacing her tone makes my own heart hurt, and I reach over and brush my knuckles along her cheek. "Whatever happens, Mik, we'll be okay. Because we'll be together."

Leaning across the SUV, I pull her in for a kiss. It won't fix everything, but she seems to draw at least a little comfort from the contact. "Take me home, Austin. I want to be home. With you."

IF I THOUGHT we'd be safe, I'd take Mik out for dinner. Woo her properly. Despite never once in my life having use for the word *woo*, with Mikayla, I want to do this right.

But as we park in her driveway, she stifles a yawn, and I take a good, hard look at her. "You're exhausted, sweetheart. Why didn't you say something?"

"Because it doesn't matter." She's out of the car before I can help her, and headed for her front door.

"Mik, wait. Let me go first."

Freezing with her hand on the knob, she stares back at me, a haunted look in her eyes. "The cameras...?"

"Are necessary. But as good as Wren and Royce are—and they're the best—no piece of technology is completely tamper-proof. Let me clear the house, and then we can relax. I can draw you another bath?" With a quick wink, I open her door and pull the Beretta from the holster. Now that I know the layout, it only takes me two minutes to verify we're alone, and once I send Ronan back to his hotel, I flip the deadbolt and scoop Mik into my arms.

"Austin!" she protests with a weak laugh. "Put me down."

"Nope. You're going to relax if I have to take you to bed and worship your body until you don't know your own name."

Her mouth opens and shuts so quickly, her teeth snap together. "Oh."

Carrying her into the bedroom, I lay her down on the bed and straddle her, sealing my lips to hers and offering her everything I am. Watching her work with a deadly poison was almost more than I could handle, but it was also sexy as hell. Her confidence. Poise. The way she took control of her space and her work and just expected me to listen.

"Mikayla, I need you," I manage as my dick strains against my zipper. "But—"

"But you also need to know what's on that drive," she says, reading me so easily, I wonder if I've lost my edge. The tight control I've always kept over my thoughts, fears, emotions.

"Is it that obvious?" I ask, sliding off her and getting to my feet.

"Yep." She reaches out and cups my hard length with one hand and my cheek with the other. "Both parts."

I'm shocked at her new-found confidence—even more than I was last night. "One day, Mik, things will be...normal."

She catches my mistake before I do and offers me a weak smile. "But then, Austin, we'd have to move to Alabama. Or Kentucky. And my work is here."

We. She said "we."

The idea that Mik's decided there's a "we" is staggering, and I rub my hand over my chin, the day and a half of stubble rasping against my palm. "No, ma'am. There's no need to move to Alabama or Kentucky. Maryland's just fine by me."

Neither of us move or speak for a full minute. Maybe two. Even though we haven't said the words, I feel them. And from the sparkle in Mik's eyes, she does too.

"Did we just...?" she asks.

"I..." Before I can figure out the right words to say, my phone beeps with an incoming text message. "It's Wren. She wants us to call her."

"She found something." Mik swings her legs over the side of the bed, but before she gets up, she flexes her left foot a couple of times. Dammit. I should have known she was still in pain.

She protests when I pick her up again, but I shake my head. "We're calling Wren from the couch. After I get you an ice pack and a pillow so you can elevate that ankle. I'm being a piss-poor boyfriend at the moment."

With her cheek against mine, the heat of her blush seeps into my skin. "I didn't know we'd picked a...label."

"Honestly," I say when we reach the bottom of the stairs. "I never really liked the word 'boyfriend.'"

"You, Austin Pritchard, are definitely *not* a boy." Mik's smile and teasing tone reassure me, despite the exhaustion rimming her eyes. "And 'manfriend' makes you sound like a male escort."

"Partner's getting pretty popular these days." I can't see her face anymore. Not while I'm rummaging in her freezer for an ice pack or bag of peas or *something* I can use to help with the swelling.

"Partner. You realize what that means, though. Right?"

I toss a bag of frozen corn kernels into the air on my way back to the couch and shake my head. "Besides the obvious? That we're...together?"

She lets me pull off her shoe, check her range of motion, and lay the bag over the swelling. Before I turn my tablet on, she rests her fingers over my wrist. "It means we're equals. That you respect my skills. My passions. And I respect your instincts. Those gut feelings that have been so on point the past week."

"Mik." I cup her cheeks, staring into her warm brown eyes and finding an emotion neither of us is willing to name, but we agree on, nonetheless. "Seeing you today, in your element? It was the sexiest thing I've ever seen. You know your shit, and if I ever make you feel like you don't, if I *ever* step over you, talk over you, ignore your expertise, I expect you to give me hell for it. And put me in my fucking place."

"So, partners?" she whispers, her eyes glistening.

"Partners." If I could tell her right now, I would. If Wren weren't waiting for us to call. If worry over what's on that USB drive wasn't eating a hole inside of me. If I didn't *need* to know how safe we are more than I need to breathe. I'd tell her I love her. That I've fallen so hard and so fast for her, even looking at her takes my breath away. That she sees all the broken parts of me and somehow...she's starting to put them back together.

"Call her," Mik says with a light kiss to my cheek. "Maybe she'll have good news, and we'll be able to enjoy the rest of our night. In bed."

CHAPTER TWENTY-FIVE

Mikayla

Austin drapes his arm around my shoulders after he taps Wren's contact card to start the video call.

I glance up at him, but he shrugs. "Wren's...family."

"And she's married to—"

"Ryker," Wren says on screen. She holds up her left hand and wiggles her fingers. "It's been nine months and I still can't believe he actually proposed."

Austin scoffs. "Pretty sure Ryker McCabe's heart started beating again the day he met you."

Wren's cheeks turn bright red and she stares down at her keyboard. "You have some explaining to do, Austin. Once we untangle this mess."

Now I'm the one blushing, and I try to scoot away from Austin, but he doesn't let me go. Wren looks like she's staring directly at me, but...that's not how webcams work. Is it? Usually, I feel like I'm looking at a person's forehead the whole time.

"Mikayla," Wren says, concern in her voice. Everything about her is...sweet. A little motherly. But, as soon as she starts tapping on the keyboard, she's suddenly all business.

"Mik. Friends call me Mik."

Her gaze shifts to me for a moment, and she smiles. "Family too?"

Oh, crap.

"Wren's...family."

Is it that obvious? That I'm falling for Austin? That we practically agreed to *move in* together just five minutes ago?

"Mik?" she asks.

"Y-yes. Family too. Well, my parents call me Mika, but they're the only ones. They think Mik is a guy's name."

"Well, we've got Joey and Dani already, so you'll fit right in." With a wink, she returns to typing, and Austin's tablet screen splits with Wren's face on the left and a passport photo on the right.

A shiver runs down my back as I whisper, "Martín."

Austin squeezes my shoulders gently. "Go ahead, Wren."

"Well, Martín Salvador isn't his real name. Arturo Lopez doesn't exist either. Turns out, these two jerkwads are actually from Peru. That's why it took me so long to track them down. The Peruvian government uses an antiquated system that... well...let's just say they don't build them like they used to."

"Wren, you're the best in the world," Austin says. "You mean to tell me an out of date system—?"

She scowls, and Austin snaps his jaw shut. I don't blame him. This woman has a fierce side to her I don't ever want to mess with. "You try pulling data from a system with the speed of a 1200 baud modem."

"Wait. That's...ancient. We had one of those growing up. Like...more than thirty years ago. I remember my parents trying to get email messages from my grandmother in Aleppo, and they'd take half an hour just to download a paragraph."

"See?" Wren shoots me a look I think might be respect. "Mik gets it."

"I'm sorry. We haven't exactly had a lot of sleep and I'm being an ass," he says. "Go on."

"You forget who I'm married to. Plus, family. You don't need to apologize. Just listen. Because this is about to get interesting."

The screen shifts, and suddenly, there are five more photos on display. "You recognize any of these guys, Mik?" Wren asks.

"Only Arturo and Martín," I say. "Who are the others?"

"The board of directors of a Nozanita Pharmaceuticals. They're based in Peru. Small. Virtually unknown. The whole company is only worth two billion."

"Only?" At my side, Austin frowns. "That's not nothing, Wren."

"It is for big pharma," I explain. "The researcher I'm working with at Johns Hopkins? He thinks the drug he's developing would have been worth a hundred times that if anyone else had realized a use for the phytotoxin first. Remember that guy who tried to boost the price of some crucial medication a few years ago? I don't remember what it was for, but he was all over the news and went to jail eventually. His company bought the patent for the drug and the pill went from like five dollars each all the way to seven hundred bucks a dose overnight."

Wren beams at me. "Don't lose her, Austin. I mean it. She's smart."

He readjusts his arm, sliding it around my waist instead. "Not planning on it. Ever."

Oh God. I don't know if I can handle all this talk about forever when I'm staring at the faces of the men who tried to murder me, but Austin's warm and solid and *real* and maybe this is exactly what I need right now.

"So they're small potatoes," Austin says. "What does that have to do with anything?"

All the pieces fall into place. "They know what the phytotoxin's used for."

"Gold star." Wren claps her hands a couple of times, then zooms in on the pictures of the Nozanita board. Arturo's real last name is Garcia, and Martín's is Alvarez. Also, Martín is dead. So there's one bad guy you don't have to worry about anymore."

She says the words to matter-of-factly they take a moment to register. "Dead?"

"Yep. His body showed up in a morgue in Tuxtla Gutiérrez this morning. At least *some* countries take photos. If he'd died in Peru...I doubt we'd know."

"How did he die?" Austin leans closer to the tablet and lowers his voice. "I stabbed him in the chest before..."

"Austin, I was there. Remember?" I elbow him gently in the ribs. "Not saying they're fond memories, but you whispering isn't going to take them away."

He lets out a heavy, resigned breath and nods. "I know, sweetheart. I just..."

"Want to protect me."

Somehow, in the last few minutes, I no longer care that Wren can see us—or hear us. Or that she's clearly a little impatient to tell us the rest of what she's found.

When she clears her throat, though, we tear our gazes away from one another and stare back at the tablet.

"You didn't kill him, Austin. His neck was broken. The stab wound to his chest would have been fatal though, because the coroner's report shows he had..." Wren furrows her brow, "a tension pneumothorax. I looked it up, and basically, air gets trapped in the chest cavity, compresses the lungs, and can eventually end up stopping the heart. Super painful. Ultimately, someone put an end to him. Quickly."

I'm not sure what answer Austin was hoping for. That *he* killed Martín or that he didn't, but I can feel the tension radiating off of him.

"What about Arturo Garcia?" he asks. "Any evidence of his whereabouts?"

"No. The smaller airports around Chiapas don't have surveillance cameras I can tap into, and facial recognition is only getting me so far. I *am* running scans on all of the main entry points to the United States within two hours of Edgewater, but if he came in like you did, on a private plane, there might not be any record of the flight."

"Fuck. So we have no idea if Mik is still in danger. None." Pushing to his feet, Austin starts to pace, and Wren huffs.

"First of all, Mr. GrumpyGus, I'm not done. Second, Ripper got some info on that crate that showed up at Mik's lab, so you sit your butt down and listen." Despite her words, she winks at me and mouths, *"Men,"* before Austin takes a seat again.

"I'm running full bios on every single member of Nozanita's board. Friends, family, recent travel...all of it. Plus, searching for any patents they've filed recently. If they're after that phytotoxin stuff, I'll know about it. Soon. But my computer power's limited right now because Ry has half of my home office torn up and there's not enough electrical in the main room. Ripper's at Hidden Agenda setting up a server farm so we can work faster, and he's been on this with me since this morning."

"And third?" Austin asks. "There's a third, isn't there?"

Wren's expression softens. "There's always a third. Mik, how well do you know a guy named Walter Ulreet?"

The name sounds vaguely familiar, but I can't place it, and tell her so.

"He works at Johns Hopkins. With Dr. Brian Branch."

"Oh!" How could I have forgotten about him? Probably because Brian always called him Wally and I never made the connection. "He's a research assistant, I think. Right?"

"Yep. But here's the thing that worries me." She leans closer to her screen, her expression grim. "Over the past seven months, he's flown down to Lima, Peru four times. The last time was two days ago."

"Goddammit." Austin runs a hand over his jaw, then turns to me. "Mik, if this Nozanita is trying to beat anyone else to market with this Parkinson's drug, they'll be able to set the price and make a fuckton of money. Enough money to be willing to kill for."

Austin

Everything's starting to make sense now, and I don't like it one bit. Scratch that. I hate it. With a passion I usually save for human traffickers and terrorists.

"Wren, what did Rip find out about the shipment to Mik's lab?" She reaches for my hand, and I thread our fingers and hold on tight.

"It was sent from the hotel the morning after she was attacked. Paid for with cash."

"Fuck."

"Hold your horses, Austin. There's more. It cost 5,337 pesos to get that box to Maryland. So Rip searched all the banks in the area for withdrawals between four and six thousand pesos that same morning. He got a hit." She taps her screen, and the image of the Nozanita board vanishes, replaced with a grainy security camera image of Corey Larkin.

Mik sucks in a sharp breath. "I still don't understand why Corey would send those to me. Especially that morning. He didn't even know if I was alive."

"Maybe he did, sweetheart. All we know about Arturo and Martín's whereabouts that day are that they kidnapped Li and Isaiah at noon. What if they checked the cliff at dawn and didn't find you?" I cup her cheek, brushing my thumb along a fading bruise. "It makes sense. They went after your students when they thought you'd survived. One person's easy to shut up—or discredit. Three? That's a hell of a lot harder."

I pull the USB drive out of my pocket and hold it up so Wren can see it. "This was in the box with samples from the hybrid orchids."

"And?" Wren asks. "You haven't plugged it in yet?" When I shake my head, she mutters, "Amateurs. Hang on." She types for a full minute, and a black box with green text flashes on my screen for a split second before disappearing. "Okay. Plug it in. I just installed a secondary firewall in case there's some sort of virus on there."

Mik gapes at the screen. "How'd you learn all of this?"

"How'd you learn the proper way to handle toxic orchids?" Wren challenges, but she's smiling. "My brain works a little differently from everyone else's. Upside? Computers make total and complete sense to me. They're logical. Easy to predict. To understand."

"And the downside?" Mik frowns. "I mean, if you want to tell me."

Wren runs her hand over her wrist, and a faint clicking carries over the call. "Massive, almost uncontrollable anxiety with some OCD—obsessive compulsive disorder—mixed in. I don't leave home much. Heck, before I met Ry, the only places I felt truly comfortable were my apartment and Second Sight."

"And now?"

"Our apartment, Second Sight, Hidden Agenda, a few friends' places. My hair dresser." She inclines her head, a hint of resignation in her voice. "I'm not agoraphobic. Not by a long shot. I go to the grocery store, we've gone on a few weekend trips, that sort of thing. I take my meds every day and just... hope for the best." Brightening, Wren adds, "I wouldn't change it. Any of it. Anxiety sucks the big one, but I love what I do, and with Ry...everything's...easier."

"Okay, Wren. The drive's plugged in. You want to take the lead?" I ask.

"Yep. Let's see what Larkin sent you." But when she tries to open the file, nothing happens. "Fudgsicles."

"Fudgsicles?" Mik asks. "What the heck does that mean?"

"It's Wren's code for fuck. You two have that in common," I say nudging Mik's shoulder. "She doesn't swear either."

"I *do*," Wren says as she narrows her eyes at her screen. "Just very, *very* rarely. My mom was a teacher."

"My parents are Muslim," Mik says quietly. "They never allowed swearing." From her tone and the tension in her shoulders and back, she's worried about Wren's response, but the redhead just glances up at her.

"I have all sorts of replacements. Spit-snacks, crackerjacks, son of a biscuit, fudgsicles... Last time we were in Boston though, we went to this coffee shop and I heard a brand new one that might be my favorite so far."

"What is it?" Mik asks.

"Son of a motherless goat."

Mikayla chuckles and relaxes against me slightly. "I like it. All I ever use is dang and crap on a cracker."

"Don't discount the effectiveness of a good crap-cracker." In the next breath, Wren says, "Shit."

"Wren? What is it?" I've never heard her swear before, and according to Ry, she only lets loose with the s-word when she's either royally pissed off or terrified.

"The data's corrupted."

Mik drops her head into her hands. "We had to disinfect the drive with a chlorine solution. Did we ruin it?"

"No, no, no." Wren waves her hand, dismissing Mik's worry. "If anything, I'd suspect heat damage. That's about the only thing that'll damage one of these drives. Hang on." A few more keystrokes, and she sits back with a sigh. "I'm sending a courier to your house, Mik. He'll be there in an hour to pick up the drive and fly it out to me in Seattle. Make sure you ask him for the password. It's 'Cracker Jack.'"

"Seattle? Why?" she asks.

Wren runs her fingers through her red curls. "I could try to repair the damage from here, but honestly, having to do that over an encrypted cell connection is going to be slower than molasses in January. Even with a five hour flight, it'll be faster for me to work on it directly."

"You've used this courier service before?" I don't like letting the drive out of our possession, but I trust Wren, and if she says she needs it, then she needs it.

"Yep. All the time." She looks directly at the camera, her expression as serious as I've ever seen it. "Austin, you're family. Like it or not. What you did for Ripper...then Trevor?"

"Wren, I—"

"Don't," she says. "Dax is getting a full report, and if need be, Trevor can be there in under two hours. I don't think it'll come to this, but Ry, West, Inara, and Graham are on standby."

Mik sucks in a sharp breath. "Do you really think there's that much danger? Are we safe staying here?"

"As far as I know? Probably," Wren replies. "But probably isn't good enough for family. I have to go. Rip's been trying to get a hold of me for ten minutes so we can finish setting up the servers at Hidden Agenda. Stay safe, and I'll be in touch soon."

The video call ends, and I pull Mik into my arms. She's shaking, and I rub her back gently, but I don't have any words to reassure her. Things just got a hell of a lot more complicated.

CHAPTER TWENTY-SIX

Austin

Mikayla's hair tickles my shoulder, and she curls her arm around my waist and makes a soft, contented sound. Peering down at her—or trying to in our intertwined position—I watch for signs she's waking up, but she doesn't move again, and her breathing evens out.

I've been awake for an hour, but this feels so perfect, so right, that I won't disturb her if I can help it. Trevor's already messaged me, even though it's barely 8:00 a.m., and he wants to come to Edgewater. I guess I'm not getting out of that *talk* he demanded we have.

At least Mik will be able to meet him. Last night, after a solid two hours in bed discovering each other, Mik curled against me and trailed her fingers over my chest, tracing scar after scar. "I'm scared," she said.

"Of what?"

"That this is all too perfect. That I'll wake up in the morning and you'll be a dream. Or worse. What if I'm still out on that ledge? What if the past few days have been all in my head? I could be dying. Dreaming of what could have been." Her voice took on a sultry tone—the result of several screaming climaxes—and she tipped her head up to meet my eyes. "I want this to be real."

"It's real, Mik. You keep saying I'm too good to be true, but you're wrong. *You're* the one who's perfect. You see all this darkness inside of me and you don't care."

She propped herself up on an elbow and stared down at me. "I care, Austin. If I could take that darkness away, I would. Because I know you hate it. But I don't. Everything you are, that's what led you to Mexico. To me. How can I not accept it when it gave me...this?" She pressed her lips to mine, and after that, neither of us felt much like talking.

"You're thinking," she murmurs now, snuggling closer. "So hard, I can hear the wheels turning in your head."

"Sorry, sweetheart. Trev texted a little bit ago. He wants to meet up later today. I owe him one hell of an explanation for going dark for so long."

She sits up, and her well-worn t-shirt clings to her breasts in a way that makes me want to shut out the world and worship her for twenty-four hours straight. Though, that'd probably kill us both.

"You're going alone?" Fear roughens her voice, and she fiddles with the sheet.

Fuck. "Some of the shit we have to talk about...what Trev went through in Venezuela... I want you to meet him. Hell, I *need* you to meet him. But give me an hour with him? There's a Dunkin' Donuts ten minutes away on Solomons Island Road. And Ronan will take over surveillance. Either inside the house or sitting in the car out front."

She worries her lip between her teeth, and shit. I feel like a total asshole. "Forget everything I just said. I'll tell Trevor he has to come here."

"No. Trevor needs you. And you need to talk to him, too. I'll be fine with Ronan." Her hands aren't totally steady, but she smooths the covers back before she gets out of bed. "I need a shower. Want to join me?"

Hell yes. I'll join her anytime, anywhere if it means I get to see her naked, touch her, take care of her. When we're done, I'm going to call Trevor and tell him we'll have to meet here. There's still too much we don't know about the men who are after her.

By the time I join her in the bathroom, she's naked, the spray cascading over her back. The deep purple bruises have started to fade, turning a sickly yellow, but they don't pain her as much as they did. Small victories.

"I could get used to this," I say as I wrap my arms around her waist and score my teeth over the shell of her ear. "Showering with you every day..."

Mik turns in my arms and smiles. "Move in."

My mouth must drop open, because Mik laughs and nudges my chin up with the crook of her finger. "Wh-what did you say?"

"Move. In." She rests her head on my chest, and her next words are muffled. "It's too soon. I know. But...you said it yourself. You don't have a home right now. No apartment. No house."

I'd hoped. Hell, our whole "partners" talk last night...we did everything but say those three little words. But I didn't think she was ready for me to *live* here.

"Now it's my turn to ask you to forget what I just said," she whispers, her voice barely audible over the sound of the shower. "I should have—"

"Yes."

"Wh-what?" Hope shines in her eyes, and she holds her breath.

"Yes. I'll move in with you." Cupping her cheek, I touch my forehead to hers. "Mik...my retirement pay is...good. Twenty-three years in the Air Force, retiring with the rank I did... Money isn't a huge concern for me. Provided I find a job."

"I don't need to run your credit, Austin," she says, pinning me with a hard stare. "You flew us—all three of us—back to Baltimore in a private jet."

"No, it's not that." I spin her around, then spill some of her shampoo into my hands and start massaging her scalp. She moans softly, and fuck. It's one of the sexiest sounds in the world. "What I'm trying to say, sweetheart, is that I'll stay with you. Hell, I'll stay with you forever if you'll let me."

At her tiny gasp, I worry I've said too much, but her smile... that's all contentment and joy.

"If you *ever* want me to leave—need me to leave—all you have to do is ask. If living together is too much, I can find an apartment in town somewhere and we can slow the fuck down. Try to date like a nor—err—typical couple."

"We're not typical people," she says as I tip her head back, one hand supporting her neck, the other combing through her hair to rinse out the shampoo.

"No. We're definitely not. And I wouldn't have it any other way. Would you?" A tiny kernel of fear tightens in my gut. What if she says yes?

Draping one of her arms around my neck, she kisses me, and when she pulls back, light dances in her eyes. "Definitely not."

Mikayla

The idea of staying here by myself shouldn't be so scary. Ronan will be right outside. This is my home. Being alone has never bothered me. Until now.

Austin cleans up the breakfast dishes—pancakes this time—and I check my email. Li and Isaiah are staying at his place—their place now—and the surveillance detail has been discreet the one time they went to the store for groceries.

She wants to come back to the lab. They both do.

Li,

You're not missing anything at work. I went in yesterday to talk to Dr. Lowenstein, but there's nothing else we can do until we know why Corey did all of this. You and Isaiah will get full credit for this semester, don't worry. You've earned it.

-Dr. Mik

Austin pulls his comms unit out of the case and tucks it in his ear. "I know you don't want to wear one, sweetheart, but I'd feel a lot better if you did."

"I don't want to listen in on your conversation with Trevor," I protest. The idea of wearing something that lets me talk to Austin any time is tempting, but he and Trevor need privacy.

"You won't be." Taking out the second device, he tucks it gently into my ear. "If you double-tap the unit, it'll send a signal to all the other units paired to the main receiver. Listen."

Austin taps his own earbud twice, and a single, low-pitched tone sounds in my ear. "Tap once to turn it on."

When I do, it's like I can hear the air conditioning twice as loud as it usually is. "See?" Austin says.

The shock of hearing his voice so quietly in my ear while still hearing him from five feet away sends me stumbling back a step. "Wow. Okay. I'll wear it. But I want it off. In both directions."

He grins like he just won the lottery, then arches a brow. "Why? Are you planning on singing showtunes off-key the whole time I'm gone?"

"No." My cheeks feel like they're on fire, and I fiddle with the bracelet he gave me. Really, it was less than week ago, but it feels like I've worn it forever. In a good way. "I'm going to call my parents. They should know...about you."

For a moment, Austin's so still, I'm actively worried about him. Until something breaks the spell, and he strides over to me and hugs me so tightly, I push against his hold. "Austin, I need to breathe!"

"Fuck. I'm sorry. I just... Mik, I—lo"

His tablet rings with a tone I now recognize as being unique to Wren. Austin rushes over and taps the screen. "What is it?"

The look on her face is pure, unadulterated triumph. "That drive was in bad shape."

"But my *wife* is a fucking genius," Ryker says from somewhere behind Wren.

"Hey. Whose win is this, soldier?" She throws a pillow off screen, and Ryker's deep, rasping laugh follows. "Go punch something. And say hi to the team for me."

"I love you, little bird."

"Love you too."

Turning back to us, she rubs her hands together. "Are you ready?"

"Yes," we say at the same time. Austin has his hand on my shoulder, and the contact helps me focus on my breathing. I woke up this morning with a hint of tightness in my chest, and even though I'm not planning on leaving the house while he's gone, my rescue inhaler's in my pocket, just in case.

My heart stutters as Corey's face appears on screen. The

video's a little glitchy, but he clears his throat and stares directly into the camera.

"Dr. Mik, I hope you see this. It's been, um...fifteen hours since Arturo pushed you off that cliff. I...I'm so sorry. I tried to go after you, but Arturo punched me—hard—and when I came to, we were already halfway back to the Hotel Centro." Corey rubs his neck and swears under his breath. "I'd just called the local *Policia* when I heard that guy outside your door. Pritchard."

After a pause, Corey stares into the camera again. "I lied to you, Dr. Mik. My dad...he *is* a drug addict. But it's worse than that. He got himself in deep with the Gutiérrez Cartel. Half a million dollars. I didn't know what to do. They were going to kill him. And then...you had that call with Dr. Branch. Back in April? When he said this drug could be worth billions..." He tears up a little and swipes at his eyes. "Dr. Branch's research assistant, Wally? I had drinks with him, and by the end of the night...he asked me to help him."

The video cuts out, static filling the screen for a full thirty seconds before the image clears again. "...analyze the samples I'm going to send you. The cartel thinks the hybrids are substandard. That only the Blushing Note orchids are viable for medical research. But they're wrong."

Another few seconds of static, and Corey's face is suddenly right next to the camera. "If I'm lucky, I'll have enough time to send the hybrid samples—and the protocol I used to create them—to the Smithsonian. I don't know if you're alive, but shit. You gave me a chance when no one else would. And I'm so fucking sorry."

I turn to Austin. "I have to go to the lab. Right now."

CHAPTER TWENTY-SEVEN

Austin

This is a terrible fucking idea. Especially since I was supposed to meet Trevor ten minutes ago.

"You saw how secure everything is," Mik says. "The assays —the tests—I have to run will take at least a couple of hours, and I have to slice the samples, mount them on slides, document every stage of the process... You'd be bored out of your mind and just sitting in the corner in full protective gear doing *nothing*. This is the best solution."

"Leaving you alone is *not* the best solution."

"You'll be two miles away. I'm wearing the comms unit." She taps her ear twice and a little beep sounds in my unit before she turns it off again. "And Ronan will be right outside."

Pulling out my phone, I force myself to unclench my jaw. Trev's messaged me twice since we left Mik's house.

Where the fuck are you?

Don't you dare stand me up, asshole.

Mik leans across the SUV and rests her hand over my heart. "Austin, go see Trevor." She presses a key into my palm. "This is yours. If you don't want to talk at Dunkin', bring him back to the house. I can even have Ronan drive me home."

I stare at the small piece of metal and what it represents. Like my dog tags, it's more than just one thing. More than a key. It's our future.

"Hey." Mik's soft voice pulls me out of the fog, and I swallow hard.

"You're really sure about this." It's not a question, but she answers anyway with a nod. "You're sure about us."

"You're not?" There's worry in her gaze now, and I hate that I put it there.

Sliding my fingers into her short hair, I pull her in for a kiss. "I'm sure, sweetheart. The words whisper against her lips, and fuck. I can't get enough of this woman. "But I've been trained to make quick decisions. Ones my life depended on. In my world—or what *was* my world anyway—there's no room for error. I was sure about you the night we spent in those old ruins. Hell, probably even before I left the hotel to find you. I want a future with you."

"Then why...?"

"Because I won't *ever* let you feel like you don't have a choice. I won't pressure you. I *can't* because I know how I can be. I have more than two decades of absolute certainty in me. More than twelve years in command. What happens with us... don't misunderstand. I absolutely *will* fight for us. But I'll also fight for you. I'll fight so that you always have a choice. So you always feel heard. Respected. By others, but especially by me."

Mikayla's eyes shine in the sunlight, and she offers me a smile. "Too good to be true. Again." After another kiss that leaves me aching, my dick throbbing against my zipper, she slings the strap of her messenger bag over her shoulder and gets out of the SUV.

"Tell Trevor I can't wait to meet him," she says. "And don't worry about me. I'll lock myself in the lab and let you know when I'm done."

And then she's walking away, her ass swaying in ways that make me want to run after her, scoop her up in my arms, and bring her right back home. Our home.

But then Trev sends me a message with more expletives than anything else, and I thumb out a reply.

I'm five minutes away.

THE IDEA of having a painful conversation in a Dunkin' Donuts doesn't sit well with me, so as soon as I walk in and see Trev, I jerk my thumb towards the parking lot.

Coffee cup in hand, he follows, scowling the whole time. "What the fuck, man?" he says when I unlock the SUV.

"Just thought we should have this convo somewhere else." I pull out my phone and text him Mik's address. "It's ten minutes away."

"Austin." The look on his face stops me cold. "Just tell me you're all right."

"I'm good, brother." Smiling feels...odd. The last time we were together, we were both in such a bad place, I couldn't imagine a world in which we'd both be anything approaching happy.

But under Trev's worry, there's a hint of contentment in his gaze, one I recognize. Because for the first time in my life, I feel it too. It's love.

"Where are we going?" he asks as he fiddles with the key fob for his rental car.

"Mikayla's house. She's at the Smithsonian with Ronan parked outside. The kid's pissed as hell we keep making him sit in a black SUV in this heat." I offer Trev a wry smile. "But he's grown up a lot since Venezuela."

"He's still an angry son of a bitch," Trevor says.

There's respect in his tone, though, and when we get to Mik's house, he's shed some of the frustration from the coffee shop.

"Nice place." He scans up and down the street, then zeroes in on one of the trees lining her driveway. "Clive did a good job with the cameras."

"I walked the whole property yesterday." Unlocking the door, I step inside with my hand on the butt of my gun, but we've only been gone half an hour, and I know without a doubt Trev's carrying too. "Could only find two of the five cameras, and I've been checking the feeds. I know exactly where they should be."

Trevor peers out the sliding glass door into the backyard. "This'd be a good place to raise a family, y'know."

"A family?" I say, shock roughening my tone. "Trev...are you and Dani?"

"No. I meant you, asshole." With a snort, he joins me at the kitchen island where I'm starting a fresh pot of coffee. "Kind of hard to be 'dad' material when you never had one."

I want to say something. Offer him some kernel of wisdom that might help him see that growing up as an orphan might actually make him a *great* father. But the look on his face tells me he's not ready to hear anything I might have to offer him on that subject.

"I spent more than half of my life serving my country," I say, watching the coffee start to drip into the pot. "What the hell am I supposed to do now?"

Shoving his hands into his pockets, Trev leans against the

marble. "Could always come work with us. Dax would hire you in a heartbeat."

"Not moving to Boston." Removing two mugs from the cabinet, I chuckle. One of them has the UC Berkeley logo on it, the other's from the Smithsonian. "I'm staying in Edgewater. With Mikayla."

His eyebrows shoot up, and he stares at me like I've lost my mind. "You've known this woman how long?"

Shrugging, I fill our mugs, then slide one across the counter for him. "A week? But does it really matter? Look at everyone around us, Trev. Dax and Evianna, Ryker and Wren. Ripper and Cara. How long did any of them know one another? And fuck. How long did you know Dani? How long did you *love* Dani before you finally pried your head out of your ass and told her?"

"Too long." He runs a hand through his hair, and as the air conditioner kicks on, he shudders and moves out of the way of the vent. When I meet his gaze, he shakes his head. "Can't stand cold air blowing on me most of the time."

I kick myself, even though I couldn't have known. Trev spent three days in a prison cell in Caracas so small, he couldn't sit up or straighten his legs. Lying on a frigid concrete slab. Chained. Unbearably cold. Bright lights that never dimmed. Not even allowed to sleep.

Gesturing to the couch where the vents don't reach, I search for the right words, but they won't come. So I settle for something...simple. "How are you, Trev?"

"Been better. Been worse." He stares into his coffee cup, takes a sip, and then sits back with his legs stretched out. "Dax and I've talked a bit. Dani goes to therapy. I tried for a while, but it's not what I need right now."

He falls silent, and I mirror his position. "So...what do you need?" I think I know, but he has to be the one to say it. Just like I have to be the one to tell him my truth. When he's ready.

"Come around sometime," he says quietly. "Dani misses you." After a beat, he meets my gaze. "You're the only one I can talk to about Gil, you know."

"So talk. I'm here now, Trev. I know I went dark. I had to."

"Why?"

The single, rasping word is like a punch to my gut, and fuck. If it weren't for Mikayla, I'd still be in that solitary, tortured world I thought was all I deserved.

"Because Major General Austin Pritchard doesn't exist anymore. And until I met Mik, I didn't know who I was without him."

"And now? You've figured it out?" Desperation churns in his eyes, like he's depending on me to help answer his own existential questions. Maybe he is. I have a few years on Trev, and we're brothers—not by blood, but in all the ways that count.

"Not all of it. But I know I need to do something that matters. Knowing Mik's in danger, knowing someone wants to kill her...protecting her gave me a purpose again. Reminded me that I'm still that same son of a bitch who fought in Kabul and Kandahar ten years ago. Still the same guy who convinced a handful of generals Rip deserved a medal instead of a prison sentence. I can make a difference somewhere. Just don't know where yet."

"Somewhere in Edgewater, though." The corners of his mouth twitch into what might be a smile. "Didn't think I'd ever see you fall so hard for anyone."

"I love her." The admission slips out before I can stop it, and I shake my head. "I fucking love her."

I hold my breath, waiting for Trevor to tell me I'm not thinking clearly. That I've let my dick override my brain. But there's a knowing look in his eyes that says he has my back.

That he's *always* had my back, just like I've always had his. Fuck. I was so stupid. Going dark on him. He's my family and I won't let him down again.

"So when do I get to meet her?" he asks. "Because anyone who can get you to stay in one place...she's got to be one hell of a woman."

"She is, brother. She definitely is."

CHAPTER TWENTY-EIGHT

Mikayla

The hazmat suit rustles as I sit down at the microscope. The goggles are awkward as all get out, but from what I've learned over the past two hours, they're necessary. The phytotoxin present in these hybrid orchids is ten times deadlier than the one from the Blushing Note.

Based on its chemical make-up, its promise to make a real difference for Parkinson's patients is also through the roof.

I wish I could talk to Dr. Branch about this. But Brian and his whole team are off limits until Wren and Ripper do more digging. I can't believe he'd be involved. But I promised Austin I wouldn't do anything to put myself at risk—well, other than work with one of the deadliest plants I've ever examined—and I don't intend to break my word.

Every sample Corey collected is meticulously labeled, down to the specific plant and site it came from. Someone needs to get back down to Chiapas and harvest at least one of the hybrids for study.

"I managed to create a hybrid last year by grafting the Blushing Note to the Zebra Stripe. Once I knew it was viable, I came down here to set up the greenhouses so we could reproduce them."

He didn't say he brought the plant with him. What if it's still in *our* greenhouse? Crap. If it is, I can divide it, study fresh samples rather than the dried, preserved ones, and start breeding the plants.

I can't get my PPE off fast enough once I've let a fine mist spray me down in the decontamination chamber, and I rush to the greenhouse. The humid, thick air is a shock to my lungs, and along with my excitement, it triggers the tell-tale band around my chest that almost always leads to an attack.

No. Not right now.

I force myself to stop just inside the door, leaning against the wall and taking slow, deep breaths. I can't stay in here very long. Not today. But I only need enough time to take a couple of cuttings from the big orchid in the corner. Queenie. Corey always babied that plant, while Li and Isaiah primarily cared for the smaller orchids in the center.

You can do this. Five minutes, and you'll be back in the hall.

Snagging a sample tray and small box of tools from the cart by the door, I head for the corner. My legs feel like they weigh twice as much as usual, but at least the chest tightness is easing a little.

The root system on this plant is bigger than a small child, but with so many of the greenish-brown tendrils hanging down, the temperamental orchid shouldn't mind me taking a couple of cuttings. Except I forgot my gloves.

"Drumsticks," I mutter, and as I turn, the door beeps. What the heck?

"Lowenstein said you weren't coming in today." Brian and his research assistant, Wally, stand just in front of Arturo.

Regret pinches Brian's features, and I yelp and take two quick steps back.

"B-Brian? You're...oh God. You were in on this the whole time?" Wheezing, I reach up to tap the earbud, but my vision starts to tunnel, and Arturo grabs my arm.

"Oh, no you don't." Fingers dig into my chin, turning my head, and he swears under his breath. "Fucking bitch."

Plucking the comms unit from my ear, he throws it on the floor and stomps on it. My stomach pitches, and gasping for air, I can't hold myself upright any longer.

Not again. This is so eerily similar to finding Corey and the poachers at the site, and tears spring to my eyes.

Arturo lets me fall, and I fumble for my inhaler and manage to get a hit of Albuterol before he kicks it out of my hand.

"Wait," Brian says. He crouches down in front of me. "The plant will be a lot safer if she helps us transfer it."

"Thought you...were my friend," I manage. Wally retrieves the inhaler from across the room and thrusts it at me, and I take a second puff. I'm already starting to shake from the meds, but my airways are opening, and with the extra oxygen, my thoughts no longer feel quite so addled.

"I am, Mikayla. My work? Developing this drug? I could *cure* Parkinson's. Don't you understand that? And if I do it in Peru, I can skip all the red tape the US government puts in place. Lives could be saved in under a year! Not five. Join me. Things don't have to end—" he gestures to Arturo, who looms behind me with his arms crossed over his chest, "—like this."

I don't have any way to get in touch with Ronan or Austin. Unless...could I send a message to Austin that he'd understand?

"Give us a minute," Brian says as he waves Arturo and Wally back. "I'm sure she'll do the right thing. Think of Dr. Lowenstein, Mikayla. You *know* he can't wait five years.

Human trials in three months. That's what Nozanita's promised me."

"Wh-what did you to do Corey?" I ask.

Standing, Brian offers me his hand, and I let him pull me to my feet. "He left the hospital before we could get to him. But as long as he doesn't cause trouble, I promise you, Mikayla. He'll be safe. Help us get the plant, then show me all the samples you have of this hybrid. We need them all."

"Transferring the orchid," I say, my voice husky from the meds and my own fear, "will take a while, and when my partner dropped me off here today, he made me promise to call him every hour. I need to check in. If I don't, he's going to get suspicious and show up here to find out why."

"No fucking way," Arturo snaps. "You're not talking to anyone, bitch."

"A text. I can just send him a text." My heart hammers against my chest, so hard I'm afraid the men will be able to *see* it. "I'll even let you type it in."

I hand Arturo my phone. "The unlock code is 422321. Text him this. 'Dropped a whole fucking tray of blank slides in the lab. I'm fine, but I have a hell of a mess to clean up. Won't be ready to go for another two hours.'"

Scowling the whole time, Arturo types my words, hits send, and pockets my phone. "I'll keep this. Now get to work."

Austin

Mik just swore. In a text. "We need to go. Right now," I say as I snatch the keys for the SUV from the counter. Trevor follows me without question, and I double tap my earbud. It beeps when it starts transmitting, and then I hear Ronan's voice.

"What is it?"

"Something's wrong. Mik's in trouble. Get the fuck in there now. Trevor and I are on the way."

The SUV barrels down her residential street, and there better not be any cops between here and the lab, because I'm so far over the speed limit, they'd throw my ass in jail for sure.

Over comms, I hear Ronan arguing with the security guard. It's not Thom today, but a different voice, and then the distinct sounds of a scuffle reach my ears.

"Fuck."

"Talk to me, Austin," Trevor says as he flips the safety off his Glock and chambers a round. I've never been so fucking glad to have him at my side as I am right now.

"Mik doesn't swear. Ever." I pass him my phone. "She's not answering on comms. Do me a favor. Send her this. 'No worries. How about I pick up sushi for dinner?'"

He shoots me a look of total and complete confusion, but sends the message, and I careen around a corner on two wheels. "Ronan? Talk to me, man."

There's a groan, and he whispers, "I'm down. Fuckin' good Samaritans. They're goin' to take me to some security office in the basement and call the cops."

Shit. We're less than three minutes out, and I tear through a red light, narrowly missing some guy in a Tesla who gives me the finger. "Stall," I tell Ronan. "We're close."

Trevor clears his throat. "She said, 'Sounds great.'"

"Mik hates sushi. Ronan's down and the police are probably on their way. There's one security guard in a booth at the entrance. But everything else in that place is secured. So we need the guard's access card, and there are apparently some civilians in the lobby who bested your guy."

"So, going in hot, multiple hostiles, and none of them are even the bad guys." Trevor cracks his knuckles, and grins. "I haven't felt like beating anyone up in months. This should be fun."

The SUV screeches to a stop right in front of the Smithsonian's doors, and Trevor and I race inside, guns drawn. "Everybody down," I shout, then turn to the security guard standing over Ronan. The man's on his stomach, his hands bound with a zip tie behind his back. "Keycard. Now."

Trevor keeps the other five guys in the lobby in his sights, directing them to the far corner where hopefully, they won't be able to stop us before we get to the stairwell.

As soon as the guard hands over his access card, I motion for him to join the rest, then pull Ronan to his feet. "Trev will get you out of those in a minute."

"Fuckin' hell." Ronan's jaw is already starting to swell, and his green eyes hold a lethal mix of anger and shame. "What do we think is happening?" he asks when the stairwell door shuts behind us and Trev pulls out his pocket knife to cut the zip tie.

I'm already halfway to the second floor. "No idea, except for trouble. Be ready for anything."

Bursting into the hall at a run with Trevor and Ronan right behind me, I head for the lab.

"Down!" Ronan shouts, and I hit the floor as a shot rings out. "Fuck," he groans.

I return fire, hitting a tall man I don't recognize standing in front of the lab door. He crumples to the ground, the bullet hitting him center mass, and his gun falls from his hand.

"Ronan, status!" Trev orders.

"Go. I'll live."

Before we take more than two steps, Arturo bursts out of the greenhouse with his arm around Mikayla's neck and a gun pressed to her temple. "Lower your weapons now," he says, "or I will kill the doctor."

Two other men follow them. Fuck. Brian Branch and his

research assistant, Wally, are both part of this thing, and Wally has a giant plastic tote balanced on his shoulder with orchid roots spilling over the sides.

"Austin," Mik rasps. "D-do what they want. Once I give them the samples from the lab, they'll leave."

She's terrified. I can see it in her eyes. "No, Mik. I won't let them hurt you."

Trevor used to be a sniper. If I give him an opening, he can take out Arturo. The doctor isn't a threat. I could probably snap him in half without even breaking a sweat. Wally? Who the fuck knows.

"Please. I'm going to take them into the lab. I processed all the samples earlier. They're ready to go. It'll be okay after that." She and Arturo have reached his dead compatriot, and Dr. Branch drags the guy away from the door. Wally sets the tote down, takes a keycard, and swipes it over the reader.

Arturo shoves Mikayla at him and aims his weapon directly at me. Fuck. We missed our chance. Wally, Branch, and Mik are already at the next door, and Wally has his hand around Mik's throat.

They're not stopping to put on protective gear, and suddenly, I realize that's exactly what Mik's counting on. She's going to dose them all with the phytotoxin. But she can't do that without dosing herself too.

Atropine. She showed me where it was. "Trev, do it." I take my finger off the trigger and point the Beretta at the ceiling.

"The fuck?"

"Do it. Now." In my periphery, I see him follow my order.

"Put 'em on the ground," Arturo says, and we lower the guns slowly, then, at his direction, kick them away. He motions for us to move towards the greenhouse, backing into the decont-amination chamber as we pass, not giving us an opening to tackle him.

Trev and I take slow, deliberate steps, and as we pass the door, I see Wally shoving Mik towards a lab bench. She stumbles and crashes to her knees.

"Where are the samples?" the doc asks.

"In cooler two." She locks eyes with me for a split second, and the regret in them...she knows she might not survive this.

"On your knees. Both of you," Arturo says.

"I don't kneel for anyone," I snarl. "And when I kill you, I'm going to make it hurt."

"The cops are probably here by now," Trevor says. "How do you think you're going to get out of here?"

His eyes widen. "Hurry the fuck up," he shouts. "These assholes called the cops!"

"Goddammit!" Branch snaps, grabbing Mik by the arm and pushing her towards the coolers.

Enough of this shit. I just hope Trevor understands what I'm about to do. "Remember that time in Kabul?" I ask. Everything about that mission was ass-backwards and upside down, and right now, that's our best hope.

"Yeah..."

"Go high," I shout, and both Trevor and I drop and roll as Arturo aims where he *thinks* we should be—at least three feet above us. Trev tackles him, and I come up at a dead run as metal crashes in the lab and Branch groans.

The dust cloud surrounds the two men inside, and it takes me interminable seconds to find a mask and a pair of gloves while Wally, Branch, and Mikayla start to cough. At least Mik pulls her shirt up to cover her mouth as she stumbles toward me, but the Atropine is *inside* the lab, not out here.

Collapsing just inside the decontamination chamber, she curls into a ball, and goddammit, I am *not* going to lose her. Wally and Branch are clawing their way to the door, and I kick

Branch in the head, yank open the glass door to the cabinet, and grab the whole tray of Atropine syringes.

As soon as I reach Mik's side, I hit the button to start the decontamination spray, which seals the door to the lab, trapping the other two inside. With all the Atropine out here. I should feel bad. Feel *something* for them, but I'm too worried about Mik.

"Please, sweetheart. Fight for me." Jabbing the needle into her thigh and depressing the plunger, I pray I won't lose this woman before I ever have the chance to tell her how I feel.

She coughs weakly and blinks up at me. "You...got my...message."

"A whole fucking tray? Yeah. I did."

Trevor comes up behind us, his phone pressed to his ear. "Make the call, Dax. Or we're all going to be arrested in under two minutes." Glancing at me, he continues, "That big asshole is dead. Snapped his fucking neck."

Two minutes was being generous. Five police officers come tearing down the hall, and I cradle Mik in my arms. "Call a fucking ambulance!"

"Let the woman go and back away," the lead cop orders. "Now!"

"Officer, I'm Major General Austin Pritchard with the United States Air Force." I don't care that it's a lie, that I'm not that man anymore. I just need him to believe me until the EMTs get here. "This woman is my girlfriend, and she's bradycardic. Her heart rate is dangerously low, and she needs an ambulance immediately. I'm unarmed, and I'm not letting her go."

They grab Trevor and shove him to his knees before cuffing him, and Ronan gets the same treatment, despite the blood staining his gray shirt at his waist.

"I'm not going to ask you again," the cop says.

Mik struggles to sit up, and I help her, but don't let go. "He's telling the truth," she says. Her voice is so shaky, but her words are clear. "He saved my life."

"Bowers!" another officer calls out. "The chief said Pritchard, Moana, and Murphy are off limits. Stand down." He focuses on me and Mikayla. "EMTs just arrived on scene. They're on their way up now."

Thank God. I cup Mik's cheek. "You're going to be fine, sweetheart. Just stay with me, okay?"

"Uh huh," she says with a weak smile. "Have to stay. 'Cause I love you."

I don't get a chance to say the words back to her because the EMTs rush over, and I have to move aside. It's the hardest thing I've ever done, handing her over to them, but once she's stabilized, I'm never letting her go again.

EPILOGUE

Austin

Sitting in the hard plastic chair next to Mik's hospital bed, I can't stop thinking about just how close I came to losing her.

Trevor's standing guard outside the room, with someone named Tank from Second Sight on the way, and Ronan's already been released—against medical advice, but the man refused to stay after they stitched up his side. He lost a fair bit of blood, but the wound wasn't serious.

My own heart rate was a little on the low side, but the doc who examined me doesn't think I need anything other than a mega-dose of caffeine unless I start to get dizzy or experience tunnel vision or muscle weakness. So I drain the fourth cup of coffee I've had in the past hour and watch Mikayla sleep.

There's a soft knock at the door, and then Trevor slips inside. "Tank's here," he whispers. "He'll stay all night. I assume you're not leaving her?"

"Would you leave Dani?"

"Fuck no." He turns back to the door, but I stop him before he can open it, my hand on his shoulder.

"Trev..." I don't have the words to thank him for what he did for me. For Mik. Putting his own life in danger, risking arrest, fighting the demons I know are haunting him even now.

"No. You will *not* thank me. This is what family does, Austin. I didn't have one for a long time. Or...I didn't think I did. As much as your parents welcomed me into your home, all the nights I had dinner there, spent spring breaks in New Haven, Christmases...I didn't see it. I was the orphan. The kid you invited along because you pitied me."

"We never pitied you."

"I know." One corner of his mouth pulls up a little, and he huffs out what might be a chuckle. "Now. Took me a long time to come to terms with it. A solid eight months. Hell, Dax and Ford remind me at least once a week. Or they did until I started to open up to them a little. Talk about what happened in Venezuela."

"Soon, if you're up to it," I say, nervous as fuck I'm going to hurt him with my next words, "we need to talk about Gil. About everything that went down five years ago. We never really..."

"I know, man. Once things settle down," he nods towards Mik, "you say the word and I'll come back. After all, I still haven't *met* her. Or, you can bring her to Boston. She's part of the family now."

"Yeah. She is, *brother*." I still have my hand on Trev's shoulder, and I pull him in for a quick, hug. "Tell Dani I love her and I'll call her tomorrow."

"Will do. Get some rest."

When the door snicks shut and I return my focus to Mikayla, her eyes flutter open, she smiles, and holds out her hand. "Hey."

"Hey, yourself." Returning to the chair, I link our fingers. Hers are cold, and the heart rate monitor still beeps too slowly for my liking. Or her doctor's. "Did we wake you?"

"No, that was the blood pressure cuff. I hate hospitals." She closes her eyes, and I think maybe she's fallen asleep again, but she squeezes my hand gently. "You can't sit in that chair all night."

"I can. Because you need to rest."

"I'll rest." She pins me with a hard stare, despite the exhaustion in her eyes. "If you hold me."

There isn't a single thing I won't do for her, so I lower the bed rail and stretch out next to her. "Your wish is my command, sweetheart. Now and forever."

"That's better," she says, but her body's still tense.

"Mik, what's wrong? And don't say nothing." Pressing a kiss to her forehead, I breathe in her scent, and though it's marred by antiseptic and the smell of the decontamination mist from the lab, it still calms me.

"I don't remember much," she says quietly. "After he...after Wally dragged me into the lab...it's all a blur."

I can't take away what happened. I can't magically raise her heart rate or get her discharged early. I can't take her home no matter how much I want to. But this? This, I can do.

I talk until she falls asleep in my arms, telling her how Trevor, Ronan, and I got up to the second floor, how Trev took Arturo down. How Wally and Branch died sealed in the lab because of how much phytotoxin Mik had managed to throw in their faces. About the cop threatening to shoot me. Dax's lightning fast phone call.

Once I know she's out, I close my eyes and let myself drift off next to her. I still haven't said those three important words to her, and I don't know if she remembers saying them to me. But I know they're true. And deep down, I hope she does too.

Thirty-six hours later

I RUSH AROUND the SUV to open Mik's door and she scowls at me. "Austin, I'm *fine*. Clean bill of health. No lasting damage. I can get out of a car by myself."

"Not while I'm around, sweetheart. At least not yet. My father would rip me a new one if he found out I wasn't taking care of you well enough." Scooping her into my arms, I ignore her protests and manage to carry her all the way inside and to the couch before I have to let her go.

"You do realize I'm going back to work in a week, right?"

"I do. And for the next seven days, I'm going to pamper you until you're sick of me." I head to the kitchen and flip on the coffee maker, then rummage around in the cabinet for Mik's favorite chocolate bar—fair trade and organic—a tin of home-made snickerdoodles from Evianna, and a bag of veggie chips.

I hated leaving her at the hospital for even a few hours, but retrieving her softest yoga pants and Berkeley t-shirt and receiving Evianna's delivery were worth it. Especially when she gapes at the tray of food I set on the coffee table.

"Holy crap, Austin. When—?"

"Evianna baked the cookies—Dax's wife?—and Li told me what chocolate to buy. Oh, and there's one more thing." I grab the flat box next to the couch and set it on her lap. "That's from Wren."

"Seriously?" Mik pulls the top off the box and breathes a faint, "Oh." The blanket looks like someone skinned a yeti, but it's soft as fuck and Mik runs her hand over it with something approaching reverence before she pulls it from the box. "I don't understand..."

Tucking the blanket around her, I take the opportunity to

kiss her—really kiss her—for the first time in days. We spent most of her hospital stay watching old movies on the small TV and just being...together. But I couldn't find the words to tell her how much I love her. Or explain what she's gotten herself into with me.

"You're part of the family now." The coffee maker spits out its last drops, and I return to the kitchen to pour us each a cup.

"But they've never even met me." Mik accepts the mug from my hands and breathes deeply. "Oh, God. That hospital coffee was *awful*."

"I know." After a generous sip, I settle back against the cushions and wait for her to mirror my movements. "Dax, Ryker, and Ripper always considered themselves brothers. The three of them were captured by the Taliban six—no—seven years ago. They spent months in a place called Hell Mountain, tortured for information they never gave up. That's where Ry got his scars, where Dax lost his sight, and where Ripper..." I shake my head. "Where Ripper disappeared."

Mik listens as I explain as much as I think I should. So many of the stories belong to the men and women they happened to. But before I tell this intelligent, beautiful, and slightly haunted woman that I love her, she needs to know what she's signing on for if she decides to love me back.

It takes two cups of coffee, a whole chocolate bar, and four of Evianna's cookies. But when I'm done, I hold her hand and draw circles on the inside of her wrist with my thumb. "You said you didn't remember anything that happened after you threw that vial of phytotoxin in Branch's face. But...you said something to me."

"I love you." There's no hesitation in her words. No doubt. "That, I remember. But...you never said it back." Uncertainty swims in her eyes, and I take her in my arms and drag my knuckle along her cheek.

"Mikayla, you are the love of my life. I have never met another woman who challenges me like you do, who trusts me like you do, or who can hold her own against...well...*anything*. I love you. Now and forever."

"Forever?" The single word escapes on a whisper.

"Yes. I don't do things halfway. I want to spend the rest of my life with you, Mikayla Salim. We don't have to get married. Unless you want to. But now that I know what it is to have you in my life, I don't want to let you go."

For a full minute, Mik doesn't say a word, and half a dozen scenarios run through my mind. Her kicking me out. Her telling me she can't be with me because I let Branch and Wally die. Her telling me two solid days of closeness was just too much.

"So, when do I get to meet all of these people?" Mik asks. "This new...family of...*ours*."

"Ours?"

"Yes. Ours." She cups the back of my neck and pulls me down for a kiss, and for the first time since I walked out of Hidden Agenda's headquarters exactly one year ago today, my life makes sense.

My name is Austin Pritchard. I protect my family. Even when that means going rogue. And I love Mikayla with everything I am.

Whatever comes next, we'll face it together.

THANK you for reading Rogue Protector. Austin's story was one that I've wanted to tell since he first showed up in *Fighting For Valor*, and you'll definitely see him and Mikayla again in future books. In fact, he has a pretty important role to play in the next book in the series, *Rogue Officer*.

Want to know more about Griff? You can start reading Rogue Officer now!

And what about Ronan? He's such a fascinating character—has been ever since *Call Sign: Redemption*. He's getting his own book in the *Away From Keyboard* series, *Protecting His Target*. You can preorder Ronan's story now! Dax shows up a little bit, as does Tank from *Second Sight*. You don't want to miss this!

THE END

ACKNOWLEDGMENTS

Writing a book might seem like a solitary affair, but I assure you, it isn't. This book in particular took a small army—or at least a village—to complete.

JW: You read my books when they're still half-finished ideas, rough and ugly. And then you read them again when they're done. That's a lot of reading. Perhaps even more importantly, you deal with all of my random insecurities and panic attacks when life gets in the way of...everything.

JF: We've had this discussion too many times to count. But even though, yes, I **can** write emotions, when you edit for me, you always seem to find that perfect place to add that perfect word or phrase at least a couple of times in every book.

Special thanks to my beta team for this book. You were amazing and everything you did? All your help? Above and beyond anything I could have asked for.

Donna, Sadie, Kari, and Kayce...I can honestly say this book would not have been done without you.

ABOUT THE AUTHOR

I've always made up stories. Sometimes I even acted them out. I probably shouldn't admit that my childhood best friend and I used to run around the backyard pretending to fly in our Invisible Jet and rescue Steve Trevor. Oops.

Now that I'm too old to spin around in circles with felt magic bracelets on my wrists, I put "pen to paper" instead. Figuratively, at least. Fingers to keyboard is more accurate.

Outside of my writing, I'm a professional editor, a software geek, a singer (in the shower only), and a runner. I love red wine, scotch (neat, please), and cider. Seattle is my home, and I share an old house with my husband and cats.

I'm on my fourth—fifth?—rewatching of the modern *Doctor Who*, and I think one particular quote from that show sums up my entire life.

"We're all stories, in the end. Make it a good one, eh?" — *The Eleventh Doctor, Doctor Who*

I hope your story is brilliant.

You can reach me all over the web...
patriciadeddy.com
patricia@patriciadeddy.com

facebook.com/patriciadeddyauthor
twitter.com/patriciadeddy
instagram.com/patriciadeddy
bookbub.com/profile/patricia-d-eddy

Rogue Defender

Dark PNR

These novellas will take you into the darker side of the paranormal with vampires, witches, angels, demons, and more.

Forever Kept

Immortal Hunter

Wicked Omens

Storm of Sin

By the Fates

Check out the COMPLETE By the Fates series if you love dark and steamy tales of witches, devils, and an epic battle between good and evil.

By the Fates, Freed

Destined: A By the Fates Story

By the Fates, Fought

By the Fates, Fulfilled

In Blood

If you love hot Italian vampires and and a human who can hold her own against beings far stronger, then the In Blood series is for you.

Secrets in Blood

Revelations in Blood

Holidays and Heroes

Beauty isn't only skin deep and not all scars heal. Come swoon over sexy vets and the men and women who love them.

Mistletoe and Mochas

Love and Libations

Restrained

Do you like to be tied up? Or read about characters who do? Enjoy a fresh COMPLETE BDSM series that will leave you begging for more.

In His Silks

Christmas Silks

All Tied Up For New Year's

In His Collar